BROKEN

A NOVEL BY
R. GASKINS

OPAL BOOK PUBLISHING

Copyright © 2013 by Rita Gaskins

Editor: Kelsey Tate

ISBN 10: 0-9727011-7-6
ISBN 13: 978-0-9727011-7-4

Printed in the United States

Opal Book Publishing
www.obpublishing.com

Acknowledgements

First and foremost, I would like to thank *JESUS CHRIST* for all that he has done and continues to do in my life. It is in HIM that I live, move, and have my being. I also like to give a huge Thank You to the love of my life, my husband, my best friend, and prayer partner, *Terrence*. You told to write and baby, I did. I hope I have made you very proud. I love you more than words could ever express. To my children, *Terrence Jr., Tahjia, and Trinity*, you are my gifts and my greatest inspirations. To my mom and my mom in love – thank you for simply being who you are. My sisters *Sheila; Clairessa; Aleshia; Tonya; and Rhonda* and my brothers *James; Dre; Anthony; Andre; and Hunter*, you know I love you! To my aunts, uncles, cousins, nieces, nephews and God children ~ I know you love me and it means the world to me. Thank you all for always being there to hold my hand. *Vernale* (Vee), I have to say thank you from the bottom of my heart. You were the first person to read the manuscript of **Broken** before it was completed. You've also encouraged me to keep writing. God bless you and I love you! To my sisters that GOD have blessed me with - *Shelly; Jasmyen; Naticia; Tonya; Sharon; Dolores; Tasha; Robyn; Sherrie*, and the rest of you ladies, (you know who you are), You have no idea how much I love you all!!!

To all of my family and friends – even if I didn't call you by name, do know that I love you with all my heart. Thank you for being a part of my life and allowing me to be a part of yours. To everyone that have previewed *BROKEN* and told me to keep going – your encouragement is priceless! Again, thank you so very much for sowing your time into my life to help me accomplish a dream.

To my Pastors – I wrote this book before I became a part of your church, but being there forced me to "Get My Faith UP!! I love and appreciate you more than you can ever imagine. And last but not least, to my Publisher, *Corinthia A. Kelley* and the *Opal Book Publishing* family– you are truly a blessing and I thank GOD for you. Thank you so very much for believing in me and helping me to accomplish my dream. You are priceless! I pray GOD's continuous blessings upon your life.

To my readers – words cannot express the gratitude in my heart for you.
If you promise to keep reading, I promise to keep writing!

BROKEN

WHEN I WAS NINETEEN!

As I sat here staring into the woods out of the kitchen window of my home, I couldn't help but reflect on my life and think about all that I went through to get here. Sometimes I wondered if I even deserved all that I had been given. I'm now in a place that years ago I would have never imagined I'd be. This was a place of happiness and joy, but it's not because of what I have gained materially, although the material possessions sure was nice, I'm happy because I have become a whole person and I truly like the person I now see in the mirror. Looking into the woods made me think about when I was 19...

I met a young man who I think I fell in love with the moment I laid eyes on him. He was six four, the color of a fresh baked chocolate chip cookie, big beautiful hazel eyes, and a body that demanded my attention from the moment he stepped onto the field at summer camp. Camp Over Comers was my summer internship, my advisor thought it would be a good opportunity and great experience for me, since I was an Education major with a minor in Psychology. I was leaning towards working in a school, somewhere that would allow me to specialize in teaching, or counseling children with emotional problems. The children at the camp were physically normal, but a lot of them had emotional issues due to either physical, sexual, or mental abused by a parent.

Tre was a young man with an interesting past. He had been brought up in the system himself and was all too familiar with the camp

1

due to earlier camping. Once he turned eighteen, he decided that he would do his best to work at the camp since the counselors and staff there had encouraged and changed his life during the many summers that he'd spent there. He was now a Business and Music major at Phillip College, which coincidentally was a thirty minute drive away from Thurman University, the school I was currently attending.

To say the least, I think I caught his attention too, but seeing as though I was just one of the many girls at the camp that noticed him, I think he surveyed his options before he even acknowledged my presence. Since it was the first day of camp, only the counselors and staff were present, and we were all being orientated to what the next six weeks would be like. Coach Jefferson was the man in charge and very serious about what work needed to be done. He made sure that we understood that the campers came first and that this was not our vacation. It was work. He let us know that we should spend the next two days getting to know each other, the camp site, and reading over the materials and schedules for camp. He even made sure that we each had a copy of every campers profile. It was important that you understood each child's issue so that you knew how to respond to their individual needs.

Nera, one of the counselors who had worked at Camp Over Comers the year before, noticed me watching Tre and leaned over me and whispered *'his name is Trevon. He's gorgeous, but strange. I think he's gay because last year was his first summer as a counselor and all he did was work, write music, play basketball, and hang out with these kids. I mean every girl working here had their eye on him, and he ignored all of them. I mean he was nice and polite, but didn't make a move on anyone.'*

I thought to myself, *'so because he was focused, you think he is gay? I would be terribly disappointed.'*

Nera was a cute girl. She was tall and slender in stature. She worked here because the pay was decent and she was saving money for her demo. She had a voice that would melt your heart and her dream was to be a star. Therefore, she spent all her time working anyplace she could to save money to pour into her music career. She attended Allen School of the Performing Arts in New York. I just summed it up that Nera didn't know what she was talking about, and that girls like me knew exactly how to get any man we wanted no matter what the situation was. Since I prided myself on being a lady and made it my priority never to chase a man, I just decided that I would let nature take its course. What would be would be, but he sure was nice to look at.

As we were all going over to Bing Hall, which is where we ate, I noticed that Tre was talking to a couple of the other guys there. I wondered what they were talking about, but as I walked by, he grabbed my arm and asked, "Are you new? I have never seen you here."

I kept walking, and now I'm thinking, *"He's not that cute because that's not how you approach a lady."*

He followed me and asked, "Wassup? Why you keep walking?"

"That's because I had no reason to stop. All that you asked was if I was new and I am, so good observation."

He laughed and replied, "not only is you fine, but you're feisty too. I like that. I apologize, I'm Tre and you are?"

I must admit, that fine comment was a good start, so I looked up at him and answered, "I'm new and I know your name already."

As he laughed, I giggled and replied again, "I'm just kidding, my name is Nia."

For the next few weeks Tre did just what Nera said he would do. He worked really hard, and he was great with the kids. It was like he knew how to relate to every last one of them and it was so strange for a young man to be that way. When he was not working, he was somewhere to himself writing music, or on the basketball court with the other guys. One thing was different though. He stopped by every day to say hello to me during lunch, then he would come by every night for about five or ten minutes to see how my day was and say good night. A couple of times I found flowers at my cabin door which meant a lot because there were no stores nearby. This led me to believe that he must have gone out and picked them out just for me. I also got a handmade card that he did with the kids to say he was thinking about me. Needless to say, Mr. Tre had my attention and of course I was flattered to be getting any of this. I gained some haters though for no reason, other than the fact that the other girls sure noticed that he'd been noticing me. It was strange to have a man that fine to be so flattering but distant at the same time. We talked a little and he always smiled at me. When he smiled, it was like he knew something about the future that I didn't know. His smile was comforting and it made me feel warm inside. He was always very polite, but he never touched me. There was no hand holding, kiss on the cheek, nothing... which I thought was very strange. Camp would be over soon and I was hoping that before it ended, we'd at least get more than just ten minutes together.

Week Six...

　　　This was the week that camp was ending and everyone was starting to get the goodbye blues. Working with the children here had changed my life as well as my way of thinking completely. I was so grateful to have a good mom, although my Dad didn't do anything for me. My mom was a blessing and I was very grateful for her. I met a set of twin boys here who ended up in the system because their dad strangled their mom. Her family was so messed up that the court would not grant custody of them to any other relative. These twelve year old boys witnessed this man kill their mom and erased their world as they knew it. Yet and still, they were so well behaved, smart, and had such determination to make something good out of their life. They spoke often of their mother, and it seemed that their determination came from the mere fact that they wanted to make her proud of them. What huge motivation for these twelve year olds to have. I also met a fifteen year old girl who was here because she had a baby two years prior. Her parents put her out and she went to stay with her baby's daddy's family. The family was good to her and the baby, but her boyfriend decided that he wanted to try the fast life. He pissed off the wrong person and they shot up the house and one of the bullets killed their baby. Needless to say, she was pretty messed up by this experience, but over the past few weeks, she seems to have opened up some and began to heal. All I could think was what an experience to have at the age of fifteen.

I sat back and just looked at all of these young boys and girls here. Some of them told me about things that they had done that at age nineteen that I still couldn't see myself doing. These kids had experiences not only with violence, but with sex that I still couldn't fathom. I found myself thanking my mom for being so strict, because if you are doing all these things by the time you were sixteen, which was the maximum age of the campers, what are you going to do at eighteen and twenty? Or even when you decide to get married?

One young man informed me that girls in his neighborhood would do anything for a pocketbook or a pair of designer jeans. He said he had girls call him and offer him favors just to get gifts. I thought to myself *'our world is sick, these babies are so lost. I'm so fortunate. I'm only a few years older than they were and I had managed to keep my virginity.'*

I always kept it a secret that I was a virgin. I did this because people made fun of it like it was a bad thing. So I lied to keep from being teased or forced into sex. Only my best friend knew the truth and I guess the guys I dated just thought they didn't make the cut. I was suddenly proud of it, just from hearing about what these kids had been through in their lives with the sexual abuses. Some of them had no self-respect, they had done things in private and in public places that just seemed disgusting to me. But when I thought about where they lived and what their lives were like, I suddenly couldn't judge them. I felt love and compassion for them instead because it told me that they were lost. All they were really trying to do was fill the voids they had in their lives. They had no parents, no friends, no family, violence, and being abused. They were all really just looking to be loved and cared for and it was their human nature to do anything to feel loved and wanted.

At the end of my last counseling session, I walked away from my group and I began to think about the fact that Tre had been a camper here. What was his story? Why was he here? None of the counselors knew and the staff would not tell you. I was feeling really nosy and wanted to sneak in the office and pull his file, but Nera had already told me that they only kept records of the campers for this session on site. If I wanted to know his story, he would have to tell me himself. I have to admit, I did wonder if he really liked girls or if he was fronting. I may not have been a movie star, but I am fine. I mean, I got all the equipment, even if it still has the tag on it!

Last Night for the Campers...

Well tonight is the last night for the campers and there was going to be a big party down by the lake with a bon fire and all that other jazz. The kids were really excited. It's been a great six weeks, and everyone seems to have made great progress. The coach informed us that it was not our party...it was theirs, therefore, we were still working. Since it's the last night, the campers sometimes tried to get out of hand, so we needed to keep an eye on them so that there was no sneaking away from the party to do ANYTHING! We all knew what that meant...

The music was pumping all night and I learned a ton of new dances to take back to school. I must say I think I had more fun at the party than the kids had. Everyone behaved mostly, except Russell, who we knew we had to watch. Russell had been a fifteen year old male prostitute and he loved what he did. Although he had been taken off the street and was no longer prostituting, he would try to lure girls into paying him for acts if they would listen. He was in counseling for this and his therapist thought camp would be good for him. He behaved most of the time but he thought the party would be a good place to make a couple of extra dollars, so he got caught harassing a couple of the girls and asking them obscene questions about what they liked, and how much they would be willing to pay for it. We just sent him to Coach, we figured he could handle it.

The party was ending and the DJ decided to play a couple of slow jams to end the night. You know the older campers loved this as well as some of the interns. There had been quite a few love connections over the last six weeks. I saw Nera link up and spend a lot of time with Jay. He was a basketball player for Bailey College. They seemed to be getting along very well and she was hoping to get him alone before camp had ended. I didn't think it was a good idea though. He had beady eyes that were close together. I never trusted people whose eyes were close together, but she didn't listen to me. She kept pursuing him anyway. Renee hooked up with Clarence, who she said she liked just because he was light skinned and had curly hair. He was something just to do during the summer because she had a boyfriend back home. Too bad he didn't know, but he said the same thing about her. She thought she had it going on. This is why I kept my stuff new with the tags still on it! I didn't trust men…they were liars. When I decide to give up my cookies, it will be with my husband after we had gone down the aisle. At least I hope that I could keep it that long.

Anyway, the DJ starting playing slow jams and all the bumping and grinding started, or at least as much as everyone could get away with. I sat off to the side on a blanket and saw Tre wondering around like he was looking for someone. He spotted me and came over and asked me to dance.

'Wow', I thought to myself. *'He's really going to put his hands on me.'*

He pulled me up off of the blanket and walked me off to the side of the lake where we could still see everyone and hear the music, but was a little more private then being right in the midst of the party.

We began to dance to Jodeci's, *All My Life*.

"This is one of my favorite songs", he told me. "I requested it and then I came to look for you."

I just stared at him, and then I had to ask, "why me and why this song? You've been really nice but we haven't really spent much time together. Ten minutes here five minutes there, that's not a lot of time."

He looked down at me. Did I mention he really had to look down at me because I was only five foot four?

He answered, "It doesn't take much time to know what you want, especially when you know what you want." Then he smiled and of course that made me feel warm all over, before stating, "you are really short", which made us both laugh.

"Well, if you would have gotten close to me before now, you would have known how tall I was."

He pulled me closer to him and rested his chin on the top of my head. He felt so good in my arms. He must of work out a lot, and he smelled so good. How did he pull that off out here in the woods? I mean I had on Victoria Secret to help me out, but what did he use?

After dancing to Jodeci, they started to play Usher, and we just held each other. Being in his arms was so different from any other boy that I had ever let get close to me. He just seemed perfect and it was so weird because I didn't really know him, or did I. It was like reuniting with someone you knew a long time ago. It was like I didn't need to know anything about him to know that I really could be with this man.

Once the song ended, we decided to just walk around the lake and talk. We discussed the fact that he was only thirty minutes away from my school, however, our homes were about eleven hours apart. He told me he had his own car and was getting an apartment this year and living off campus. He had saved enough money to get studio equipment, so he was getting his own place so he would have a place to set it up.

"Well, I'll be living on campus", I told him. "I can't afford an apartment yet, but I do have a car. My mom got it for me for graduation. Not sure on how she did it, but she did."

He looked away, "It must be nice to have a mom to take care of you", but that's all he said.

I didn't know if I should ask about his parents or what. So I decided to let him tell me when he felt comfortable to do so.

He grabbed my hand, "I think you are special. There is something about you that I trust and that doesn't happen often. Can I really trust you?"

"Yes", I replied.

The next thing I knew, Mr. *'I don't touch no one'*, grabs me and lifts me off of the ground and kisses my forehead.

'What the heck was that?' I thought. I wanted to feel those beautiful lips on mine. The forehead thing was nice, but my lips would have been better. I hope he ain't playing games or I'd be pissed!

He told me he didn't have a girlfriend at school because he didn't want to be distracted by a relationship – unless of course he found that special someone, then asked if he could write and visit me when camp was over if I was not seeing anyone.

"Of course…" I blurted out, "I don't have a boyfriend, and I do have friends but no one special".

He looked down at me strangely, "friends? What does that mean?"

But the look on his face was weird.

"Guys I hang out with, but nothing special", I replied.

This guy who I only spoke with for ten minutes at a time and who after six weeks had just decided to touch me, seemed bothered by the other guys, almost intimidated by the thought that there were other men in my life.

So I just looked up at him and said, "I'm not screwing them if that's what you are thinking. They ain't partners!" He then had the look of relief on his face. What in the world?

"I understand. I mean you are beautiful and I'm not just talking about that phat body you got either. There is something about your spirit that brings peace", he said.

He sounded so much older than he was. He sure did know how to make a girl melt, but I was playing it cool and just listened.

He then asked if we could have lunch tomorrow after our closeout meeting for camp. I agreed to meet him in the parking lot where we would drive some place for a nice lunch afterwards.

The Last Day...

When the meeting was over, Tre came to my cabin to help me carry my things to my car.

"Which car is yours?" He asked.

"The black Saturn."

"Oh, that's nice. It's a cute little girly car."

"Whatever", I laughed. "What do you drive?" I asked him.

He pointed, "That black Escalade over there."

Now I'm really thinking he's fine. He has an Escalade and no woman? What the heck is really going on?

He just grinned, "I don't sell drugs. I bought it with insurance money from my mom's death. She died when I was younger and I got money last year when I turned eighteen."

"Oh, okay. I'm sorry about your mom", I replied.

He stares off for a bit and then put my things in my car and told me to get in and follow him.

We stopped off at a place called *Star Diner.* He said he always ate there when he left camp and the food was good. We went in had lunch and talked for hours. He told me he was the only child, no mom and no dad or at least he hadn't heard from his dad. He didn't know if he had aunts, uncles, or grandparents. He was in foster care from the time he was about ten and until he was thirteen, then he was in a group home until he went to college.

"So where's home when you leave camp?" I asked.

"Nowhere really. Sometimes I go back to the group home", he replied softly.

Ms. Agnes was the lady who ran the home. He told me that she was very sweet to him and all of the other the kids, so that was why he goes back there. A lot of the kids come back there on holidays and summer breaks.

"She always makes room for us and makes it feel like home." He said.

I thought, '*wow, how awful, but he seemed so calm about it though.*'

14

"That's why I'm getting an apartment. I need a place to call home as well as a place for my equipment. I'm going to be famous one day, and I want to give the woman I marry everything she could dream of. I want a son. One that I can love and give everything to that I never had."

At first I was thinking, why is he telling me this? However, all of a sudden he just seemed to really open up to me and tell me all his dreams. That's the day I found out that Trevon Whitmore was not only tall dark and handsome, but that he was smart, gifted, and determined.

He was in school for business and music, but on a music scholarship. He played keyboard, drums, and the saxophone. He said that he taught himself how to play them all and when he was in high school, he learned how to read music.

I told him how I was an only child. How I had no idea where my dad was. I grew up in the city, but my mom made sure the hood stayed on the outside and how I was grateful that she made me go to church. I also told him how my mom worked hard and later bought us a house in a small suburb right outside the city. It wasn't the greatest, but it was nice. It was a good place to grow up in. I let him know that I was an Education and Psychology major, but that I came to school on a dance scholarship and was part of the band.

"So you wear those little outfits on the field and shake your goodies in front of the world?"

I giggled and asked, "is that what you think of dance?" He shrugged his shoulders.

"Well, I guess I do if that's how you look at it", I replied.

"You are so beautiful. Your body is amazing", I blushed of course. "You dance, so I know men are always after you. Why are you single?"

"You are fine, talented, and got cash…why are you single?", I replied sarcastically.

He just laughed, "I see your point, but I don't think I'm single anymore."

"Oh really," my heart skipped a beat for one minute. I kind of liked the fact that he was so assertive in a quiet kind of way. "Not single? Who are you hooked up with?"

This man looked into my eyes as if he could see my soul and answered, "You! You are my wife and I'm going to put the world in the palm of your hands."

I had no words at all. I was speechless. I just looked at him and shook my head.

"Nia, I'm not crazy. I just know what I want and I want you. I've never even kissed you, but I know kissing you will take my breath away. I knew it the moment I saw you. I know it sounds crazy to you and you don't have to believe me, just let me show you."

All I could say was "okay."

Then he said, "say okay to one more thing."

"What's that?" I asked.

"Say that you aren't single any more", and of course I said with a little hesitation, "okay".

We sat there for a while longer, "you know this is all pretty quick for me. I mean we are going to be a couple! I feel like I've known you forever, but it's only been for a summer and this just doesn't seem like it could be real."

"Nia," Tre said, "it's real and it's okay. There is no time limit. I didn't say you had to do anything except let me show you that I really like you and that I want to be with you and that's it. That's not crazy or hard."

Again, I just replied, "Okay. Well, it's getting late and I have three hours to drive home, so I better get going."

We walk outside and as we are hugging and saying good-bye, Tre lifts me off of the ground with my head a few inches over his, presses his lips on my neck and slowly lowers me until he gets to my lips. He landed his lips on mine so gently and our first kiss began. It felt so good as his tongue moved inside of my mouth. It was a feeling I'd never felt before. He was so good at this that it seemed unreal. I was hoping that he couldn't feel my heart beating because this kiss seemed to have lasted forever. Then he slowly lowered me back to the ground and it took a minute for me to open my eyes again. But when I did, I felt light headed. He pulled me into his arms and I could hear his heart beating. I think he was a little excited too,

"Wow" he said, "I'm one happy brother."

I just giggled. But at that moment I thought, *'I think I love this man.'* But is this possible? Can it be real? I'll just keep that thought to myself. He opened my car door and I hated to get in and leave him, but I knew I had to be getting home, especially since my mom was expecting me.

"Be safe", I told him.

He winked at me and handed me an envelope with the words, *DON'T OPEN UNTIL YOU ARE HOME AND IN BED THINKING ABOUT ME!* He kissed me on the forehead, waved, and got into his truck and we headed our separate ways.

At Home…

When I pulled into the driveway, the porch light was on and I can see my mom looking out of the window. She opened the door and ran to the car, "Nia, I'm so glad you are home."

She helped me get my things out the car, filled me in on all the family and the neighborhood happenings, kissed me on the cheek and turned in for bed later that night. All in all, I felt like it has been a good day. But before letting her go to bed, I first mention to her that I met a guy at camp.

"That's great!" she said. "I hope he goes to church."

That's all she ever said. Sometimes I think to myself, *'if she only knew that half the boys I meet that claim to go to church, still tried to take the tags off my goodies! Oh well, she's just being a mom.'*

I unpacked my things, took a shower, and brushed my hair. Then I hopped on my bed and pull out my envelope. When I opened it, it was a letter that read:

Dear Nia,

I just wanted to write you so you would know that over the past six weeks, I have watched you and enjoyed every minute you allowed me to spend in your presence. You have been my summer joy, and joy is something I haven't felt in a long time. I know you think I'm moving fast, and believe me I normally don't, but I just couldn't let you out of my presence without letting you know how I felt. There are so many things about me that I want to share with you. Some I will write, some we can talk about over the phone, and others we should discuss in person. I know Nera told you she thinks I'm gay, and that's cool, but trust me I'm not gay. I just didn't want those girls and I'm not about flings. My mom had a fling and it got her killed. Yeah, my mom was killed. I love women and yes, I've had girlfriends, but when you are young, the relationships don't last. I'm just careful about who I spend my time with. You seem so special to me and I hope I'm right about you. I think I am. Please take the gift that I left you in the enclosed envelope and prepare yourself for school. I will see you in two weeks if I can't stay away. Please call me after you have read this.

Peace,
Tre

I opened the envelope and its five hundred dollars! The questions that went through my mind were *'What? Do I keep this? What in the world is going on? Is this man crazy?'* This was almost half of what he made from working at the camp. He gave me half of his paycheck. This is WILD. When I call what was I to say?

The Phone Call…

I get my phone and I dial his cell phone number and there was no answer. It was late, but I wasn't going to start tripping. I hang the phone up, and about ten seconds later, the phone rings and it's Tre.

"Hi Nia, sorry I was checking into a hotel when you called. I decided to go back to North Carolina instead of going home to Georgia. It was too long of a drive and I needed to find an apartment, so I drove to here and got a room. How are you?" He asked.

"I'm fine. Thank you for the letter, but the gift was a bit much though. Although I appreciate it, I don't know if I should keep it."

He was silent, "I'm scaring you aren't I?"

"No I'm not scared. I just don't want to move too fast."

There was silence again, "well, I tried not to move fast by not touching you for six weeks. Nia, do you think that was easy for me? I was just trying to respect you so you would know that I was sincere and serious. I apologize if the gift was too much. I'll slow down."

"Thank you" I said. "Are you sleepy?"

"No. I'm still thinking about that kiss. I have to take a cold shower though. I can't get those lips off of my mind."

I didn't say anything, but I was thinking the same thing. I have never had a kiss that made me feel like that before. I felt that kiss in my toes. If his kiss was like that, what was the rest of him like? I think I will have to tell this one I'm a virgin. I really like Tre and I want this to be an honest and trusting relationship. I hope us being at separate schools was not a problem.

I asked him if he wanted to talk about what happened to his mom, since he put it in the letter.

"Well, my dad is in jail. He got locked up on some serious drug charges, but my mom was a decent woman. She worked hard and we lived pretty well. She went to see my dad for a while, but I was two when he got locked up. By the time I was five, she had stopped going to see him. I don't even know where he's locked up at. She never had contact with her parents. I don't know what happened between them."

He continued, "She dated this guy for a while and he was cool. At least he seemed to be, but my mom was a very attractive woman and a bit of a flirt. After a while, he couldn't handle it anymore and he became a very jealous man."

That was all he said before changing the subject, so I didn't push it. I just left it alone. But I sure was curious to hear the rest.

"How many girlfriends have you had?" I asked.

"Not many" he replied quickly. "And you?"

"Only a few," I answered back. "I mostly have male friends that I hang out with."

There it was again, that weird silence. I asked, "Tre, does that bother you?" I just knew that he wasn't insecure, as fine as he was.

"Well it doesn't bother me as long as you are always honest with me about them, and not accumulate any new male friends during our relationship."

"Deal", I confirmed. "How about you?" I asked him.

"I got a best friend and his name is Nick. He's cool. I don't have any close girlfriends though. They can't handle being my friend. They always get it twisted. So if I ain't dating them, I leave them alone."

"Good, so I don't have to worry about chicks playing on my phone."

"None of that! I ain't having it." After a while, we ended our conversation and went to bed.

For the next two weeks we talked on the phone every morning and every night. I think he wanted to come and see me, but didn't want to overdo it. I did get flowers sent to my home though, with a card that simply said, *'for my Joy'*. My mom was very impressed, so he got mega cool points for impressing my mom. Oh, and he sent me a cell phone, for which he planned to pay the bill. That was cool, I thought, since he is my boyfriend. Wow...I have a *boyfriend*.

DAYS AT THURMAN UNIVERSITY

As I walked down the hall into the study and see the many books we have accumulated, all the awards on the wall, the degrees I have gained, I thought back on all the knowledge, wisdom, and understanding that each stage of life brings, and realized that life itself is a university. You never really graduate from it, but with each stage, if handled correctly, there is a reward or an award. This study reminds me of my days at Thurman University...

Tre drove to my house to help pack up my things and take them back to school. We loaded up my car and his truck, kissed my mom goodbye and hit the road. We only had about a five hour drive, but decided we would stop off and have dinner together before checking into my dorm. I was a couple of days early, so I figured it shouldn't be a problem getting settled in. There weren't going to be many people there anyway.

During the drive, Tre called on my cell phone and asked if I was up for some Chinese food.

We pulled over into the mall area and we grabbed a table at Changs.

"I love this place!" I told him.

"So do I. They've got the best spring rolls."

We ordered our food and sat for a moment while he just stared at me. His looks made me feel as though he could see right through me, which kind of always gave me chills. I tried to keep that to myself. I didn't want to tell the brother that he was giving me chills after only dating for a few weeks.

"Why are you looking at me like that?" I decided to ask.

He just grinned and looked away.

"I'm sorry," he apologized, "I can't help it. I've never been like this before. I don't even know why or what it is about you, but you just turn me on. I mean not just sexually, but in every way. You make me wanna be something, just by looking at you. I have never felt like this. I..." he paused.

He seemed like he wanted to tell me something but was holding back.

"You what?" I asked, eager to know.

"Nothing, I...I just like looking at you. But if it bothers you, I won't do it again."

"It's okay," I told him. "I sure don't want you starring at anyone else."

Our food arrived and it was either really good or we were really hungry, because it wasn't long before we were looking at the dessert menu. The waiter came back over and we ordered dessert. While we were waiting, we started talking about our friends back at school. He mentioned that he didn't have a lot of friends he hung out with.

"Friends are people you can trust and I don't trust anybody really."

"I hope you trust me," I said as he smiled.

"My one and only friend Nick, we grew up in the group home together and he plays trumpet. Watch him when you meet him. He thinks he's a player, but he's cool though. He was in the home 'cause his folks got locked up for running a drug and prostitution ring. His dad was a pimp."

We both laughed at the pimp comment, "I guess that's why he thinks he's a player. He got it twisted though. He doesn't know how to treat women, so I keep him away from my female friends. Or at least the one I like."

I made a mental note not to be too friendly with Nick. "Well, I have a roommate name Natalie and she is sweet. She's really smart and a church girl. She doesn't party much or anything, so it's cool having her around. She keeps me focused. I also have a best friend name Wayne and we grew up together. We've been friends since we were about eight. We walked to school together every day until we graduated high school and we prayed to get into the same college together ..." I paused, noticing that while I was talking, Tre stopped eating his dessert.

I continued, "We've been through everything together, girlfriends, boyfriends, break ups, grandparents dying, we've always been together."

"Wow" he said with almost no expression. "So why is he not your boyfriend?"

"Umm…" I hesitated, "we just never went that route. I don't think I was his type. I wasn't fast enough for him. Plus, he liked the red and mixed girls, and I didn't fit that portrait."

"What's his last name?"

"Nelson…Wayne Nelson." I answered.

"Nelson? The basketball player that everyone is talking about going pro?"

"Yep, that's him."

"Nia, what's that like? I mean, being his best friend?"

"It's cool. It's like it has always been. Guys get intimidated by it and girls either try real hard to be my friend or they hate me. But it's all good. We were friends before all this, so it doesn't even matter."

"Okay…" he ended.

We finished our meal and headed back to our cars. He kissed me on the cheek and closed my car door,

"I'll follow you," I told him.

Once we were about an hour away from my school, my cell phone rung.

"Hey princess, I wanna ask you something."

"Sure, what is it?"

"Will you stay at my place tonight?"

"Umm…" I hesitated while my heart started to race. Then I hear that strong voice on the other end say, "We don't have to sleep together. I just don't want to be without you tonight. I'll take you to school in the morning."

Before my rational thoughts set in, I heard myself say, "I guess so."

"Cool then." he said before hanging up.

For the next hour, all I could think about was, *'Oh my God, what am I doing? I'm not ready yet for this. I sure hope he is really a gentleman.'* I picked up my cell phone and I called my friend Wayne.

He answers the phone, "Who is this?"

"It's me boo,"

"What number is this?"

"My new boyfriend got me a new cell phone."

"Oh, the music man?" He said sarcastically.

"Yeah…" I said. "Listen, I'm staying at his place tonight. Here is the address. If I don't check in tomorrow, come looking for me." I was in panic mode.

"Umm Nia, does he know you are a virgin?"

"YES…" I said in a stern voice.

I hear Wayne ask again loudly, "You are a virgin aren't you?"

"Yes Wayne, I would have told you otherwise."

"Alright Nia, no secrets, no secrets boo!"

"I promise, love you."

"Love you too," I hung up.

We arrived at Tre's apartment, and the complex was really nice. It had a beautiful courtyard, pool, tennis courts, the works.

"This doesn't look cheap," I said. "It's not the typical college man pad."

"Nah," he said, "I wanted to be away from the hoopla so I can stay focused."

I grabbed one of my suitcases from my trunk and followed him to his door. He put the key in the door and turns toward me and said, "Okay, it's a bachelor pad, not much furniture yet, so know that alright?"

"It's cool." I said.

He opens the door, and it was nice. There was no living room or dining room furniture, but it smelled good and it was clean. There were two bedrooms and a den. The den is where all the music equipment was, and the bedroom set was really nice. It was black lacquer and cast iron furniture, with a silver and black comforter set and red pillows.

"This is really nice. You picked it out?" I asked.

He laughed and replied, "Yes and no. I just went to Stravens and bought the bedroom set that was on the display."

"Oh, okay."

Nera's words were about to resurface in my thoughts. The bathroom was clean, but there were no decorations though. The bathroom had just a shower curtain, toilet paper and some soap.

"Make yourself comfortable", he yelled from the den.

Did I mention that there was a huge TV and stereo set in the living room, but no furniture? Typical guy.

"You can shower if you like. There are towels and wash cloths in the linen closet."

I looked in his closet and it was pretty organized and I noticed he's got some really nice clothes.

I wondered to myself, *'how much money does he really have? This place can't be that cheap. He's doing pretty well for himself.'*

I opened my suitcase and tried to pick out something appropriate to sleep in. Didn't want to look like a prude, but I also didn't want to be a tease and get myself into something I wasn't ready for either. I hear him in the den playing the keyboard and laying down tracks. He sounded really good. However, I turn on the TV and try to find something to watch so I didn't disturb him.

After about thirty minutes, he came into the room, "I can order some pizza. I don't have any groceries or else I would cook."

"You can cook?" I asked him jokingly.

"A little bit, not much."

He picks up the phone, orders pizza and drinks, and then said, "I'm gonna take a shower. I'll be out in a minute."

He was awfully comfortable with me being here. I wondered if he'd done this a lot.

I hear the water running and the radio on in the shower, after about ten minutes, he emerges from the bathroom with a towel around his waist, water dripping off of him. This man has got to be one of the sexiest men I have ever seen. He looked so good to me, but I had to turn my head.

"Sorry," he apologizes, "I forgot to take my clothes in the bathroom."

He goes to the dresser, gets his gear and goes back into the bathroom. He comes back out with some basketball shorts, boxers showing from underneath them, and no shirt. This man must work out all day because he had muscles in all the right places. I notice a small scar on the lower right side of his stomach, which was actually kind of sexy.

My thoughts were telling me that I just found the man I hope to marry, because I would love to give my virginity over to him. I couldn't believe I had these thoughts because I usually have way more control than this. But this man was not just fine, he was sexy and nice, a perfect combination.

Before I went into the shower, he looked at me and asked, "is that ponytail yours?"

"What?" I responded.

"Is it yours or did you buy it? For the entire summer you've had either had a pony tail or had your hair braided straight back. I mean you look pretty like that but I was just wondering if it's yours or not."

"Yes this is my hair," I tell him. "I decided to let it grow a few years ago, and so…"

"Wow," he said. "Most girls with hair that long bought it or they're mixed."

"Well," I tell him, "I ain't mixed and I got a perm, but it's my hair,"

"Then take it down when you come out the shower. I wanna see what you look like with it out."

"Okay!" I tell him.

After my shower, I put on my VS lotion and body spray, let my hair down, and exited wearing a tank top with no bra that stoped right above my belly button. My girls were a perky C cup, so I figure while they look this good, I better make use of them since I hear it don't last always. I also had on some night shorts, short enough to be sexy, but not to let my butt cheeks hang out from them. I figured this was safe enough.

When Tre heard me come out the bathroom he yelled, "Princess, come out here, the pizza has arrived."

There he was, sitting on the floor with the TV on and the pizza on a blanket. He looked up and took a deep breath, one that I could feel, and he just stared.

"Tre," I said. "What's up?"

"Why you say that," he answered slowly looking at me from my head to my toes.

"Cause you're staring!"

31

"Nia, you are so pretty to me. You look so good. I hope that I can keep it together, but I don't know."

I just smiled and sat down, "you look good too baby," I said to him.

We ate pizza and never even noticed what was on the TV, and talked. I figured this would be a good time to talk about our past. These days you gotta know where somebody has been, and who they've been with, or else you could be killing yourself. We shared small talk for a while before going into the bathroom to brush our teeth and exchange some childish play before retreating back into the living room on the blanket.

I got right to the point, "I have a question for you. How many girlfriends have you had?"

"I have only had two serious relationships," he said.

"Two?" I asked thinking of another number, "as fine as you are?" I was hoping that it wasn't from him having a small penis or anything like that. Otherwise, what else could it have been?

"He looked at me like he was reading my mind… "There's nothing physically or mentally wrong with me. I have had two serious girlfriends and I had sex with only one of them. I'm only nineteen and I'm proud of that fact. My mom was shot and it was done in front of me by a boyfriend that she tried to break up with, but he couldn't let go and didn't want to see her with anyone else. He came to our house, barged in, pushed her on the couch, tied her up and tied me to a chair at the dining room table. He made me watch him sexually assault her and then he shot her in the chest, shot me in the abdomen, and then shot himself in the head. The neighbor heard the gun shots and called the police. They arrived in time to get us both to the hospital, but my mom only lived a few hours after that from what I was told. I was unconscious for a while and lost a lot of blood, but was blessed that the bullet missed most of my vital organs. I was only ten years old. When I left the hospital, I was sent to a foster home. I don't even know how or where my mom was buried. Because my dad was in jail, I knew nothing about her next of kin. I'm telling you this so you understand that for a long time I thought sex was something you did to hurt women, and because I saw my mom suffer, I didn't want to do that to a female. My mother taught me at an early age what it meant to be a gentleman and what she taught stuck with me. It's something that I hold onto dearly. I don't want to do anything that would dishonor her memory because of how she lost her life. Please know that my lack of partners has nothing to do with desire, just respect."

All I could think was '*Wow*'! He had to have been messed up really bad behind all of this. He went on to say that he started going to Camp Over Comers at the age of thirteen and it really helped him heal a lot and understand what being a man was about.

"I do have issues Nia," he admitted. "I'm not perfect, but I work on it. If I ever do anything that you don't like, you have to tell me."

So I asked, "What happened with your ex-girlfriends?"

"Well I had my first real girlfriend at fifteen. She was a sweetheart, but was really fast. She taught me all about oral sex and some other things, but we never went all the way. I played basketball, and one night after a game, I went by her house to see her, and ask why she was not at my game. She'd never missed one before. She informed me that we had to break up 'cause she was pregnant. Needless to say, my heart was broken and I didn't ask any questions, I just walked away. I didn't sleep with her, so she had to have slept with someone else. I guess I was too slow for her. My next relationship started a little after my sixteenth birthday and lasted until I was about eighteen. I thought she was my soul mate. I was her first and she was mine. I really loved this girl, but we were going in two different directions. She wanted to get married after high school and I wanted to go to college. Therefore, she had a 'best friend' that was out there living the life. He liked her the whole time that we were together anyway, so I guess he filled her head with promises. The next thing I knew I couldn't find her half the time, and he would answer her phone and everything. We ended up having a really bad argument and went our separate ways, and that was that. I never felt pain like that in my life and it wasn't until I saw you that I thought about getting into another serious relationship. I have been on dates, but just no real relationships."

He was so open and honest with me that it was strange and just as I was thinking that, he looks at me and said, "I really want this to work with you, so I think that we have to be really honest with each other. That's why I'm telling you all of this."

"Okay," I assured him.

Then he asked, "What about you?"

"Well," I said hesitating, "I've had three somewhat long term relationships, but..." I hesitated again, "I've never had sex before."

His mouth dropped open, "you a virgin," he said and sits up and looks into my eyes like he's trying to see if I'm serious.

"Yes" I said.

"I have had three boyfriends in my life, one I really thought about sleeping with, but I just couldn't. I didn't want all of the issues that came along with it, so I never did it. I use to lie and say that I wasn't a virgin, so I guess the guys just thought I didn't find them attractive, but I did. I just wasn't ready. I got my heart broke those three times though, because the brothers couldn't handle it, so they cheated after about six months and it always took until about the eighth or ninth month for me to figure out that there was someone else."

"Wow Nia. I don't know what to say. I can understand the brothers being frustrated. That's only because you are sexy and a man is going to want to be with you. But I promise that I will always be honest with you, and if you want to wait, I will wait until you are ready. I can't promise you that it will be easy, but I can promise not to hurt you."

He laid back on the floor and pulled me over on top of him and started kissing me. I'm telling you, this man kisses like he won't get another one, and I can feel it from my head down to my toes.

As this kissing went on, I felt his hands on the small of my back and he began to caress my lower back and the top of my behind. It felt so good and I was really enjoying this after a few minutes of laying on his chest. I could tell that he was enjoying it too cause his heart started to pound as he lift the lower half of my body away from his and rolled me over. My guess was that he didn't want me to feel what was going on below his waist line.

He looked down at me and said, "girl you have got the softest lips I have ever felt," he smiled. "I have never dated a dancer before...you wanna dance for me?"

"Tre," I said. "You think that's wise?"

"He laughed and laid down. "Umm...nah you right. I better quit right?"

"Yeah," I said, "maybe a little later. I'll give you a dance, but if you just want to see me dance, you are more than welcomed to come by my rehearsals when you have time."

"Okay," he said. "I would like that."

It was getting late and I was pretty tired. "I'm going to go to bed now."

"You can sleep in the bed. I'll sleep out here and close the door," he said with a smile on his face.

He stood up to walk me to the bedroom. Once inside, he picked me up and stood me on top of the bed, "what are you doing?" I asked.

"Nothing," he said softly as he slid my shorts off. "Don't worry baby, I just had to see what you looked like under those shorts. Besides, I can see the G string anyway."

I started thinking for a minute that this was getting dangerous. He placed my shorts on the nightstand and laid me on the bed, leaving the covers off and my body exposed. He then turned off the light leaving the television on, and kissed me, "good night princess", and left the room. I heard him go into the den and play music for about another hour and I just listened. Before dozing off, I said to myself, *'this is just too good to be true.'*

When I woke up, I see the bedroom door opened but I didn't see Tre. I went into the bathroom to wash my face and brush my teeth. Then I walked into the living room, but I still didn't see him. I heard music coming from the second bedroom so I walked over and stood in the doorway and there he was, lifting weights. He put the bar down, walked over and kissed me on the forehead. "Good morning baby…please do me a favor and put your shorts on. You're trying to mess me up early in the morning."

We both giggled, "I'm sorry, I didn't even realize it. I wasn't use to waking up in the house with a man."

"I hope this is something you can get used to," he said.

I walked away and I could feel his eyes all over my backside. I'm glad I'm in good shape. I went back into the bedroom and put on my shorts.

"What's for breakfast?" I yelled from the room.

"Whatever you cook," he said laughing.

"What? Who told you I can cook?"

He laughed again, "Your mom told me."

"Fine," I said. "But you have no food!"

"Oh yes I do. I went to the store this morning while you were asleep."

"Alright! I guess I can, but nothing elaborate."

I decided to make omelets, toast, and bacon. He gobbled it down like it was his last meal and smiles.

"Girl, you are a bad chic. You fine and can cook? That's the best combination."

"Whatever," I said. "I gotta get to school."

He got quiet again, gets up and said, "Okay, we can leave when you get dressed."

After arriving to the school and checking in, I start to get the stares from my fellow students. Rosa, the bold nosy girl from across the hall, sticks her head in my door and loudly asks, "who in the world is that man carrying all your stuff and where you get him from? Girl ain't too many of them floating around."

"Bye Rosa," I said.

"Not til you tell me who he is."

"He's mine," I said.

"So, what is his name?"

"His name is Tre," I told her.

"I bet Wayne don't know about this one."

"Yes he does, now please mind your business."

Rosa turned and headed back over to her room. Once I get settled with my bags, Tre came with one last bag and tells me that he has band practice this evening so he had to get back to school.

"I understand, I have to work out and be ready, my practices start tomorrow," I replied.

He kissed me passionately, "please call if you need anything,"

"I'm fine," I tell him. "I have no needs."

"I mean it Nia, call me if you need anything."

"I'm straight…go to school baby. I will talk to you tonight." He kisses me again and leaves.

He's plays Drum and I Dance…

Over the next couple of weeks, we both are very busy with practices, classes and my job, where I wait tables at Frankie's. We talk every night, but have not seen each other since school started. Our first game is coming up, so we decided to come to each other's game to see the performances and meet friends. I'm looking forward to seeing him.

Tre's game is on Friday, so I planned all week to go to the game and spend the weekend with him since it has been three whole weeks since I've laid eyes on him. I was really, really missing him and according to all the phone calls and messages, he misses me to. I have to figure out what to wear to his game. I gotta be cute, but not too cute.

His Game…

It's Friday and I packed my things to go to the game at Phillip College and to spend the weekend at Tre's. I let Natalie know where I was going, and of course she lectured me about being safe, which I did appreciate. I called my mom and left her a message to reach me by cell phone if she needed me.

I hopped in my car and drove to Phillip College. The crowd was hype and the game was pretty good. By half time, Phillip was winning by one touchdown, so the crowd is in a great mood and ready for the band to perform. They hit the field and were pretty good, although of course, I didn't think their dancers were as good as we were, but they had it going on. The band was fierce but I thought that the drum line was the best.

Once the game was over, I headed to my car and drove straight to Tre's house. We'd already discussed that we would just meet at his apartment because it would be too much of hassle for him to try and find me after the game. When I arrived, I didn't see his truck so I sat in my car for a while. After about twenty minutes, I saw his truck pull up and it's filled with a few guys and one girl. He stepped out of the truck looking just like I like him to look…baggy shorts, tennis shoes and a wife beater, sexy as all get out. He walked over to my car and apologized for being late.

"A couple of my friends parked their cars here so I had to collect everyone to bring them back to their cars."

"I'm cool," I tell him and step out of the car.

He looked at me strangely but doesn't say anything. At that moment, his friends walked over, "so this is princess?" one of them said. I extended my hand and a tall slim, light skinned gentleman takes my hand kisses it and introduces himself as Nick.

"Oh," I said, "Hi Nick, it's nice to finally meet you."

He looked at Tre…"Hey man I understand!" Smiles and walked away. The others introduced themselves and walked away to their cars. The girl was the last one to introduce herself and she did it with a bit of an attitude.

"Hi, what's your name?" She asked.

"Nia."

"Oh, I knew your real name couldn't be princess."

"I'm Toni. I had to meet the woman who got Tre, cause he don't fool with nobody. He's a hot commodity girl…you better keep your eye on him."

"Whatever," I said under my breath, got my bag and walk to the door.

"Go on girl," Tre tells her. "You always acting a fool. Get yourself on out of here," and he waves her off.

"Sorry baby, she is just crazy."

"No problem," I tell him.

We walk inside and I go to the room to put my things down. He looks at me and said, "Princess, where's the rest of your clothes?"

"What do you mean?" I ask.

"I mean you look good but umm…those shorts kind of short and you got a lot of cleavage, I mean, all my friends were looking at you."

"Tre," with a raised eyebrow while speaking, "I have on a halter top and some shorts, is this a problem?"

"Nah princess, I'm sorry. I'm just tripping. I don't see you a lot and my friends were really staring at you. I guess it just got me for a moment. You can wear whatever you want. I apologize."

"It's okay," I said before jumping up on him with my legs wrapped around his waist and kissing him. This was just to remind him of why he was feeling jealous in the first place.

"Woo," he reacted, "girl you are my joy. I have missed you so much."

After jumping back down off of him and he said, "I'm going to shower, be back in a moment."

After showering, he comes out in only a towel, this time he sits on the bed. I gather my things to take my shower afterwards and come out in my nightgown with my hair up in a clip and Tre is still sitting on the bed in his towel.

"Are you hungry", he asks.

"Not really."

"Okay, well I am."

He gets up and heads into the kitchen and emerges with a sandwich, some chips, and a soda and comes back to the room and sits back on the bed.

'Why is he not getting dressed?' I'm thinking to myself as he's eating his food. I then decided to lean over to take a bite of his sandwich. He kind of looks over at me, but doesn't say anything.

He puts his plate on the nightstand and lies back on the pillow.

"That's a nice night gown you got on."

"You like," I said. "It's not much, nothing special."

"Nia, it don't take much at all."

I smiled, "can I see you without that towel?" I asked.

He frowns and kind of laughs at the same time, "uh…are you asking me for something?"

"Yes, I'm asking if I can see you naked."

"Nia, I'm surprised, what are you saying?"

"I ain't saying anything except I wanna know what's under that towel."

"Then what?" he asked.

"Nothing, I just want to see you naked."

"Okay," he said. "You gonna take that gown and those panties off?"

"Why?" I said.

With a devilish grin on his face, "I'm not getting naked by myself."

"Alright, I'll play with you, but it's just getting naked."

"Girl you crazy, you playing Russian roulette. If you get naked in my bedroom, I can't make you any promises about how I'm going to react. You know, it's been a while since I've seen a completely naked woman in my bedroom. Especially one that I care about."

"Yeah, I know. But for real, I really want to see what's under that towel."

"Okay, so I'll go first because I don't want to be embarrassed to take off my towel if you go first." He laughs.

Tre stands up on my side of the bed and removes the towel then looks me dead in my eyes.

'There is a GOD' is the thought that ran through my mind. This man had everything a girl would and could want. There had to be something wrong with him, but from what I could see in front of me, it sure wasn't anything wrong with his body.

"Okay," I said. "Nice."

He smiled, "I'm glad you approve."

Tre pulled me up close to him and said nothing but takes the clip off my hair and lets it fall around my shoulders and down my back. He then stuck his hands under my nightgown and slowly removed my panties. For a moment he just stood there like he was trying to prepare himself for what was next.

"Are you okay with this? If not, I can stop."

"I'm okay," I said, "I think."

He paused for a moment then lifts my nightgown over my head and lays it on the bed. He took a step back and just gazed at me.

I started to get a little nervous.

"It's okay. You are so beautiful" he tells me. If I promise not to lose control, can I touch you?"

"I don't think that's a good idea," I told him.

He goes to the drawer and puts on a pair of boxers, walks back over and asks me to lie on the bed. I lay down and he takes his finger and rubs my neck down to my belly button, then turns over and sits up on the side of the bed.

"Are you okay Tre?"

There was nothing but silence, but I can hear him breathing. I walked over to his drawer, took out one of his tank tops and put it on. He just sat there.

"I'm sorry baby, I shouldn't have asked you to do this." I told him.

"Nah princess, it's okay. I'm just trying to get it together"

He left the room for a moment to get a drink from the kitchen and comes back and lies on the bed staring at me.

"Tre, I really apologize."

"Nia, I gotta tell you something."

"What baby?"

Straddling me across his lap, he looks into my eyes, "I'm really in love with you. You don't have to say anything, but I need you to know that I love you. I've felt this way since camp. I didn't say anything because I didn't want to scare you and I know it seems really fast, but I think about you all the time. I smile when I hear your voice. I have never fallen for anyone like this in my life. I have been in this world alone for a long time and I don't feel alone anymore. Even when you are not here with me, I feel like you are. I hope I'm not scaring you, but I'm so excited to have you in my life. It's been so long since I had anyone that I could love and I love you. I really do and I enjoy loving you."

I looked at him and I said, "I love you too! I knew I loved you since camp as well. I get chills every time you are near me, but I have to admit that I am scared, only because this doesn't seem like its real. I'm just waiting for something to go wrong."

"It won't Princess, I promise."

I think to myself – I think I just gave my virginity away. I start to kiss him on his neck and chess, and I feel him start to get excited and pull away, I look at him and say "you don't have to stop."

"No," he said. "I want you to know that my loving you has nothing to do with sex and as bad as I want you, don't do this because I told you I love you." I have to admit I was feeling like I had to because I

46

had this man strip naked and I let him touch my nude body – I didn't want to be a tease.

"I love you Tre and really I'm not ready for sex yet, but I want to make you feel good"

He looked at me and smiled, "I do feel good. Knowing that you love me feels good. I need a cold shower, but I'm okay."

He gets into bed with me and we fool around for most of the night but no sex. Finally we fall asleep. It was a great night, at least I thought it was.

In the morning I'm awakened by lips between my legs. It felt so good that before I could open my eyes, I gasp. I've never had this done before and now I knew what all the hype was about. I'm not sure how to feel. I felt somewhat embarrassed cause I couldn't help but to moan and I felt like I was about to explode in any minute. I couldn't be still. I felt my heart rate rise and rise and something on the inside feels like it was spilling over. The faster his tongue moved, the faster my heart was beating, until I couldn't take it anymore. My body was convulsing and I think I screamed. I couldn't even catch my breath, and then Tre sat up and smiled at me. I felt great and embarrassed at the same time. My first orgasm and it was great. Now I was hooked. But now what? What am I supposed to do for him? I can see he is very excited by what just went on and I know he wants me to do something, but what?

Tre goes into the bathroom, comes out and then lays next to me and kisses me then said, "Good morning princess."

"Good morning," I said. "What was that for?"

"I just wanted to make you feel good."

"You did a good job."

"Was that your first time?" he asked me.

"Yes."

"So, you are a real virgin?"

"Yes, I told you that before. This was my first experience with oral sex and my first orgasm."

"Did you like it?" he asked.

"Yes," I said blushing. "So now what?" I ask.

"Nothing, unless you are ready for something."

"Tre," I said to him shyly, "You have to tell me what to do."

"That's cool," he sat on the side of the bed and then asked, "What are you ready for?"

"I want to try what you just did."

He sits on the side of the bed and puts me on my knees in front of him, then directs me like he's directing a movie.

"Nia first you lick right here, then you put your hand right here, and you suck like this."

I'm a smart girl, so it only took a moment for me to get the hang of it. After about three minutes, he just looks at me with this awe in his eye.

Since it had been a while since he'd had sex, it didn't take long for him to explode and without notice. I was not ready for that part.

'*Yuck*', I thought, '*what the heck is this?*' I gagged really bad, but he was calm about it. He just collapsed back on the bed and laid there while I ran to the bathroom to spit and rinse out my mouth.

When I came out, he was laying on the bed, staring at me,

"You sure you've never done that before?"

"Yes Tre," I said. "I'm sure. I just learn fast and I'm open to new things, plus I'm really comfortable with you."

"I see," he said.

But it almost seemed like he was mad that I was good at it and it was my first time. I think I gotta say something to make him feel better. I leaned over and kissed him, "You're a great teacher."

He smiled and seemed to feel a little better. I gotta admit that after this experience, I really wanted to know what sex was like with him. I think he was thinking the same thing. We get up and shower, get dressed and decide to grab a bite to eat and catch a movie. We go to Millers to eat lunch and then we hit the mall. I'm going to have to ask how much insurance money he's got because he likes the stores like Lord and Taylor, Neiman Marcus, Macy's the Prada Shop and the list goes on. And here it is, I'm over here looking for bargains!!! He offers to buy me all kinds of stuff and I declined, but he buys a couple of things anyways. After shopping, we decided to go and rent some movies, get take out, and go back to his place and chill. We rented two of my favorite movies that he'd never seen because he said they were Chic Flicks. We watch Love and Basketball, eat Japanese and chill. Then we decided to take a break after it went off to take our showers and get more comfortable then we watch Love Jones. After the movie, he asked me if I would like to decorate his apartment for him, picking out the living and dining room set.

"Sure," I said. "Sounds like fun to me."

"Okay, then we can do that tomorrow."

We go into the bedroom and I noticed that now I guess we sleep together, because there was no more of him sleeping in the other room.

"Nia, I want to make love to you so bad right now that I can hardly see straight."

"I think I'm ready," I tell him. "But please take your time with me."

He sat up. "Before we do this, you have to understand that because it's your first time, it's going to hurt and you may bleed."

"What?" I asked. "How do you know that "

"I told you," he said. "I had sex with a virgin my first time."

This wasn't a turn on conversation for me and now I was scared. He pulls me close to him then looks at me, "I assume you are not on the pill."

"No," I tell him.

"I've been tested in case you were wondering, although I've only slept with one person. You can't trust anybody these days," as he reaches to grab a condom from the nightstand.

"Thank you for being that responsible." He turned on a slow jam CD that he made, and we danced for a while. He pulled my gown up and over my head. He picks me up, carries me over to the bed, and lays me down gently. The lights went off and I felt him start to kiss me from my neck down to my toes.

Wow, here comes that feeling again! I must have been ready this time cause it didn't take long before I was exploding. He slid himself on top of me and pushed my legs up and opened. I felt him trying to slide inside of me and it felt like someone was prying me open.

He slowed down and asked if I were okay, since he could hear my breathing getting faster, and if I wanted him to stop, in which I didn't want him to.

Once he was inside of me, it felt like I had been pried apart. But it was strange, painful, and pleasurable at the same time. He really took his time with me. Didn't move to fast or too hard, and didn't expect too much from me. It was an experience like nothing else I had ever had.

Once he reached his climax, he stayed there for a while and then he eased his way out of me and rolled over, putting his arms around me. I just laid there I was in so much pain, but emotionally I felt really good and really connected to him.

"Nia, I love you and thank you because you just gave me a very big part of yourself. I really enjoyed you," he whispered in my ear.

After getting up and going into the bathroom, I can hear the bath water running. He comes back into the room, picks me up and places me in the tub. Thank goodness for that because I swear I wasn't able to walk.

The water felt so good. He sat on the side of the tub while I soaked and we talked for about thirty minutes.

The next day we got up and went shopping for furniture. I stuck with the black theme and chose black leather furniture, a table with silver chrome bottoms, and a silver and black dining room table with a black bakers rack. I also brought red and purple pillows and vases. He loved what I had picked out and according to the sales man it should all be delivered by early next week.

Once we were done shopping, we went back to his house and I started packing up my things. I remind him that I can't spend every weekend with him because I had to work and had to get someone to cover for me this weekend, or I wouldn't have been able to come.

"Nia," he said smiling, "you don't have to work if you don't want to. You are in school on a scholarship, your car is paid for, and if you need spending money or whatever you need, I can give it to you."

I sat down next to him and had to ask, "Tre, I don't mean to pry, but how much money do you have?"

He laughs and said, "It's a lot."

"Okay, how much is a lot?"

"Enough that I could buy a house and cars if I wanted to, but I don't want to buy a house until I'm married, I want my wife to pick it out."

I tell him "this is unusual, why you have so much insurance money?"

He takes a deep breath and begins to explain that his mom was very responsible, and had a policy on herself for five hundred thousand dollars.

"I think she did it because she wanted to make sure if anything happened to her, that I would be fine because she knew there would be no one else to take care of me. Well the boyfriend that killed her was a police officer, so the social worker I had sued the state on my behalf because number one, he shot her with his service gun and two, because of the trauma it caused me, we won. So they set up a trust that matched the insurance policy, and in total and after taxes, I got about nine hundred thousand. I got half at eighteen and I'll get the other half after I turn twenty one, and graduate from school. I got to keep it all cause I don't pay any tuition since I'm in school on scholarship."

I was speechless, and he could tell.

"NO ONE ELSE knows this, so please…"

"I won't say anything," I told him.

He gets up and gets his check book. He writes me a check for five thousand dollars and said, "This should get you through this semester and you can concentrate on your classes and dance, and you won't have to work."

I don't know if taking the money was a good idea, but I sure took it. I thought, *'Shoot, I gave him my virginity, five thousand dollars was nothing.'*

I kissed him goodbye and reminded him that our first game was this Friday. We agreed that he'd come to the game and meet me at my car after it's over and we'd drive back to his place. So I guess this means, I'll be spending just about all my weekends at Tre's place.

I drive back to school, stop at Frankie's, and quit.

When I arrived back to my room, Natalie was up watching TV.

"Hey Nat."

"Hi Nia," she said. "You stayed the entire weekend huh?"

"Don't start with me," I tell her and she giggles.

"You knew I would say something."

"Okay Nat, go ahead."

She looks at me, and said, "you had sex with him!"

"Dang Nat, no beating around the bush huh?"

"Nope," she said. I just looked at her.

"Well," she said, "I knew you would. I knew you had feelings for him. This is our second year living together and it's the first time you have ever spent the weekend with a guy outside of Wayne. Just keep praying Nia about the men in your life, it's important that GOD be the one who puts them there."

"I hear you Nat, I hear you."

I grew up in church, so I know prayer is important. I need to get back to that place and I'm sure I will.

I hit the books because I haven't studied all weekend and I have a scholarship to keep. I have to admit it sure feels good to know that I don't have to work anymore. I wonder what my mom would say. I don't know if I should tell her.

I sat down to study for a while, and then I called Wayne. The phone rung and I got no answer so I left him a message… *'I gotta talk to you.'*

In about fifteen minutes, there was a knock at my door and it's Wayne.

"Hey boo," I said

He picks me up and kisses me on the cheek, "I have missed you girl," he said.

"We got a lot to talk about."

"Yes y'all do," Nat said from her corner of the room.

He walks over and hugs her, "hey Nat" he said. "Good to see you."

"You too," she said.

I know Natalie liked Wayne and I think he liked her too, but he knows she ain't giving up the cookies, so he's just nice to her.

Wayne asked me to take a ride with him so we can talk. So we drove down by the lake and parked.

"I think at the end of this year, I'm going pro," he told me.

I smiled, "I figured that."

I have to admit I felt sad, cause I feel like it's the end of an era. If he goes pro, I won't see him every day and there will be so many girls that I'd be on the back burner.

As if he could read my mind he leans over and lies on my shoulder, "Nia, we have been best friends forever, and money won't change that. I'm going to take care of you and I'll still keep in touch. We'll always be friends."

I hear him, but I just don't know.

"You didn't call me this weekend. This is the first time you ever spent the weekend with a guy and you didn't call me the whole time. I mean, I never even met this guy and I know you didn't just play cards the whole weekend."

"You are right. A lot went on this weekend and yes I did sleep with him."

Wayne got quiet. He didn't say anything at all and it was as if I told him someone had died. He sat up and looked at me and the look in his eyes said something I didn't want to deal with. He'd never looked at me like that before, or maybe I'd never noticed that he did. He asked if I was okay.

"I'm great, don't worry about me. Tre is a good guy. You'll meet him after the football game on Friday." We talk for a while longer and then he drove me back to my room.

Her Game…

It's the first game of the season for the Thurman football team so everyone is hyped. The team played well but we are down by three points at the half, so the band had the chore of lifting everyone's spirits.

The band played several of the newest dance songs and the Thurman dancers were known for turning up the heat and always had a flock of male admirers hanging around after a game or performance.

When the game ended, I hugged my fellow dancers, gave out some hugs and hellos to other band members and the football team. I looked for Tre but didn't see him, so I assumed he would be waiting next to my car.

As I'm walking, I see Wayne and some other basketball team members heading in my direction. He started running towards me and almost tackles me.

"You look good girl, Wow."

"Quit playing boy," I said. "You've seen me in this gear before."

"Yeah," he said, "But you grew in some places over the summer."

"Whatever," I said.

So I hug the other players and they all follow me over to my car.

As I approach my car, I see the Escalade pulling up next to where I'm parked. Tre parks and gets out, but he has a look on his face that I haven't seen before. I hug him and he hugs me back, but not like usual. I introduced him to Wayne and they do the get acquainted chat for a few and I hear Wayne say, "Tre it's nice to meet you man. Please take good care of Nia. She's my best friend man, she is very special."

Tre just listens and nods his head.

When we decided to leave, he asked if I wanted to just get in his truck and he would bring me back to school. So, I yelled for Wayne to come back and take my car back to my dorm and park it since I was going to be riding with Tre.

"Okay," Wayne agreed.

There was silence for the first fifteen minutes of our ride and finally I look over at Tre.

"Baby, I missed you. Is there something wrong?"

He just stops the truck in the middle of the street and loudly asks me what the hell did I have on.

I'm very quiet cause I'm thinking to myself, *'Was he at the game? Didn't he know I was a dancer? He's in the dag on band so he knows what dancers wear.'*

After he starts driving again, I politely said, "I still have on my uniform did you come to the game?"

"Yeah," he responded without even looking at me. "I saw the game and I saw you shake your butt like there was nothing to it. Then I saw all those guys hollering at you."

He just shook his head and kept driving. My uniform was pretty tiny and it was a strapless body suit that tied in the back with lots of sparkles and glitter and dancing shoes. But, I choose to stay quiet and not respond.

After we pulled into his complex, he got out of the truck, snatched my bag out the back and walks around to open my car door and slams it behind me. By this time I'm feeling very hurt, cause I don't understand what I did wrong.

We get to his apartment and he opens the door. Wow, the furniture I picked out arrived and he did a good job arranging it. It looked really nice in here and the colors were great.

I went into his room and took off my uniform and put on one of his T shirts. I see him flipping through menus, looking for something to order to eat. I said nothing and just sat on the couch. Finally I turned towards him, "why are you being so mean to me? You haven't seen me all week and I didn't do anything to you."

"Nia," he said. "I can't handle it. I saw you shaking all over that field and it turned me on so much that it made me angry. And if it turned me on, what were all those other guys thinking? And then if that wasn't bad enough, I saw all those guys trying to talk to you when you were leaving. If I had a gun, I could have shot all of them! Then I see you hug the entire basketball team…man I'm trying to be okay with this, but I don't like it. I don't like anybody trying to talk to my girl. It brings out the worst in me."

I knew it was too good to be true. This man is crazy.

"Are you crazy? What do you want me to do? I have to dance, that's what pays for school."

"I can pay your tuition," he said.

"No Tre, I won't do that. You have to accept what I do. I accept you being in the band with all your gyrating and you always got some girl in your face. I trust you and you have to trust me."

He doesn't say anything. He just picks up the phone and orders food. I go in and get myself cleaned up and more comfortable.

The food arrived and we sat at the table and ate. After about an hour, he finally calmed himself enough to apologize and then to ask me how Wayne took my car back if I didn't give him the key. I was waiting for that. I knew he had paid attention to that.

"He has a key," I told him.

"I suppose you have a key to his car too?" he asks.

"As a matter of fact I do."

There was silence again, "Wayne makes me uncomfortable Nia, I know he's in love with you."

"No he is not! You are being crazy Trevon, you just met him."

"Nia, I know what a man looks like when he is in love with a woman and he loves you very differently from what you think. I know you told him we had sex…what did he say?"

"He didn't say anything," I responded, but really I was thinking about the look of hurt and sadness that was on his face when I told him. I wasn't even going there.

"Trevon, you need to stop and if you don't change your attitude, I'm leaving."

He jumped up quickly and yelled out, "YOU ARE NOT LEAVING NIA! Don't play with me like that. And what's with the Trevon?" He asked. "You always call me Tre."

I looked at him as if he'd just lost his mind, "You're about to be called something else if you don't get it together."

"You know what? Forget Wayne, forget those dudes at the game, forget all this arguing…forget everything! Let me show you something."

He grabbed me by the hand and pulled me into the bedroom. He throws a blanket on the floor, takes off all his clothes, and my t-shirt. I wasn't wearing any underwear because I was hoping for a replay of the week before. He lays me on the floor on my stomach and proceeds to lick me from the base of my neck, all the way down to my ankles. My whole body is tingling and then I felt him lift my lower body with one hand and enter me. There was a little pain, but a lot more pleasure than last time. We started on the floor and ended up in the bed. This man was like the energizer bunny. He rolled over next to me and pulls me in closely, looks

61

in my eyes and tells me to understand that I belong to him and he just can't imagine me with anyone else.

At this moment, all I wanted to do was sleep from the exhaustion of his energy and then he tells me that he has a present for me. He gives me a box and it's a key to his apartment with a key chain that said *'Anytime'*.

"Wow Tre!" I said with excitement. "What does this mean?"

"It means I want you to come here any day at any time you want to. You don't have to be invited and you don't have to call first. I want to see you all the time, so when you can or whenever you want to, you can just come. Come and go as you please."

I think about all the events of the night, and then sum it up that I just have a man that really loves me. He's a little possessive, but he loves me. At least I hope that's all there is to it.

For the rest of the weekend, we spend a lot of time in and out of the bed and talking. On the drive back, Tre looked over at me and said, "Princess, I think you should get on the pill or patch or some form of birth control." So, I agreed and decide that I'll make an appointment on Monday.

For the next month, Tre and I both got very busy with classes, performing, and traveling with the band. We continued to talk every night, sent lots of text messages and emails. On several occasions, I got deliveries of flowers and teddy bears. We only got to see each other about twice after the last game in September, when I spent the night at his house. I'm really missing him and he said he feels like he's going to pass out if he doesn't see me soon. Veterans Day was coming and the band he played for had a gig on Friday night, so we agreed that we'll meet up that Saturday. I think I'll surprise him by going over on Friday...now that I had a key.

The Surprise...

On Friday, I run to the mall to find a gift for Tre. I just wanted to get him something to say I appreciate him. I picked up a watch and ran over to *All Things Remembered* and had them to engrave the words *Anytime* on it. I thought that was cute, since that's what he put on my key chain. I go back home to pack my things and then I take Natalie to the airport so she can go home for the weekend. I decided to stop by the grocery store and pick up a few items so I could make dinner for him. I thought that will be a nice surprise. I grabbed some candles while I was there as well. He said he should be home by midnight so I'd have everything ready, including myself by the time he got home.

When I arrived, I can see a light on from the balcony. It was strange because he never leaves the lights on. Although he has money, he was very frugal about bills, and doesn't believe in any kind of waste. I didn't think anything of it so I grabbed my things, balancing bags on my shoulders, wrists, and in my hands and headed into the building.

I can hear music as I approached the door. Now I'm really nervous, because I didn't need any surprises right now. I really have fallen in love with this man, and anything other than a radio left on by mistake would devastate me.

I turn the key and walk into the apartment. The music is kind of loud, but I don't see anyone. I drop my things at the door and walk to the bedroom and there is no one there. As I turn to come back into the living room, I see Nick emerge from the second bedroom, where the weight equipment and futon were. I jumped because I'm wondering why he was here. He looked at me all crazy, and he's wearing shorts, no shirt and is sweating.

"Umm…hello Nick," I said. "What are you doing here?"

He stutters and said, "sup girl umm…I was here earlier waiting for the cable people. The cable was messing up and Tre had things to do so he asked me to wait for them."

Now I'm thinking to myself, *'that had to be way earlier in the day so why you still here?'* But instead, I just looked at him and said nothing.

"We were just working out," he stated. Then a few minutes later, this football player looking guy emerges from the room wearing some shorts and a tank top.

"Nia this is Jeff," He introduced us.

This was really weird and I was just silent. I didn't know him like that and I wasn't comfortable in this house with these two guys.

Jeff walks over towards me and shakes my hand, "Nice to meet you" he said.

I left them standing there and start putting my things away and then I go to the kitchen. They go back to the room together and get dressed. About ten minutes later, they decided to go out to the club.

"You and Tre should come to Club Z when he gets home," Nick said.

"Okay…" I responded and kept on preparing food for Tre's dinner.

Nick walked over and said, "You sweet Nia. Tre is lucky to have you. I know he really likes you cause he don't be bothering with no one else. You and I are all he has. He would be devastated if he found out anything hurtful about either of us."

I just kept chopping lettuce for the salad and though… *'What the heck is he talking about?'*

He walks really close to me and tightly grabs my arm and said, "I'm glad you and I are here for him."

I just looked at his hand on my arm and kept chopping. He looked me up and down, "you almost sexier than Stacy," which was his girlfriend. He then leans over, kisses me on the ear, and they both leave.

What a strange experience that was. I'm not sure what he meant, but I didn't like how it felt.

I prepared shrimp Alfredo, French bread, and a salad for our dinner. I set the table, put out some candles, set his gift on the table, and go into take a shower. I decided to take my hair down just the way he liked it. I found this cute little two piece see through night set from my favorite store. I sprayed on some Very Sexy, put on a little make up, not too much, and retreated to the couch until he came in. If I'm right, he'll be here in about ten minutes.

I flip channels and then decide to go fill the CD player with my favorite slow jam CD's. I turned the music on and picked up my cell phone to see where Tre was. He answered and said, "Hey Princess, it's good to hear your voice."

"Where are you?" I said.

He tells me he is outside of his apartment, getting ready to come inside.

"Okay," I tell him. "Call me once you get settled."

"Okay," he responds. I'm going to find something to eat. I didn't eat at the club and I'm starving."

"I guess he didn't notice my car, but that was fine.

He opened the door to slow music, candles, and the scent of food. He drops his bag down, slowly closes and locks the door and stands there for a moment, kind of in shock.

"Princess," I hear him call as he walks toward the bedroom.

"I'm in the kitchen." He walks in the kitchen with that smile that always melts my heart, and just stares for a moment.

"WOW girl…you are a sight for me. You look so good. I feel like I haven't laid eyes on you in months."

He lifts me onto the counter and kisses me like he's been waiting to do this for a long time. I hope we make it to dinner.

"Thank you so much baby," he said. "This is the bomb."

"Good," I tell him. "Have a seat."

He sits down and I serve dinner. He eats half the plate and said, "I can't eat no more."

He jumps up from the table, grabs me by arm and takes me to the shower, turns the water on, takes off all his clothes, and pulls me in with my lingerie on, "Tre, I'm dressed."

"I know," he said, "I wanted to see that body wet through that outfit."

He slides off my clothes, and before I could figure out what was going on, my legs were around his waist and my breasts were in his mouth.

We proceeded to bump in the shower, grind on the bathroom floor, on the dresser in the room, on the floor by the bed and finally ended up on a blanket in the living room by the stereo. We dozed off for about thirty minutes and were awaken by a siren outside. I decide to get up and go take a shower because there was sweat and a whole lot of other stuff all over the place.

"Girl, you sure caught the hang of doing the nasty real fast. If I didn't know any better…" he said jokingly.

"Whatever!" I responded, "You inspire me."

"Tre, when I got here, Nick was here."

"He was?" he asks with a frown on his face.

"Yes. and he was with a guy named Jeff."

"They were in here with you?"

"Yes." I tell him.

He sits up looking very concerned, "What happened and why was he still here? I didn't know Jeff was with him."

"Well, I'm not really sure. They said they were working out, but it was weird and they had music playing," I continued explaining the entire situation. Finally I get to the part about him grabbing my arm and kissing my ear, and all of a sudden I see real anger on his face. I mean fury. He jumps out the bed, grabs the phone and calls Nick, but there was no answer and it was now four in the morning.

"Baby lay down," I told him, "talk to him tomorrow."

"I'm not sleepy," he said. "Baby are you hurt? He put his lips on you and I'm going to find him."

Why did I tell him that part? "It's okay Tre, I'm not hurt so calm down."

This man was furious. He almost looks like he is either going to cry or explode.

Trying to calm him down, "I have a surprise for you."

He doesn't even acknowledge my statement at all. So since he didn't notice it during dinner, I got up to get the watch and bring it back to him.

He looks at me and opens it.

"Read the back," I tell him.

Finally, I get a half smile. "Thanks," he said. "This is really nice. No one has ever really given me a gift just for no reason."

"I have a reason," I tell him… "I love you."

That at least gets him to lie down in the bed with me before asking not even five minutes later, "What were they doing working out at my house? I don't trust that guy Jeff. He seems suspect to me and I told Nick don't have him in my house."

"Well, I don't know." I said. "But they seem awfully close for two brothers."

"Nick ain't gay if that's what you thinking."

"I don't know, all these brothers on the down low now days, you can't be so sure."

"He's not gay…I don't know what they are up to, but that ain't it."

"Well, why did he act so funny about me telling you? It was almost threatening…like you would be mad if you knew what they were doing."

Tre sat up in the bed, "Nia, he was probably saying that because when my insurance money came in I kind of helped him out a little. Well you know, I did it because I know what his life has been like. I mean we grew up in the same home, but now it's like he expects me to support him."

"And you do it?" I ask.

"Nah, not really…but if he gets in a bind, I help him out. So I guess he don't want you saying anything that would mess that up. But now I'm pissed and concerned about what they were doing in my house, and why he put his hands and lips on you. You best believe I'm going to find out though."

"Lay down and get some rest baby. We can talk to him in the morning, I said."

"Not we," he responds, "I will."

We ended the night by turning the television on and falling asleep watching movies.

Confronting Nick…

When I got up around nine in the morning, Tre was gone. I got up and went to the kitchen to get some juice, picked up the phone and called Stacy.

"Hi Stacey…this is Nia."

"Hey Nia, sup girl? Why you calling so early on a Saturday? You trying to go shopping?"

"Maybe later," I tell her, "but right now I need to tell you something that you may be mad about."

"Okay. Go ahead," she sounded concerned.

"Well, I surprised Tre last night and came over without him knowing, but when I got here Nick was here with a guy named Jeff."

She takes a deep breath, "What! He told me he wasn't hanging with that guy any more. Nia, did they do anything to you?"

"Nah just made me uncomfortable."

"Stay away from him. Nick is about to mess things up. That guy Jeff is trouble. He's a dealer."

"He selling drugs?"

"Yep," she said. "And who knows what else he does. He is not in school and he met him at a club when school started. I think Nick bought some weed or something from him and then they hooked up. I know Tre don't like him."

"Well Stace..." I hesitated for a moment and decided not to tell her about the kiss on the ear thing yet. "Well Stace...Tre is pretty pissed. So I don't know what things will be like from here on out."

"Well Nick didn't come by last night, so I'm about to call and see where he is and I'll call you later."

We hung up and I headed straight for the room they were in. I look around but nothing was out of place. Maybe they were working out. I looked in the closet because Tre said Nick leaves his things there sometimes, so I continued to look around and still saw nothing.

Then I notice a black gym bag under the futon. I pulled it out and open it and it was filled with weed, pills, and rocks. So I guess they were in here separating their stuff. Tre is going to be pissed and I'm getting a towel and wiping my prints off of this bag.

I called Tre on his cell phone, "Nia?" he answers, "I'm on my way back there. Nick is on his way there too. He said he left something."

"He sure did."

"You know what it is?"

"Just get back here before he arrives, please."

I hang up, go in the room, and put on the largest sweat pants and T-shirt I could find. Tre comes in the door, kisses me on the forehead, and sits on the couch still looking pissed after I told him what I found in the black bag under the futon.

About two minutes later, there is a knock at the door. He jumps up, opens the door, and before Nick could open his mouth, he puts his hands around his neck, pulls him in the door, and pushes him against the wall. Nick is yelling and I can see a real fight is about to start.

"Stop baby," I beg. "Don't hurt him and keep the noise down! The neighbors gonna call the police"

"Hold up Tre man let go. I can explain."

He lets him go for a moment and Nick starts to talk real fast.

"I can explain everything. First, I'm sorry Nia for touching you and Tre sorry for Jeff being here. Nia I know you called Stace."

Tre looks at me. I'm sure I'll hear about that after Nick leaves.

"Tre sit down man, let me tell you wassup. I was a little buzzed last night on X."

"What?" Tre asks, "Man, you crazy? You in my house doing drugs? Dude you know I don't play that…for real Nick."

"Well…I wanted to make some extra money, so I've been doing some things for Jeff and the money is good. For real Tre, man you can get in on this."

"No thanks," Tre responds. "Man you gotta go and don't come back no more."

"What?" Nick said, "You trading me in for this trick you dating?" To my surprise Tre stays calm.

"Nick you my boy, but you pushing it. We've been like brothers most our lives so I'm a let you live, but you got ten minutes to get your stuff out of here and go."

"Man I told you I'm not living like a punk."

"You want money you get a job," Tre said.

"You didn't work for your money!" Nick yells.

"Okay dude, and you worked for all you got? Whatever man, just go."

Nick goes in the room gets his stuff and his black gym bag and leaves.

That was about to be deadly I thought, then I feel bad because I feel like he was kind of choosing me over his best friend and that was never my intention. He laid on the couch for a few minutes, then goes into the den and starts to play music. He called me in and told me that he met another producer that told him he liked his stuff, so he may start working for him soon.

"Cool," I was excited for him.

We talk a little more and I go to the computer and decide to do some shopping on the net and sort out my thoughts about all that just went on.

FIRST HOLIDAY TOGETHER

As I look out my front door and see the snow begin to fall and all the decorations that are going up all over the place – I think about how much joy the holiday season brings. This time of year always brings up so many different emotions. It can make you happy, sad, joyous, and lonely all at the same time, but with all these emotions come the reality that emotions are a large part of who we are and they are important. Sometimes they show us things we didn't even know were there, I look at all this and I remember, our first holiday together…

Tre informs me that he got a call that Ms. Agnes wasn't doing so well so he would be going there for Thanksgiving break. Well, my mom informed me that she has been dating a "nice man" and he'll be at our house for Thanksgiving dinner, so I have to be home. So this meant that we wouldn't see each other for Thanksgiving.

Tre goes home to Georgia and I go back to Maryland for a very interesting Thanksgiving dinner with my mom and her new friend. Dinner was very weird to me and there was no one there but the three of us, which was not my kind of holiday. I wanted to see aunts, uncles, and cousins. Dinner was quiet and brief. We prayed, ate, and then my mom and her new man decided they were going to the movies, which was something my mom never did. I didn't want to tag along, so I just went into my room and watched cable and prayed that Tre would call soon.

It was around eleven that night when Tre called and told me that Ms. Agnes was not doing so well. She was on all kinds of medication and goes to dialysis twice a week, but she still managed to cook dinner for all of them. He said he missed me and was sorry to hear that I was alone. As he was talking, I could hear all kinds of folks in the back ground and there sounded like there was almost a party going on. I know I heard Nicks voice too.

"Tre, is Nick with you?"

He pauses and then said "yeah, I brought him."

"Oh, okay"

"Look Nia," he said. "I don't want him in the house cause you are there and he understands that, but he is the closest thing to family I got so..."

"Alright Tre, it's your business, just be careful."

I didn't care about Nick right now. I heard a ton of women in the background as well. I wanted to know all about that, but I had no questions. Thanksgiving was nice, and it goes by slow and I was ready to get back to school and to see Tre.

When I returned to school, I had so many engagements and papers that were due that I didn't have time to just take the thirty minute drive to see Tre. Instead, we just did a lot of talking on the phone and emails. He was also busy with school, the band, playing at the club on Fridays, and working with this new producer he met. He was really serious about this music stuff.

My mom informed me that she and her new man were going on a cruise for Christmas and that I could come along if I wanted. I wasn't interested because I really didn't like him too much, so I declined her invitation. I planned to spend Christmas with Tre instead. I'm sure he'd like that.

Christmas...

When school breaks for the winter holiday, I'm thrilled. I haven't seen Tre since before Thanksgiving. I have been shopping and am really excited and nervous. I have never spent a holiday with a man before, so this should be fun. Plus I get to make dinner for us. He'll get to see my true skills in the kitchen. I give him a call after my car was all loaded and let him know that I was on my way. Tre has already informed me that Stacey went home and that she and Nick had a fight, so he'll be coming over for dinner and maybe one or two other people. That was cool, I guess. I kind of wanted to spend it with him, but I have to understand.

Over the next couple of days Tre and I spend a lot of time shopping, decorating, and getting ready for our first Christmas Dinner. I must say it was a lot of fun. According to Natalie, I was just playing house, but it felt good. I was really letting go with this man. I feel like he just swept me off my feet and I was enjoying this. We'd talked about a lot of things, but he never said much about his time at Ms. Agnes house for Thanksgiving.

On Christmas Eve, I started cooking and Tre seemed so impressed, but so sweet. He came in the kitchen to help and reminisced about helping his mom cook holiday meals when he was younger. I have to admit, I wanted to impress him so I decided to really cook! I made turkey, stuffing, fried chicken, ribs, potatoes salad, greens, mac and cheese, sweet potatoes, rolls, pound cake, sweet potato pie, cherry cobbler, and I baked cookies to just have in the house. He was very impressed. He could not wait for his friends to come over for dinner.

What a Christmas Dinner...

Christmas Day started off really nice. I cooked most of the food the night before and when I got up, Tre was up making breakfast for us and then I started to finish the rest of the meal. He calls me over to the tree, but we had decided to wait until everyone got here to open gifts. But he said he had a couple of things he wanted to give me before everyone arrived. I went over to the tree and sat down. He pulled out a rectangular box, and I opened it up. It was a check card and a check book, with both of our names on it.

"A joint checking account?" I was speechless!

"Tre, what is going on?"

"Nia, I put some money in it because I don't want you to worry about anything. What I have is yours. I want to discuss something else with you after dinner tonight, but that's later."

I couldn't wait for this conversation. I was about ready to cry. He leaned over and gave me another little box. I opened it up and it was a platinum locket with the words *Lovers and Friends* on the front and a picture of us on the inside. It was beautiful. I think this was the best Christmas for me ever. My little gifts couldn't even compare.

"I have more, but we can open them when everyone else arrives."

"I do have one special gift for you that I want you to open. It's not much, but I got it for you."

I pull out a medium square box from under the tree and he opens it. It's a brown leather book with the inscription - *Music from my heart.*

"It's for you to write the words to your songs in," I told him. He was amazed. You would have thought I'd given him a million dollars.

"Baby, thank you so much!"

"It's just a book Tre."

"No," he said. "To me, it said you have faith in my dreams and that means the world to me, thank you so much."

He grabbed me by the back of my neck and kissed me and slowly laid me on the floor by the tree.

He took a bow and placed it on my forehead, "Nia you are the best gift I could ever have and I'm so grateful for you."

We got our Christmas morning freak on for about forty five minutes. We couldn't spend all day with it because we had folks coming over. The phone rung and Tre answered. It was Nick saying he was on his way and he was bringing a friend with him. I wondered who that friend could be and why he coming so early.

So, I jumped up to get showered and dressed. As I'm in the room picking out clothes to wear, Tre comes in and said wear this…it was a beige off the shoulder shirt that slanted at the bottom. It was really cute and had slacks that matched.

"Why are you picking out my clothes?"

"I know you Nia. You're sexy and you know it, but I want a good day and I need you cute, but covered up."

I just rolled my eyes, but I put it on because it made him happy. I curled my hair and pulled it up in a curly ponytail and put on my locket.

Once I get dressed and looked in the mirror, I thought to myself… *'I'm sexy in whatever I put on'* and I walked into the kitchen. Tre looked at me from the couch and just shook his head.

"Dang girl, I'm gonna have to put you in a sheet." He said jokingly.

I continued cooking while Tre put on some Christmas music. The Temptations and the Jackson 5, of course, are two of his favorites. He also pulled out the PS3 and the X Box 360. He sat back on the couch and began writing in the book I gave him. He hasn't opened anything else yet.

I walked over to the couch. When he saw me coming, he put the book down so I can sit on his lap.

"Who else is coming to dinner?"

"Lance, from the Jazz band I play with. He couldn't afford to go home so I told him to come here."

"Did you buy him a gift?"

"Yeah," he said and looks at me like I was crazy. "And Peaches."

"Peaches? Who is Peaches?"

"She grew up in the home with us and goes to one of those private colleges around here.   She couldn't go home either so I told her to come over also."

"When do you talk to her?" I asked.

"I speak to her often Nia, we grew up together."

"I was just asking. I've never heard you speak of her before."

Inside I feel kind of upset, but I'm not planning to let anything ruin this Christmas so I hop up and go back to cooking.

My cell phone rings and its Wayne.

"Hi Boo!" I said loud and excited. That of course caught Tre's attention, but he doesn't say anything.

"Merry Christmas...I miss you," I tell him. "This is the first Christmas I won't get to see you."

"I know. I miss you too, but you got a new man now. I guess you don't need me anymore," he said laughing.

81

Wayne was at home which was two doors down from where I lived.

"Your mom ain't here."

"I know," I tell him. "She is on a cruise."

He laughs, "Umm Ms. Renaye doing her thing huh?"

"Yep," I tell him. "All is well."

"I heard that! You don't have to worry, no one can replace you."

"Did you get me a gift?" I ask.

"Yes," he said. "I sure did. All you have to do is check your email."

"Really?"

"Yes, but do me a favor though and check it later when you are alone."

"Sure, did you open the gift I sent you?"

"Yes," he said with a lot of love in his voice. "I got it and I really like it."

I got him a watch to and the inscription said *"Friends for Life"* with a little heart and my name.

"Good, I'm glad you like it. So what did Lisa get you?" I ask him.

Lisa is Wayne's girlfriend. They have been together since high school and despite the fact that he does dirt on the side, he is crazy about her and wouldn't trade her for anything or anyone. He said he's going to marry her. For a long time, she didn't like me. But after about the second year of them dating and me not going anywhere and his mom telling her to leave me alone, she somehow fell in love with me. Now she is almost as good of a friend as Wayne is, or at least she pretends to be. I think she would rather keep me close so she can see what I was doing. Plus she knows at this point that Wayne and I will always be friends.

Anyway I can see Tre looking a little irritated that I've been on the phone for about twenty minutes. It's only because it's with Wayne though, so I decided to end our conversation, "well boo, I better go."

He asks to speak to Tre, so I hand Tre the phone. They talked for a few and then hung up. Tre walked over to me in the kitchen and sat on the counter, "Wayne loves you Nia."

"I know this," I tell him, "and Tre I love Wayne too."

"I know Princess, I understand. It's just hard because I know that he loves you. It only took me to see him look at you one time to know that he would kill for you, and I don't like it, but I respect it. Just keep it under control."

"What are you talking about?" I ask him. "We have been friends since we were eight and he's been dating Lisa since ninth grade, so he doesn't want me."

"Oh yes he does Nia! He would be crazy not to. He just chose to keep it safe and keep you as his best friend because this way in his mind there is always a chance."

"Okay," I said. I didn't want to argue so I decided to leave it alone.

There was a knock at the door and it was Peaches. Tre opened the door and she jumps on him, wraps her legs around him, and kisses him on the lips. Now there is steam coming off the top of my head cause I don't play this mess and he is over here smiling and hugging her back. I walk up next to them and she looks at me with a frown and hops down.

"Hi," I said. "I'm Nia."

"Oh hi," she said never really looking at me. Then Tre tells her I was his girlfriend the one he told her about a while ago.

"Really," she said. "She is short, not tall like your usual women and you still seeing her? I thought you were just excited about a girl you met. I didn't know it was really going to last this long. You met her at camp right?"

"Yep," he said and walked over to the couch and sat down. She hands me her coat and sits next to him on the couch. They talk and laughed while I continued to prepare our feast. I'd decided to make some finger food to set around while we waited for dinner. I pulled out the blender and some fruit to make smoothies as well. I really wanted to make a good impression on Tre and his friends. Though I have to admit, I didn't feel very welcomed by Miss Peaches.

So I hear her asking him, "Tre, this seems pretty serious. I mean you ain't never had none of your ho's cooking for you."

"Watch it Peaches," he tells her. "I ain't never had no ho's and you know that so don't start no stuff up in here. Respect Nia! She is important to me."

Peaches just looked at him and threw her hands up. Peaches was okay in the appearance department. She was of average height, about a size ten, wore braids, and had a really cute sense of style. I got the sense that there was more to Peaches and Tre than he had told me, and I will find out.

Another knock came at the door and this time, it was Nick with some girl named Tayvia, and a guy they called Boss. They all come in and we did introductions. A few minutes later, Lance arrived. I go into the kitchen and put trays of cookies, fruit, cheese and crackers out on the table. I also set out glasses of smoothies, which everyone seemed to have enjoyed. We continued to listen to Christmas music and talk until dinner was ready. We also decided not to open gifts until after dinner.

I set the table, proudly I must say, and everything turned out really well. Before we had dinner, Tre asked everyone to bow their heads so that we could have prayer. I've heard him say that he prayed, but I've never actually heard him do it. I hear Peaches and Nick say, "oh boy, here we go…Tre gonna pray."

"Just bow your head." he said sternly and opens his mouth and begins to pray.

Father GOD, in the name of Jesus, we thank you for this day on which your son was born. We thank you for giving us the

85

opportunity to celebrate his life in which he used to give us.
Father we thank you for everyone present and we give glory and
honor to your name. We ask that you bless each and everyone of
us and ask that you continue to lead and guide us on the path
that you have laid for us. Father we also ask that you bless this
food and the hands that prepared it. We thank you GOD for all
that we have been given. In the name of Jesus...We all say
Amen.

I thought to myself, *"Wow, he prayed! That was really awesome."*

I mean I pray, I just never talk to him about it. He knows I grew up in church, but I guess GOD is something we should talk about at some point. We never have up to this point. I feel very impressed.

Dinner is served and everyone seems to really enjoy it. Even Peaches has to tell me in her smart tone... "This is pretty good Nia. I guess you can do more than one thing."

I ignore her comment, but leaned over and told Tre, "It's the last time I'm ignoring her comments and you gonna explain some stuff when all these people leave."

He actually looked a little concerned about having to tell me about their "real" relationship. We all ate until we couldn't eat anymore. Then Nick jumps up and runs to the tree. He couldn't wait no longer to see what he got as if he were a little child. So we started handing out gifts to everyone. At the end of the evening, I racked up big time. Tre's friends seemed somewhat annoyed at all the stuff I got from him. But even Nick was nice to me and bought me gift certificate to a spa, which was nice but a surprise.

Anyway, we sat around, laughing, talking, playing games, watching movies, eating dessert, and just cutting up way into the evening. Around nine that night, Lance stated that he needed to run. Said he had company coming over. He was nice. He hugged me and thanked me for dinner, gathered his gifts, and left. Boss left too, so it was now just us…Nick, Tayvia and Peaches.

Nick goes to his car and comes back with an envelope and a bag. He pulled out some Hennessey and some other stuff and he and Peaches start drinking.

Around eleven thirty, both of their true colors were coming out and Nick starts talking about Thanksgiving,

"Hey Peaches you remember Thanksgiving? We had a ball didn't we?"

She just giggles, "Tre got to see what you was working with huh?" he said.

She was like, "yeah – he know he like it."

Then she looks at me and said, "Nia, you dance right? I bet you can do this…" she starts shaking and dancing and taking her shirt off.

Tre jumps up, "alright y'all calm down."

Tayvia and I are kind of looking like what is going on.

Tayvia gets up, "Nia, thanks for everything. This was really nice.
I think I should get Nick home. I guess I'll drop off Peaches too since she
been drinking."

She tells Nick and Peaches to come on and Tre starts gathering up
their stuff and putting it in bags as these two idiots continue to drink out
the bottle and giggle.

Nick turns towards me, "Nia, I brought you some pictures from
Thanksgiving. I thought you would want to see them."

I see Tre frown, but he still doesn't say anything. They all leave
and I start to clean up...

"Nah baby", Tre said, "you did enough. I'll get the kitchen. You
just relax."

Honestly, I'm not thinking about relaxing. I wanted to see those
pictures and talk about Ms. Peaches, but I go in and shower and put on my
night clothes instead.

When I come out, the kitchen was clean and the food was put
away. The music was turned off and the only light on are the ones on the
Christmas tree. Tre was sitting on the sofa waiting for me.

"So Mr. Trevon?" I asked. "Who the heck is Peaches for real?"

"She is really a girl I grew up with from the home."

"Why does she act like that?"

"She behaves that way because..." he hesitates and then gets up
and walks to the balcony door.

"Now I'm getting mad." I tell him since he doesn't finish his statement.

"Well Princess, we never had sex, but one night we were all partying and drinking and I had a little too much to drink. That's why I don't do it and well she sucked my…"

"Never mind," I said and I got up and walked away. I don't know where I was going but I felt sick. I just cooked for a woman who knows what my man looks like naked.

"Nia," he said. "Just understand we are all we got, so we stick together."

"Yeah Tre, but that's messed up. You had me cook for her and be nice to her and she wants to screw you and yet you always on me about Wayne? He aint never had any sexual contact with me. This is stupid. You wrong!"

"Nia," he said, "Calm down. That was a long time ago."

"You calm down," I tell him. "This is not right. When we talked about partners, you didn't mention her. Honesty, remember? We gotta be honest."

"But it's not like that."

"Tre get away from me because you sound stupid."

"Stupid? Nia, now you're over reacting."

"You sound stupid!" I said loudly, "and I'm pissed off and you need to leave me alone for a few minutes."

He goes into the bathroom to shower. I sit on the couch and open the envelope. As I look at the pictures, tears just automatically start to fall. I don't even know where they came from, but in the pictures were Nick and Tre. Then I see Peaches sitting on his lap. I see pictures of her lifting her shirt in front of them. I even see some pictures that look like she stripped for them. I guess that's why Nick said Tre got to see what she was working with.

I felt so hurt and I know I was being crazy, but this really hurts. I didn't know what to think. Was this cheating? Why did I feel like this? This was a new pain. Oh my GOD, I felt like throwing up. This was scary for me that I could feel like this because of a picture.

Tre came out the bathroom with just his boxers on and I was just sitting on the sofa with the pictures spread out and the tears running down my face, and honestly, the look on his face was as if he had seen a ghost.

"Princess, what's wrong? Why are you crying?"

He walked over and stoops next to me cause I wasn't saying anything. Then he looks at the picture…"Aw man," he just looks.

"Princess it's not what it looks like. Nick had TC took those pictures, and I don't know why, but I swear I didn't touch her.

Peaches always sitting on my lap and she's a stripper. That's what she does and because I never went to see her dance she decided to strip for all of us at Thanksgiving, after she had been drinking of course.

"Nia I swear I would never hurt you."

Still no words came from me. I couldn't talk. I thought he was perfect and now I find that he is not. This really hurt, but I couldn't say anything.

"Nia I wanted Christmas to be perfect for you. I'm sorry about this. Please forgive me for behaving that way at Thanksgiving. I should have never let her sit on my lap, but that's all it was. There is nothing between us. I love you so much and I was not going to mess this up. Tell me what you need me to do so you can believe me."

There were still no words from me. I got up and walked to the kitchen to get a napkin. He picked up the pictures and tears them up and throws them in the trash. He didn't know what to say.

"Maybe I should leave until I can get myself together", I told him.

"Nia, no! Come on, please don't do this. It's our first Christmas, please don't leave. I feel like if you leave you may not come back."

He actually looked scared, "NIA please, please come on. Let's talk about this. Nia, I don't know what to say or do. All I know is that I love you so much and I would never hurt you. You've got to believe me. Nia my heart can't take you walking out that door, say something to me please. It's not that bad, it's just pictures."

Finally, I look at him and say, "Don't keep secrets from me Tre. If you have been intimate with someone, tell me. No more surprises okay?"

"Okay," he responds, but kind of unsure like he expected me to do or say something else.

I look at him and say, "I love you so much, but I don't like how this feels."

I get up and go over to the computer. I figured I could use some cheering up, so I check my emails. I open Wayne's first email and it's his official notification that he has enlisted in the NBA Draft. I screamed, "Oh My GOD! He gonna do it – this is great."

Tre walks over to the computer and leans over my shoulder and reads the notice, "That's tight." he said, "but that's your gift?"

So I scroll down and it's a ticket and hotel reservation with a note that said "I can't do this without you."

Then he wrote a little note that said: "Merry Christmas Nia Boo... you've been my best friend my whole life and I can't imagine this moment without you. Please come and stand at my side when they draft me number one!"

Tre walks away after reading that. He should have read farther down that said "you can bring Tre if you want. I just NEED you there."

I leave it up because I know he's coming back, but right now I don't care that he's mad. Wayne has never hurt me. He of course walks back over to the computer and said "I guess we are going to LA in February for the draft?"

I said nothing and go and sit on the floor by the patio. Finally, Tre comes over and sits in front of me and said, "Princess, from the bottom of my heart, I'm sorry about the pictures and not telling you about Peaches. But honestly, I have not cheated. I have been faithful. I know those pictures don't look like it, but I need you to believe me and trust me."

I just shook my head.

"Remember I told you I wanted to talk to you about something else after everyone was gone?"

"Yes," I said.

He proceeds to tell me that he knows we've only been a couple since August, which was only four months, but like he said in the beginning when its right, its right!

"What I want to know is if you'll think about moving in with me. Even if it's not right now, maybe this summer? Just think about it. I'm willing to move closer to your school if that's what you want. I just want to come home to you."

"Tre, I love you and I want to but I don't know. I really need to think about this."

"Okay," he said. He pulls me up off the floor and we cuddled on the couch to watch Christmas movies.

As we watched movies, I thought about his question and it was sweet, but I don't know about living together just yet. I think I will talk to him about how I feel tomorrow.

The talk...

I woke up in the bed, but we fell asleep on the couch. I guess Tre carried me in the room. Once I was up, I found Tre sitting at the counter eating a full plate of left overs for breakfast. He's always up first. So, I walked over and started to eat out of his plate.

"Morning gorgeous," he said.

"Good morning."

We lounge around for most of the day eating left overs and watching movies. Finally, he turns to me and says, "Did you think about what I asked you?"

"Well yes." I tell him, "but I need to talk to you about it. See Tre, I don't think we are ready to live together yet cause as much as I feel I couldn't be with anyone else but you, I think that it's moving a little too fast. I don't want to just live with a man, I'd rather be married."

He looks at me, smiles, and said, "Okay, then marry me."

"What! Tre stop being silly I'm serious! I love you and I love being with you, but I don't want you to get content just living with me. I really want to live with the man that I marry. I really don't think just living together is right."

He smiles at me and said, "Princess you're going to be my wife when the time is right. I have let you into everything I have. What more can I do to show you that I really want to spend my life with you? And yes, I am sure about this after only four months, but if you want to wait… I'll wait for however long it takes and I'll move closer to your school if you want. I'll even transfer if it means I can be closer to you. I'm loving this Nia. I love having someone in my life. Loving having someone to give to that appreciates it. I'll wait for however long it takes for you to really believe me."

I just listened to him because right now, I was still thinking about the Peaches thing...

Well Christmas break was ending and it's about time for me to pack up my things. I'm going to drive home just for the weekend to see my mom since I didn't get to see her for Christmas. This way, we'll have a big dinner on Saturday and exchange gifts. I missed her and I couldn't wait to see her.

I packed up some of the stuff that Tre got me, but a lot of things I left there since it seemed that I'll probably be spending most weekends at his place anyway.

My trip home went well. My mom was great as usual, except her new man was there every day. She informed me that things with him were going well too and that she may be getting married. She then of course reminds me that sex before marriage was a sin and that I need to be careful. She also told me the she knew I was not a virgin anymore and I must say, I appreciate how she handled it. I thought she would have flipped, but instead she said she was praying for me and that she believed that GOD would take care of me and that in due time, I would be back on the right track. I just listened to her, despite how much fun I feel like I was having, I knew my mom is right. My weekend with my mom ended all too fast and I had to leave to head back to school and back to the books.

Tre and I seem to be getting along pretty well. I get ticked every now and then when I hear that he is still hanging tight with Nick, but no mention of Peaches lately so that's good. He informed me that he had to play at the Jazz club on Valentine's Day, but that I should come and he'd make sure I got the VIP treatment and then we can do something together afterwards.

Valentine's Day ...

I went to Tre's house for Valentine's Day. This time I brought him a new drum machine for his studio. I took it to the house around nine that night since he said he would be at the club by eight. I wrapped the machine in beautiful red paper along with a nice card. I couldn't think of anything else to buy him. I thought to myself that I'd have to be the rest of his gift.

I get dressed in red, which is what he asked for. I wore this really nice little red dress that had long sleeves, but was off the shoulders. The middle part was sheer and the bottom slanted from mid-thigh to above the knee. I put on a Tiffany choker, bracelet, and earrings that I got for Christmas. I wore my hair down cause Tre really liked it that way. I also wore some really cute multicolored pumps that tied around the ankle and up my leg, with a matching bag and headed out the door for the club.

When I arrived, the band was breaking and I didn't see Tre, but Nick and Stacy spotted me when I walked in, so they waved me over to our table. I should have known we'd be spending our evening with them. Stacy hugs me and compliments my outfit, "You look pretty too", I tell her. Nick stares at me like a hungry dog looking at a bone and finally said hello to me. He hugged me with his entire body and kisses me on the neck, not on the cheek. Stacy just looks at him and motions to me that he'd been drinking. I didn't even care. I didn't trust his nasty behind anyways. And, I didn't want any trouble tonight.

Finally, Tre comes over and I can feel him looking at me as he was approaching. He pulled me up from the table and kissed me like there was no one else around. I tell you this man knows how to get me.

We all sat and talked for a few minutes before Tre went back to play. I ordered myself a soda and some hors d'oeuvres and I really enjoyed the show. Nick and Stacy got up several times to dance and I got numerous offers from guys to dance, which I thought was weird cause they had to be here with someone. At one point, Stacy stated that she was tired and tells Nick to dance with me.

"That's okay," I told him, but he insists and forcefully pulls me up from my seat.

So I reluctantly head to the dance floor with him and the band starts to play an old song called '*Two Occasions*'. Nick pulled me really close to him, closer than I needed to be and he really pushes it by placing his hand in the small of my back, really close to my butt and we start to dance. This man is breathing me in and I can feel it. It's like he was really enjoying this and then it started.

He whispered in my ear, "I know why you with Tre. I see all the stuff he gives you, but you know me and him are a lot alike. You should let me give you something that you haven't gotten from him."

"Nick," I said. "Just dance don't start this with me."

Then he pulls me close enough to him to feel his erection and I was disgusted.

"What are you doing?" I frown and ask.

He looks right in my eyes and said, "I want to know why Tre fell in love with you so fast and why you getting all his money and everything. I want you to make me wanna give you my money too. I mean I understand, I would be blowing somebody mind too if I was getting paid."

I felt hurt and pissed cause this man basically called me a slut. "I have had enough."

I back away and go back to the table. I guess I was visibly shaken because Stacy asks me if I was okay, but before I could answer she makes excuses for Nicks behavior "Nia, he's been drinking and I will admit he thinks you are attractive so I guess the liquor brings it out."

"Doesn't that bother you?"

"Not really," she said. "I know he's going to look at other women, but you don't seem like the type to play his game."

"No I'm not and I don't even like games."

She sips her wine and keeps listening to the music. Nick finally comes back to the table and sits down. The club was having a special musical guest tonight, so finally Tre comes over to join us for the rest of the evening. He sits next to me and kind of glances at me and Nick. I guess he saw us dancing, then asked if I was okay.

"She's fine man," Nick answers. "Dag you treat her like china, she ain't gonna break."

Tre ignores him and asks again if I was alright. "I'm fine," I said.

We laughed, danced and talked for most of the night, and around two in the morning, Tre decided it was time to go home and I followed him.

Once we are back at home I head into the room and he yells, "don't change your clothes yet."

So I walk back out to the dining area and there is a little box on the table. He's in the kitchen and I ask "is this for me?"

"Yes open it," he said.

I pick the box up and say, "first go look in the den."

He walks over to the den and grins when he sees the large box. He opened it and said, "Thanks, how did you know I wanted a new drum machine? You must really listen when I'm talking about the things I want to do."

"Yep," I told him, so then I open the box.

WOW I don't know how he's going to keep this up, it's an anklet with the word Princess in Diamonds. I was like, "this is expensive."

He grins and said, "It could be, but I know a jeweler."

I don't want to know any more so I hug him. Then he walks me over to the living room, moves the coffee table out of the way and throws on some Destiny's Child – Cater to You and said, "here is what I wanted for Valentine's Day – a private dance – you dance for thousands of people all the time I want a private dance, but just dance don't take off the dress or the heels yet"

So I of course dance for him until he can't take no more. The next thing I know I was bent over the back of the sofa, once we've both exhaled and he collapses onto the floor. I step over him and head for the shower. In about two minutes he joins me, then he tells me just go lay on the bed. This man comes back with a can of whipped cream and some warm caramel. He sprays and pours it all over me and proceeds to lick it off and eat it like it was a meal. He seemed to enjoy it so much that I was out of control just by watching him – needless to say this night was a good night.

I leave that morning to head back to school, but this was the best Valentine's Day ever for me. It gets harder to leave every time I spend the night with Tre, but I know I was not ready to just move in with him yet, but I was starting to warm up to the thought of it. I'll see him again in two weeks when we fly out to see Wayne in the NBA Draft!!!

For the remainder of the school year Tre and I continue to see each other on weekends and during breaks. We both have internships to do for the summer so we won't see much of each other. That's going to be hard, but it will let me know if this is really meant to be.

CRACKING THE FOUNDATION

This morning I had to call and have the pool people come out to fix the pool I think the ice from the winter cracked the foundation, I've learned over the years that you must have the right foundation not just in your relationships, but in life. Sometimes we can make decisions that shake and even crack the foundations on which we stand – but if the foundation is the right one shaking it or cracking it won't break it.

Tre and I have been dating for two years and graduation day had come and gone. I feel so blessed to have made it through four years of school including summers and I came out with a Bachelors and a Masters – Tre told me that I think I'm smart, actually I am – this dual degree program really worked in my favor. I was done with school and I was pretty proud of this fact, my mom of course is over joyed. I think part of it is because I did it on a scholarship, so she didn't have to pay for it.

Life after Graduation...

Tre finally convinced me to come to Atlanta, Georgia with him after graduation – just for the summer at least.

"Stay with me and see if you can find a job you like and we can take it from there."

I agreed, although my mom was not happy about it.

"You know it's not right," she said, "living with a man, but you grown now. I'll be praying for you."

I of course had to hear it from Nathalie too.

"Nia," she said. "I know you know better, you need to stop backsliding. Take your tail back to church and get it together."

"Back sliding," I thought. "that's not me – I still pray and go to church sometimes and I even pay tithes sometimes – I'm okay!"

Tre went to Atlanta to find a place for us while I went home to see my mom, and pack up my stuff. While I was there my mom informed me that "Mister" had asked her to marry him and she said yes. I said I was happy for her – I am happy that she has someone – I just don't want him to take my place. Anyway, I packed up, kiss my momma, and headed off to Atlanta to start my adult life.

During my drive I speak with Tre several times, but my most memorable conversation on the drive there was with Wayne –this was a conversation that I have never forgotten.

The phone call from Wayne...

Wayne calls me on my cell phone and said he needed to talk. He tells me that him and Lisa got married. I was speechless.

"I can't believe you got married without me there."

He said, "Let me explain – I asked her to marry me. You knew that I would, but she said that she needed me to do something without you. She said that all of our lives and our entire relationship it has been me, you and her. She said that I've had the best of both worlds – she went on to say that she loves you, but that she knows that I'm in love with you and that she has dealt with that all our lives. But if she was the woman I wanted to be with then I had to marry her without you there. Nia I have to tell you that I really do love you and that I think I have been in love with you my entire life. You make me smile like no one else can. You know things about me that no one else knows. You were the first girl to see me cry and remember when I first started working out. I wanted you to look at me and tell me if you thought I was sexy, so I got naked in front of you with no problem. You've been my world and I so appreciate it, but Lisa has stood by and loved me through all this and I had to think that if you didn't have anyone in your life would I have married her. The answer is no I wouldn't have – I would never have married anyone as long as you were not involved and it has taken me a life time to admit that – but I married Lisa because she understands how I feel. I know you're going to marry Tre so I couldn't risk losing the only other woman in the world that touches my heart, and if I hadn't of married her she would walk and I don't want to have all that I have gained and no one to share it with. You can call it crazy or whatever but it's how I feel."

I was speechless and in tears as we spoke.

"Nia I hope this conversation stays between us – I married her because I do love her and I am in love with her and I realize that I'll never love anyone like I love you. You're in my heart forever and I was happy about that, but I got to go on and start a life and live it."

"Wayne" I tell him, "I'm happy and sad at the same time. I love you so much, you're the first man I ever loved and you're the only man that's never broke my heart and for this I'll be eternally grateful. Thank you for loving me like you did and always have. I hope that this does not mean our friendship is ending cause I can't bear that"

"No," he said sternly. "You just need to know where we stand – so if I back off some – know that it has nothing to do with my heart."

"Nia" he said –"if you need me…"

"I know boo – I know." He hangs up.

I think I cried for about an hour after that call. WOW Tre was on the money about him. The funny thing is I know I loved Wayne, but never thought about whether I was in love with him too until now – just never had to admit it or deal with it – and now it doesn't matter. Lisa is a sweetheart, I will have to congratulate and apologize to her at some point.

I arrive in South Carolina and I was too emotionally drained to drive anymore – I get a hotel room and stay the night. I can't get Wayne off my mind so I call him and he answers the phone.

"Wayne, are you alone?"

"Yes," he said. "I'm at summer training camp so I'm in a hotel room – Nia are you okay?"

"Yes" I told him. "It's funny. I just wanted to hear your voice on the other line. When you hung up, I felt like I had just lost my best friend"

"Never" he said, "but I gotta back off and concentrate on my basketball career, and Lisa for a while that's all. I've been in the league three years now I got to get my head straight. It's funny I never realized until she said it how much I depended on you. I think having you at the Draft, and at my first game, and helping me pick out my first house did it for her ,but for me – I couldn't see it being any other way."

"Okay," I tell him. "I respect that."

He can hear the tears in my voice and I hear him sigh.

"Nia don't do this to me. I can't bear to think that I hurt you – that is not my intention – man I never thought growing up would be this hard"

"I'm sorry Wayne – you didn't hurt me – I was just hurt cause we gotta grow up. We have never had to choose between our relationships and our friendship, it's not a choice I ever wanted to have to make that's all. It's okay though."

"Nia – wow, know that this is something I have to do, or I'm going to lose it, I gotta focus on Lisa and our life together because the more I talk to you the more I want to talk to you, and the more I see you, the more I want to see. It's natural for me, it's like breathing – you been right here since I was 8. Not a choice I wanted to make either I always thought I would never have to choose. Life's been great with you – you been my safety net, but we grew up – you fell in love and you should, you deserve to. Tre is a good dude, my having to let go of you is my own fault, but letting you go does not mean I'm saying goodbye. You will always be my best friend, my heart, we just have to do things differently now."

"I understand" I said.

"Bye" and he hangs up.

I never told Tre about the conversation other than to say that Wayne and Lisa got married – he seemed thrilled.

Living Together…

I finally arrive in Georgia and I call Tre to get directions and he tells me he has a surprise and gives me directions to little suburb called Martique. When I arrive I find that this man has bought a two story condo with a loft. It's gorgeous, has a fireplace, and beautiful patio and deck, off the master bedroom, that faced a lake and woods. Needless to say, I was very pleased, he knows how to live and live well. He comes out and helps to bring my things in the house then he gives me the keys. He doesn't waste anytime handing me a key and saying if you decide to stay I'll add your name to the mortgage. This is too much right now so I just take the key and say thanks. After all this driving I just want a shower and too relax AND to start looking for a job. This man has taken care of me the entire time we've been together. I didn't have to work through school which is what helped me get that dual degree – its time I carry my own weight.

"The place looks nice," I tell him.

"All I did was hire a moving company and have them move the same furniture you picked out in here – it's just a nice place and the furniture fits perfectly."

"What's in the loft?" I ask him.

"Studio equipment," he said with a big smile.

Tre cooks dinner for us and we decide to iron out some details for our future. I hope you stay is how he started out the conversation – and in my mind I'm saying if you ask me to marry you – I'll stay – but I didn't say it out loud.

I just say, "We'll see."

"Nia are you okay?" he asks. "You seem kind of distracted."

"I'm fine," I tell him.

"You sorry you missed seeing Wayne get married?"

"Yeah, kind of."

He gets up and kneels next to me, "I understand – he must of felt strongly about it not to include you princess – you'll be okay."

I must admit I was impressed by that comment because he only tolerates Wayne, he never really liked him. He respected him, but never liked him.

So I tell him, "I'll look for a job right away."

"Take your time Nia," he said. "We don't have money issues – you know that – playing at the club did me very well, not to mention I got the rest of my money in march when I turned twenty one and I was going to tell you this later , but now is as good as any. A producer for the rapper Fuzz was at the club in NC and someone told him that I produce as well as play. Well before I left NC he dropped back by the club and asked for some samples of my work, he listened to my stuff and on Graduation Day they sent me a contract!"

"A contract?"

"Yep princess, just for tracks right now, but the pay is really good plus you know I got the job as band director at Martique High, so we're fine. Take your time baby, you have no worries at all. I will have to be gone when it's time to lay things down in the studio. I'll have to fly to NY sometimes and maybe LA depending on what's going on, but it's what I want to do Nia. I must say that praying has helped."

I was still blown after all this time when I hear this man talk about praying.

The next couple of weeks go by well and I play house wife. I cook and clean, pay the bills, decorate the house, and shop – in between looking for a job. I finally get an offer from a small family counseling center about ten minutes from our house. The pay is pretty good for a first real job and it seems like something I would enjoy. I'll be a case worker, meaning when the families come in for counseling, they'll see me at the office. I'll also be doing home visits, etc. It's the type of thing that fits me, so I'm looking forward to it.

Tre and I wanted to take a vacation, but he had no time cause he was always working. You would think he has no money – said you gotta work to keep it and that since he's spoiled me now he has to keep it up – I gotta admit, I do like this. My birthday is coming up August fifth and I want to go away and I'm hoping he'll say yes...even if it was just for the weekend.

My Birthday...

I'm excited it's my twenty first birthday I have a new career and a wonderful man so I'm pretty happy. I get a phone call and it's Tre.

"Nia pack a bag and meet me at the airport."

"For real? I wasn't expecting to go anywhere until the weekend – its Thursday – my birthday is tomorrow"

"Just meet me at the airport – take a taxi and come to United Airlines Terminal D"

"When?"

"Now," he said.

I pack a bag with a lot of unnecessary things because I don't know where I'm going. I throw on a nice sun dress, call a taxi, and I'm on my way.

I get to the airport and find that I was being whisked away to Jamaica for my birthday. We have a nice flight and once we land there is a limo there to take us to the Hilton Resort. I arrive and find myself in a huge suite with every amenity known to man.

"Tre, how in the world did you pull this off?"

"Fuzz" he said. "He hooked us up."

"Thank you baby, this is great." We walk around the resort for a while and then retreat to the private pool in our suite.

I was awakened by the smell of pancakes, fresh fruit, fresh flowers, and coffee being set on a table next to the bed with Tre standing over me singing Happy Birthday. I sit up wipe my eyes and smile.

"Come on baby it's your birthday. We have a lot to do, we only here for the weekend."

I eat breakfast and we are off for a day of horseback riding, snorkeling, and shopping. It's a very full day. We head back to the room to change for dinner. We have reservations at the resorts five star restaurant at 8pm.   After dinner we head back to our room, when I open the door there are rose petals everywhere, soft music playing, and candles all over the place.

"Wow Tre,"

We headed onto the patio which overlooked the most beautiful view of the ocean I have ever seen. There was a bottle of champagne, two glasses, and several types of desserts. Now I know why I didn't have dessert at the restaurant. We sit down and he removes my shoes for me, pours me a glass of champagne, and begins to feed me dessert. This is really sweet and I was looking around at all of this and I feel tears in my eyes because this is just unbelievable to me, but I try to keep it together. Tre gets up and leans over the balcony staring at the ocean and starts to talk to me, but his tone was very different, very serious, and very humble it was a strange combination.

He said to me, "Nia, you have become my world. You are why I do everything. I am always thinking about you and that has not changed since that day I saw you at camp. I knew you were the one woman that could change my life and you did. You make me think about things differently. You love me no matter what, you have never taken advantage of me or tried to hurt me. You have been everything to me that a man could imagine, not to mention you have to be the most beautiful woman I have ever laid eyes on and I don't just mean how you look. I told you two years ago that your spirit brought peace to me, there is something about you that allows me to rest and I don't ever want that to go away." He walks over to me and for the first time in two years I see tears running down his face.

"I can't explain what you do to my heart, but you bring things out of me that I didn't know were there. You let me be me, no worries, no fears, I can be just who I am – I can't see my life without you – it would be an honor and a privilege if you would be my wife."

He gets on both his knees and said, "Nia will you marry me? Spend the rest of your life with me and let me spend the rest of my life making you happy?"

"Yes," I answer, because that's the only word I could get out and he pulls out this little box that had a five carat platinum ring. Now I'm speechless, he puts the ring on my finger, pulls me up from the chair and kisses me like he never has before. He takes me over to the bed and he caresses by body like its his prize possession – he touches me like it's new, like it's our first time. How does he do this – I don't understand – we spend most of the night making love and talking.

Our next couple of days in Jamaica was beautiful. It was a birthday I'll never forget. Now I have to call my momma and Wayne and tell them – I'm getting married.

When we return home we see a champagne gold Mercedes truck in front of our house with a big red bow on it. Tre's face looks surprised and irritated.

"Baby" I ask. "Is this for me?"

"Maybe" he said, "but I didn't buy it."

I jump out the cab and look at it. There is a small tag on the window that said *Happy Birthday Nia – Love Wayne and Lisa* – OH MY GOD – this is the best birthday ever. I couldn't ask for anything else. Tre just pretends to be happy and takes our things out of the taxi and goes in

114

the house. For the first time I think about something – does Tre work so hard because he feels like he has to compete with Wayne? He doesn't, but I don't know how to make him understand that.

I go inside and check the messages. We get to the message from Wayne and Lisa who first sing Happy Birthday and then I hear Wayne say, "Enjoy Nia Boo I love you always."

It was something about how he said that that seemed to irritate Tre – and pull a string to my heart – but I keep cool and act like it was nothing abnormal.

We unpack and get prepared for work on Monday. It's my first day at the Center and Tre is off to the school to start band camp for the High School students. I decide that I'll tell my mom and Wayne about us getting married a little later, I'll see if he wants to tell them with me. I do call Nathalie and tell her that I won't be shacked up for long – I was getting married – but that she can't tell anyone yet. She is happy – still lectures me – but said at least you are trying. I love Nathalie. She's like the good side of my conscious.

Tre and I sit down and talk and we decide we'll get married next year around my birthday. That gives him time to get established in both his careers, and I can get established on my new job, and get used to living in GA.

We call my Momma and tell her the big news, she is so excited she screams on the phone and starts to do her praise the LORD thing. She said she was praying for this, knew she didn't raise me to give the milk away for free. My momma is crazy – gotta love her.

I called Wayne and he was happy for me and Lisa sounded relieved. Wayne and I don't say much. We don't talk like we use to ever since that phone call, but our friendship has not changed. It's strange, it's like we know where we stand and its okay. Life goes on and whatever happens in the future happens.

Tre of course can't wait to call Nick and tell him, so he calls him and said I gotta tell you something and Nick offers to come over. I hate the fact that he moved back to GA when Tre came back. I wish he would have stayed in NC, but he came back here and got a pretty decent job for some Technology firm. At least he's making his own money and he is still with Stace. Why she stays with him I don't know, we have caught him so many times with other women it scares me. He's just nasty.

Nick comes over and I speak and go upstairs to my room, but I leave the door open so I can hear the conversation.
"So what you gotta tell me man?"
Tre said proudly, "I asked Nia to marry me when we were in Jamaica and she said yes!"

"You getting married?" he asks with a nasty tone. "Man you are so stupid. That trick gonna take everything you worked for. Why are you marrying her? She been sponging off you for years and you let her. She doesn't work, don't do anything for herself, and you dumb enough to marry her!"

"GET OUT NICK! You wrong man. You're supposed to be my best friend and you never been happy about nothing I do. You jealous and I'm tired of it."

"Whatever man," he said. "You stupid"

I hear Tre open the door and yell, "GET OUT OF OUR HOUSE"

Nick was like, "alright man – but don't say I didn't tell you" and he leaves.

Tre stays downs stairs when Nick leaves. He doesn't come upstairs until it's time for bed.

Over the next few months Tre and I find ourselves working a lot. It seemed a lot like when we were in school except at the end of the night we share a bed, which is cool. He starts to travel a lot with Fuzz which is good for him because a lot of other folks in the industry are hearing his name so the publicity has been good. Not to mention our check book is increasing all the time. I don't know how he'll keep this up though, he won't be able to work with Fuzz and work at the high school much longer. I'm happy to be working though. It's nice to have something to do since he's gone all the time. Most of the time I send my money to my momma , I think it's time she had a good life.

Wayne and Lisa seem to be doing well. I got a call that Lisa was expecting, they said they wanted me to know before the tabloids got to it. Wayne has been doing very well on the court, so his name and pictures end up in the tabloids a lot. I stay away from him in public, normally I let him come and see me. I don't want to see my name or my picture in nobody's tabloid.

I notice that Tre has been mildly distant with me since Nick's conversation. I have to admit that it's been hurtful. We normally can talk about everything, but this seems to be something he has avoided. He never said anything when Nick left, but since he's been acting weird for a while, I'm going to ask him about it.

"Tre I want to talk to you," I yelled when I heard him come in the door. "I was in the kitchen."

He comes in and I serve him dinner.

"Baby – you've been a little different since Nick made those comments about me."

He looks surprised, "Yes I heard him and I thought you would say something and you didn't. You feel like what he said?"

He paused and then said "Nah, it's just that I never looked at it like that, but when he said it – it kind of bothered me. I mean I know you not trying to take advantage of me, but to hear him say it like that, it just really bothered me."

"Well, Tre" I tell him, "I'm sorry you let him upset you and after all this time you never said anything, but if you feel like you need to know that I can stand on my own two feet I can move out until the wedding and take care of myself."

Before I could finish my sentence, he was like, "Nia please, I don't want you to move out and really it's not even about you. It's about me and Nick, it's just something I have to work through. I mean most of my life the folks from the home have been my family – it's all good now though."

"Okay," I said and I head into the den to work out.

The Label Party...

Tre comes in all excited and tells me that Fuzz started a new label that will be based out of Atlanta, and that he asked him to sign on full time as a producer for the artists. He even offered him a hefty signing bonus, I was excited for him. He plans to resign from the high school, but will help out until they find someone else to fill the position. I told him he should refer Lance.

Fuzz's new label is having a kick-off party at a club called the Zone in Atlanta, so everyone who is anyone will be invited. I guess we'll be snoozing with the big dogs. Tre had been busy all week in that studio up stairs and our phone was ringing off the hook. I tell him he had to get us a private line, since everyone was using our home phone for business. I even work with him on some stuff, which was fun, but never knew I had a flare for music. I just thought I could dance. I teased and joked with him about being in a video, but he didn't think that was funny. Most of the time he ignored the comment – truth be told I was serious. I may even audition for one, who knows....

Before we went to the party, Tre felt the need to tell me that in this industry, there are a lot of women, therefore, I shouldn't be insecure.

"Whatever," I tell him. "I'm not insecure and I'm not stupid either."

He laughs, "Don't give me no excuse for you hanging out with women. I ain't having it so don't start it."

Then I remind him that there are men in the industry too.

When we get to the party there are photographers everywhere, the club looks great and there are all kinds of folks. The music is pumping and Fuzz is working the floor and introducing people to the first three artists. To my surprise I see Nera on one of the poster as a newly signed artist.

"Surprise!" Tre said, "She sent Fuzz a demo and I knew that voice anywhere. When I heard the demo I told him that I knew and we had to sign her."

"Is she here?" I asked

"If she is not here yet, she will be."

This is great I thought, everybody's dreams are coming true.

The party was going great until I saw Peaches walk in the door wearing next to nothing. Tre was off doing his thing, but I went to find him. Before I could get to him she did and she did her usual inappropriate hug and kiss, and then I walked up.

"Hey Nene, sup?"

"Hi Peaches," I said. "What you doing here?"

"I dance for Fuzz," she said. "Tre didn't tell you?" she had a smirk on her face.

"No," I said. "I guess there was no reason too."

I just look at Tre and walk away. I met a lot of people that night and tried to enjoy myself despite the fact that Peaches was there. I saw people all over the place snapping pictures. I got pulled into a few with Tre and Fuzz, but not many. I didn't know if I liked the lime light yet. At one point, I saw Nick with his camera and he pulled Peaches and Tre in front of a big sign that said Fuzz. This trick kneels down in front of my future husband, opens her mouth, and Nick takes the picture. I was pissed and I really think they both had her before, because she did whatever Nick

121

said. It ain't that much family in the world, and furthermore, Tre got one more time to disrespect me with her and we were going to have some serious problems.

GETTING MARRIED

As I stand in our family room and look at our wedding picture above the fireplace, I'm reminded of our first years of marriage and how you have to be committed because with all the joy and excitement of a new marriage there also comes some sadness and disappointments. It's important that you hold on to your vows and good times in order to get you through the rough spots. There are some trials that can make your bond stronger.

Tre and I got married in August; we had a wonderful wedding and a beautiful, but all too short honeymoon. The wedding was everything I had dreamed about and more. But now it was back to reality and back to work. He has been on me to quit working at the Center and come and work for the label. I think about it, but I kind of like what I do and I am happy that I get to help people, so we keep going back and forth about me working for the label. He said it would give us more time together, which is true – his other option for me at this point is not to work at all – cause business is great and we don't need my money.

We are in the process of looking for and purchasing another place to live. In between looking for a new house and helping my momma plan her wedding, since she put hers off until after I had mine (gotta love her), working at the center, and helping Tre sometimes in the studio, I was starting to feel worn out. His offer to quit my job is looking really great.

I think that if I quit my job – I'll start some kind of non profit organization. I don't just want to do nothing.

My Momma…

I've been calling my mom for two days now and no answer. That's not like her, I normally speak with her for a few minutes every day, and since we are planning her wedding we've been talking several times a day. I tell Tre that I was thinking of flying home in the morning if she doesn't call me back tonight. I call Mr. Gray to see if he has spoken to her, there was no answer at his house so I call the cell.

"Hi Nia" he said.

I ask about momma and he said, "I'm concerned too, I haven't heard from her in two days. I'm in Texas at a conference and she didn't come with me, she said there was too much planning for her to do so she couldn't get away."

"I'm flying home in the morning," I tell him. "I am so worried."

Tre has to fly out to LA in the morning so he won't be going with me – I wish that he was I don't have a good feeling about this. I go to the computer and make reservations on the earliest flight I can get into DCA, Dulles or BWI where ever I can get to first – I get a flight into BWI that leaves ATL at 6am. I pack a small bag and I can't sleep most the night

I'm so worried. I pray really hard that my mom is okay. I felt guilty because I hadn't prayed in a long time.

That Day…

     Tre and I kiss at the airport and I tell him to call as soon as he lands, since I'll be in MD before he gets to LA. I board my flight and I'm off. When I arrive I get a rental car from the airport and I drive home. My mom moved out of our old neighborhood and bought a new house in Badensville. She said all the money I sent her helped her to do that – I was happy to help. When I pull into the driveway, my heart sinks, because I see the kitchen light on and my mom's car in the driveway – why isn't she answering my phone calls. I jump out my car and run to the door scramble to find my key, when I turn the door I hear the TV. I see her purse on the table, and shoes at the door.

     "Momma" I yell. "You here"

     No answer. I run upstairs and her bed is made and she is not there. I walk from room to room upstairs with my heart beating faster and faster with each room I approach. Momma where are you I said to myself. I decide to go into the basement and see if she is there. With every step I take my legs feel heavier and heavier, no momma in the family room and no momma in the laundry room. I turn to go towards her office and see her feet in the door as I approach the office. My mom is laying on her side on the floor as if she had collapsed.

     "OH MY GOD."

I feel like my heart just jumped out my chest. I scream and I run and grab her.

"Momma, wake up."

I check and there is no pulse oh GOD what do I do. I run, grab the phone, and call the ambulance, and then I sit on the floor with my mom in my arms and it feels as if the tears are rolling from my toes out my eyes – I can't understand this what happened. The ambulance arrives and they pry my mom from my arms – they pronounce her dead right there in front of me on the floor. They tell me they can take her to the city morgue or the hospital and I can make arrangements from there. I couldn't move, I couldn't speak, I felt like a piece of my heart was broken off and shattered. Why my mom and why now.

I sat in that office on that floor for hours, I just couldn't move. My momma was my friend, the only parent I have. I was now an orphan – what do I do – I never thought this day would come. She's too young and was looking forward to a new chapter in her life. Should I be angry because of what she missed – do I celebrate what she lived, how do I feel – I sat on that floor for hours. The house phone was ringing, my cell phone was ringing, and I couldn't move. I didn't know what to do next. My world seemed to get really small, really fast and I realized that my momma was my rock, no matter what was going on when I talked to her, things were okay. I even thought that if things ever went wrong with Tre that's okay too, because I can always go home – now there's no home. I don't know how long it was that I sat there with my thoughts before I heard Mr. Gray come in the door.

"Renaye!"

Oh NO – I have to tell him – but I couldn't open my mouth. I hear him walk down the stairs and when he saw me just sitting in the floor – he fell to his knees next to me and asked "what happened?!"

Still I had no words – after a few moments of him shaking me and asking me where momma was I managed to say that she was gone that I found her right here on the floor. I can't imagine how he must of felt all I know is I've never seen a man sob so loud and so hard. It made me cry even harder watching him. He cried as if his future had been snatched from him. He sat there next to me for a long time before I guess he decided that one of us had to get it together, he finally got up and went to the bathroom to get himself together, when he returned he knelt down next to me and asked me, "how long have you been here Nia? It's nine pm.

I couldn't answer, all I could think is it only feels like a few minutes. A few moments later I hear Tre knocking on the door and yelling my name.

"Nia!"

James opened the door and I guess he told him that momma was gone because he ran downstairs to me and grabbed me – and for the first time that day – I took a deep breath.

"I'm so sorry baby," he kept saying over and over again and then he lifted me off the floor and carried me to the sofa. James told him that I was not saying anything and that he was guessing I'd been in that spot for hours. He seemed to be trying to be calm or strong, who knows……. I just want my momma back. Mr. Gray called the hospital to ask for an autopsy to be done, but because they were not married yet it had to come from me. All I could get out was "okay" on the phone. I guess they understood, because the gentleman on the other end said "no problem" and hung up. I finally find the strength to ask Tre what he was doing there.

"You were supposed to be in LA."

"Nia" he said. "I called you a hundred times when my flight landed in New Mexico, when you didn't answer I didn't go to LA I got on another flight and came to BWI and then I got a taxi and came here. I knew something was wrong you always answer my calls." I just lay my head in his lap and I think I cried myself to sleep. The next day was horrible – I kept looking for my mom. I couldn't think straight, finally Mr. Gray called a friend of his that was a doctor and got some sedatives for me. So I slept that day and he and Tre made most of the arrangements for the funeral, and Mr. Gray called my aunts and uncles, her job, and other family members to tell them.

Finally I get a call from Wayne who is pretty messed up himself, I guess his mom must of called and told him. Our mothers were good friends so Mr. Gray must have called and told her. Wayne tells me that him, Lisa and the baby will be at the services. He asks if I need him now – I did but I said no because I didn't want to upset Tre. I just hang up and cry some more, and then Tre or Mr. Gray hands me another pill and I was asleep again.

The services were nice if you can consider a funeral nice, I don't remember much of it at all, I just know my momma is gone. I can't hear her voice no more and my heart is broke. People came to the house after the funeral like folks do and we had them coming out of the wood works. Relatives don't have no shame, my uncle Tank asked for momma's car – I told him maybe – but can you believe it she ain't been in the ground twenty four hours and he asking for her car. My aunties want the clothes, they already took some of them, and I saw them doing it before the funeral when they were visiting during the week. People hung around until after eleven pm I guess it was around eleven thirty before the last person left. So now the house is empty and it feels cold. My momma brought so much warmth wherever she was. A lot of her co-workers came to the house. They had great things to say about her – of course they would – people always do after funerals. This all seems so strange to me, I was in my momma's house two months before her wedding and she is gone. I'm glad I said I loved her and that the last conversation I had with her was a good one. I still can't help but feel like I was cheated though. So much we still wanted to do together.

I decided to stay at my mom's house for a couple of weeks after the funeral to try and sort things out before I head back to Georgia. Mr. Gray asked for some pictures and other things that he shared with momma.I felt bad for him, so I let him have what he wanted. I asked him if he wanted to live in the house. He said no he had his own house, plus he didn't think he could bear it. He did ask me to please let him know what the autopsy said and asked if I would do him a favor and keep in touch with him, said I was all he had left of my momma. Funny thing is I didn't think I liked Mr. Gray, but over the past week I can see what my momma saw in him. He was a nice man, very humble, and very thoughtful. He was just the kind of man my mom deserved. Once he left there was just Tre and I in the house, all of a sudden the house seemed so big and so empty. I felt like I was in the strangest place. I just couldn't believe that my Momma was gone. I'm glad she saw me get married, but I was sad that she didn't have her own wedding. It's so amazing what emotions you feel after a death. I'm kind of angry I felt like this was unfair, but who could I be mad at?

Tre and I retreat to my room and fall asleep. When I get up in the morning I get a call from the coroner saying the autopsy revealed that my momma had a stroke. He said that the official papers would come in the mail in two-three days. I said thank you and hang up. I wonder what happened I knew she was on blood pressure medication, but I thought it was under control. I figure I better start calling around and canceling all the arrangements for the wedding. It was so hard for me to call all these folks and tell them the same thing over and over again.

"Renaye Harrington passed away so I'm canceling."

I said that phrase all day long until it just got to be exhausting and I couldn't do it anymore. Tre tried to help out by going through all of momma's bills and attaching the death certificate to the ones we needed to send off – I didn't want to do that. We contacted the Insurance Company and it turned out that momma had a large policy. It was for three hundred thousand dollars. I decided not to keep all of it for myself. I gave Mr. Gray a large part of it which he refused at first, but I convinced him that my mom would have wanted it that way. I gave ten percent of it to her church because she was a tither, so it just seemed right. I then gave some of it to my uncles and aunties. Hopefully, it would make their lives a little easier. I kept a small portion for myself and decided that I'd put it into an account for when I had a baby. This way, I'd give it to them and tell them it's from their Grandma Renaye.

After being there for two weeks I finally decide to go into my moms' room and clean some things up. I'm not packing her room away, and I'm not selling the house. I don't want to let go of that part of her yet. Tre told me I can keep it and we can just pay it off. I open her closet and there was her beautiful wedding gown and shoes. I sit on the floor and cry, I feel so shattered it's like my insides are torn and I feel a pain that nothing is soothing – nothing – not even Tre can make me feel better, although I'm happy that he is here with me.

I stayed home for a month . I let my momma's baby sister Sasha come and stay at the house. She recently lost her job and was just now getting back on her feet, so I told her she can stay in the house as long as she takes care of it. She agreed and moved into the guest bedroom. I felt good about that, at least when I call someone will answer the phone.

Tre told me it was time for us to go home and I thought he was being insensitive because I just lost my mom. He didn't say much just said "Fine you can stay as long as you need, but I have to go home. I have to go back to work."

My aunt Sasha told me it was time I go back to my life. I think everyone is nuts – my life will never be the same – never, not without my momma.

Back Home…

When I arrived back home, Tre had roses all over the place and big balloons that said "Welcome Home". It was nice to get back. I still felt horrible, but it was good to get home. I noticed that a lot of things had not been done around the house, so I threw myself into cleaning up my house and throwing out stuff we didn't need. I realized that we'd put looking for our new house on hold, so I went back to the computer emailed my real estate agent and let her know that I wanted to get back to work on that. Then I decided to make my husband a romantic dinner to say thanks for putting up with me. Alhough I didn't want to be bothered with the rest of the world – I was looking forward to seeing him, he is now the only family I have. When Tre arrived home he was happy to see me wearing next to nothing. He basically tackled me in the living room and it took a good forty five minutes before we were sitting naked at the dinner table and eating the meal I had prepared. I fill him in on my day and he informs me that he's had an interesting day, He said he got a letter that was forwarded to him from the home in grew up in – the letter was from his father.

"Really?" I asked. "Well what did it say?"

He got up, picked his jeans up off the floor, and handed me a letter that read:

Dear Trevon,

I hope this letter finds you well. I know you are surprised to be hearing from me after all these years, but I finally got up the courage to write to you. It took a lot of research to find you. I first want to say that I'm so sorry I got sent away when you were so young and I'm even sorrier that I was not there for your mom. I should have been there to protect her. If I were, she would still be here. I want you to know that we loved each other very much, but we were young and I made terrible mistakes and really bad decisions with my life. Your mother waited as long as she could for me, but after about five years she gave up and I understood. She was young and beautiful and full of life and I was okay with her moving on and trying to enjoy it. I hope that after you read this letter you will decide to keep in touch with me and maybe come visit. Because of a Miracle ...I'll be getting out of here soon and I hope that I'll be able to come and see you. I went through rehab and I also went to school so I've done some something with my life while I was in here. I'm just really sorry that I was not there for you. I hope you have done something with your life. If you choose to write me back I will be very happy to hear from you, and if you choose not too I will understand.

Peace to You.
Trenton Whitmore

"Wow baby, this is big news for you. How do you feel?"

"I think I'll write back," he said.

I was thinking to myself , '*How did he know that he hadn't seen his name on the back of some CD or knew about the insurance money?'* But, I decided to keep those thoughts to myself.

"Okay baby", I told him. "Just take it slow."

He just smiled and said, "I hear you princess…I hear you. It's cool. I'll take it slow."

I went back to work and gave my two week notice, I didn't want to work anymore, didn't feel like helping anyone anymore. I gave the notice and then took leave for the two weeks. I didn't even let them give me a party. I just felt like I wanted to be by myself for a while. I felt like I didn't need the money anymore because I was just sending most of it to my momma – I still can't believe she is gone. I cleaned out my office, said goodbye to most of my co-workers, wrote letters to my clients, turned off the light, closed the door, and gave the keys to the receptionist. I had a lot to think about, it seems losing my momma has just left a void and given me so much to think about, then hearing that Tre's father contacted him got me to wondering where my Dad was. I decide I'll take one more of those pills the doctor gave me and I'll get some rest – I can figure out my life later.

I was awakened by Tre calling my name and asking what I was doing home in the middle of the afternoon. I sat up and told him that I'd quit my job.

"Really?" He said, "Stop playing,"

"No seriously, I quit."

"Are you okay Nia? I mean all this time you said you wanted to work."

"I know, but I just don't feel like it anymore. I just feel sad and like I don't want to be bothered right now."

Tre looks at me with concern, "Okay baby I know you're still grieving about your mom, but you have to live. What are you going to do?"

I tell him, "I'm going to find us a new house,"

Tre smiles and said, "Good cause I haven't had time to look for anything, so for now that will be your job and Nia I don't want you just moping around okay?"

"I know" I tell him, "I'm doing my best."

For the next couple of weeks I drive my real estate agent crazy looking for houses. I have her looking, I ride around looking, I've been on the internet and I still haven't found the perfect house – I have a picture in my head of what I'm looking for and she hasn't shown it to me yet. I finally found a house on the internet that peaked my interest so I leave her a message. I get a call back from a gentleman who said she had an emergency and would be out of town for a couple of weeks, so he's taking over her clients. Fine I said, I really don't care who it is, I just want to see this house so I can get moved and settled. I think once we move, I'll figure out what I want to do with my life, I still have no idea.

I finally meet up with Ron the new real estate agent – he was a decent looking guy about five eleven, light skinned, but he had this air about him like he thought he was a gift to woman, I just wanted him to show me the house !! As he is showing me the house he's telling me about all his degrees and about his house and all his possessions and making comments that annoyed me. I just ignored him mostly. The house was beautiful, long driveway, security gate, pool and hot tub in the back yard., marble foyer, 6 bedroom, 5 full baths and 2 ½ baths, 3 fire places, it was just gorgeous and the price was unbelievable. It was a one owner home that had been foreclosed on, it was owned by some executive whose company went under, so he lost the house. I felt bad about that, but since it was a foreclosure it put the house in our price range, we only had to pay what was owed, I quickly put a contract on it. As I was completing the contract and getting ready to leave, Mr. Ron complimented me on my appearance and asked me out. I informed him that I was married and he had the nerve to tell me, I know that, but you are by yourself now so I thought maybe you may need some company. He went on to inform me that I'd be missing out by turning him down. Needless to say – I told him no thank you and left. I'm not sure if I should tell Tre, but I think I better since we still have more work to do with him.

I get home and run to the studio to inform Tre that I'd found the perfect house and then I drag him away from all his equipment to my truck and I drive him over to look at it. He loved it, then I told him that I'd put a contract on it already – he was okay with that, but informed me that he didn't want me to continue to make those kinds of decisions without speaking with him first. I understood what he meant and I apologized. I also told him that the agent asked me out. He wasn't happy about that at all and then laid his law down that I was no longer allowed to meet up with Ron if he was not going to be there. So now I had to schedule all the appointments around Tre's schedule. He had some really good news for me too, he said he would not be traveling as much anymore. Fuzz was stationing the label in ATL and opening up a club, and he would be in charge of the band. The club was going to be upscale, the band would play every night, but occasionally they would feature other artists and of course the artists on the label. He told me that I could work there if I wanted to, but that he liked having me home so I didn't have to do anything if I didn't want to.

"Right now" I told him, "I just want to do things for us and take care of you."

"That's fine with me baby," he responds. "I'm happy with that."

We decide not to sell the condo, but to keep it as investment property. I spend time looking for a renter, picking out furniture for the new house, hiring movers, changing our address on everything, balancing the bank accounts and sleeping a lot and feeling sick. I think it's those pills the doctor gave me. I'll make an appointment to go to the doctor after we go to settlement for the house.

In the midst of everything going on Tre informs me that he has decided to go see his father. I think that's a good idea I tell him, it would be great for him to get to know his Dad, I'm sure he needs that.

THE FATHER-IN-LAW

I had a conversation with a friend today and she called to inform me that she was getting married. She said her fiancé's parents were divorced and that she met the mom and that went okay, but she was nervous about meeting his father. That conversation made me remember when I first got to meet my father in law – my father in law is a sure example of how not to judge a book by its cover, it's best to get to know people for yourself.

We finally got moved into the house, it seemed like so much work even though we had movers. I spent the first couple of days having things painted, etc. and then the next couple of days telling furniture delivery men where to put things. Tre and I worked well together decorating most of the house, there are still some rooms empty that he said I'm on my own with. Once things are done we have planned to have a romantic dinner alone, and then we'll have a dinner party and invite our friends over.

I finally got the dining room set up and Tre and I will have our dinner tonight. I still need to make my appointment to the doctor I can't seem to keep anything down, I think I'll make something simple for dinner like salmon – I hope that will stay on my stomach.

When Tre comes up from the studio he is impressed with the way the dining room looks so he sits down and we have dinner. I got up to go get dessert and the next thing I knew, I was looking up at him and there was an EMT worker kneeling beside me asking me to say my name and how old I was. I felt so embarrassed and I thought, *'what just happened?'*

Tre looked terrified and stated, "Baby, you got up and just passed out."

I said, "I'm fine."

The EMT worker said that he thought I should go to the hospital, so I'm thrown into the ambulance and taken away to the closet Medical center. Two hours and several tests later, the doctor walks into my room smiling and said "Mrs. Whitmore I have some news for you. First you need to have more iron because your iron levels were low and so was your blood sugar, and secondly, you've been sleeping and sick on your stomach because you're six weeks pregnant."

"Pregnant!" I said. "I can't be, I have a patch."

Tre just looked at me like he's thinking about it and says, "Nia, you haven't been wearing it. I thought you got the shot."

I laid back on the bed and thought about it. Oh no…when my momma died, I completely forgot about anything to do with birth control the month that I was at her house and I guess when I got home I never thought about it anymore. The doctor gives me a prescription for iron pills and prenatal vitamins and discharges me.

On the ride home I tell Tre that I'm sorry, because we said we would decide when to have children together. He just looks at me and shakes his head.

"Nia please there is nothing to be sorry for. I'm happy you are carrying my baby and I'm even happier that you are not sick. You really scared me by falling out like that."

Then he laughs. "It's not funny," I tell him. "That was so embarrassing, I was trying to be romantic and I wake up on the floor."

When I get home I have to keep repeating to myself that I'm pregnant, WOW I guess I'm going to be a mommy. I sure wish I could tell my momma, but I guess I'll call auntie Sasha, she will be happy, and of course, I'll have to tell Wayne. Well I guess I'm at home for a reason now. The doctor told Tre I should rest for a few days, no activities and to go see my OB/GYN as soon as possible. I spent the next three days in bed – Tre's orders he wouldn't let me do anything except go to the bathroom. I thought this was ridiculous, I'm not handicapped, I'm just pregnant, and some women faint when they are pregnant. Since it made him happy, I did what he asked.

I decided to call Wayne while Tre was making dinner. I couldn't get him at home so I called the cell, still no answer. I just left a message for him to call me – told him I had BIG NEWS. When Tre brought up dinner he reminded me that my appointment to the OB/GYN was tomorrow morning. I ate and then fell asleep as usual.

Off to the doctors…

I'm awakened by Tre tapping me and saying, "Nia, wake up and get dressed we have to get to the doctor's office."

I roll out of bed, shower, get dressed, and Tre drives to the doctors office like I'm already in labor. This is going to be something else I think to myself. This man is going to drive me crazy. Once we arrive at the doctor's office I go through the normal exams, urine test, blood test, pelvic exam, and finally the vaginal sonogram. They spent much longer than I thought normal looking at my belly and I think Tre and I both were getting nervous.

Finally the doctors said, "Well Mr. and Mrs. Whitmore, you are definitely pregnant. Congratulations, we wanted to be sure we were all seeing the same thing, that's what took so long, but from what we can tell it looks as though you have a low lying placenta."

I just sat there and Tre asked all the questions, once the doctor assured him that if I followed their instructions everything should be just fine, he calmed down some. The doctor tells me that he wants me on semi bed rest right now and that means he is limiting activities, and that I should avoid stressful situations if at all possible. He tells me not to carry, lift, push or pull anything. Wow my life has completely changed in a matter of minutes. Once the shock wore off, I began to get excited and sad all at the same time. I'm having a baby and my momma's gone and my best friend, well he has a life of his own and a new baby, I wonder if he'll be able to share any of this with me. It's so weird not having him around – he has been in my life for every major event that I've ever had. Well I quickly get over that and find myself feeling very blessed, I really don't have anything to worry or complain about. We leave the doctor's office and head home.

Once we get home Tre decides that I should get in bed for the day. When I protest he insists and convinces me that its what's best. Since I'm kind of tired anyway I go along with it, but I'm thinking to myself – I'm not spending 9 months in bed doing nothing, if I do that, I'll be huge. I laid down and drifted off to sleep, it seemed like I had been asleep for only a few minutes when Tre woke me up for lunch. He had made me a sandwich and a salad it was nice, once I was done eating I told him that I'd had a dream while I was sleep. In the dream my momma sat next to me while I was in a hospital bed and told me that no matter what everything would work together for my good. In the dream after she told me this, she bowed her head and prayed for me, but I couldn't remember what she prayed. It was strange but comforting. Tre just listened, I asked him what he thought it meant but he had no answers. I hope things will be okay, that dream really got me to thinking and missing my momma.

Establishing a relationship with Dad...

Tre's father had been calling and writing a lot, said that he only had a few more months in prison and then he would be out. Tre keeps hinting around to me about him staying with us. I'm not saying much cause I'm not really feeling living with this strange man, but he seems like it's something he really wants to do. Finally I just come out and ask him and he tells me that when his Dad gets out he really wants him to stay with us. I tell him I don't like it, but if it's important to him, then I will go along with it.

Tre goes to visit his father on the weekend and when he got home he informed me that I won't believe how much alike they look. He said his Dad is only about one inch shorter than he is, but weighs more and that his eyes are green. He said it was weird, kind of like looking in a mirror.

"We talked a lot he was able to tell me how he and my mom met and what happened the day I was born, catching up was great."

"That's great baby," I tell him. "I'm happy you are getting to know your father."

"I want you to come with me the next time I go." He said, "I've told my dad all about you and he wants to meet you – he said you sound like you are a lot like my mom."

"I would love to meet him," I respond.

I'm thinking to myself, maybe if I get to know him before he moves in here, I won't be so uncomfortable. Tre seems thrilled that I have agreed. I decide now is as good of time as any to let him know how I feel about living with his dad.

"Tre, I want to talk to you."

"Okay," he said and sits down next to me.

"I'm a little nervous about living with someone from prison, I know he is your father, but why was he locked up and how do you know he has changed and won't do anything to bring harm to us or our family – I mean we'll have a baby soon and we have to think about his or her safety."

Nia," he said. "I know and I have thought about all of this, I would never let anything happen to you, I have talked to my dad a lot over the phone and in letters and I've learned a lot about him, I really believe that he is a changed man. He is locked up on drug charges – he was dealing when he was out and got caught with a lot of drugs in his car and he got locked up for it. No one is looking for him, he didn't snitch on anyone. He was dealing for himself and since he has been in prison he has gotten his degree and is now saved. I really believe that he is a changed man."

"Okay," I tell him. "I trust you if you say it's okay then fine, but I had to tell you how I was feeling. Thinking about it was making me nervous."

"It's okay princess." Tre said, "I won't let anyone hurt you even though he's my father if I thought he would hurt you, I would not let him move in here."

"Well I guess I feel a little better I'm sure after I meet him I'll feel much better."

I got to meet Dad...

Tre woke me up Saturday morning and asked if I would go with him to visit his Dad. He said he'll be out in about two months and he wants me to start visiting him so that I can get comfortable with him being around. So I get up, get dressed, and we hit the road. I asked him if he had been planning this for a while because I know you have to be on a list to get into a prison.

He just smiled and said, "Yes, I had him add your name to his visitor list the first time I went to see him."

Tre explains to me that his dad is in a different type of facility now that he is about to come home, so visits are "contact" which just means there won't be any glass between us. When we arrive we go through the routine check and we enter a room. The room seems nice for a jail, it had tables, chairs, several TV's, couches, snack machines, and a guard that sat by the door. I felt a little nauseous so I got up to go see if I could find a Ginger Ale in the machine. Tre sits and waits for his father to come out, I look at him and he looked like a little kid. It was kind of cute, but strange too, I wonder why this is so important to him – I guess because his mom is gone. This is making me think though, I haven't talked to my father, he was not at graduation or my wedding, nor did he attend my mom's funeral. I don't even know if he knows she is gone, maybe I should try and find him. I get my soda and as I'm walking back to the table where we were sitting. I see Tre get up and this very handsome man that looks like a lighter version of my husband is walking toward him. It was so weird, I could not believe my eyes, they look just alike. Wow I thought how amazing is this, and then I thought, I'm a blessed girl cause if this is what Tre will look like when he is older, he will be fine forever! Tre greets his Dad with a big hug and then points in my direction. When I get to the table he introduces me, and his father extends his arms to hug me. I hugged him, but it was kind of weird to hug this strange man, although he really looks like my husband.

We sit down and Tre and his father talked about everything from what this facility was like to which one of their favorite teams would be in the NBA playoffs. Then his Dad asked me about Wayne, said Tre told him that my best friend was in the NBA. I told him yeah, explained all about Wayne and then changed the subject because if I talk too much about him Tre will get annoyed. Then his father got serious on me, he asked me right out how I felt about him living with us. Oh my goodness I thought, he doesn't beat around the bush at all. I was honest and told him, I wasn't sure because he was a stranger to me. He held my hand and told me that he understood that and he would not come unless I was comfortable, but that he wanted me to know he was a changed man. He had given his life to Christ – and he wasn't living the "life" anymore, and that he knows he can't get the time he lost back with his son, but that he prays I will allow him to spend the rest of his life getting to know Tre and me . How can I argue with that I think to myself, I told him okay. Our visit went really well and I was a little more comfortable with Mr. Trenton Whitmore. Now if I could just figure out what to call him, we would be moving along fine.

When we arrive back home, we decide that we'll put his father in the guest suite at the end of the hall. Tre wanted to make sure that he felt like he was really a part of the family, so he didn't want to put him in the guest house out back. So I decide that I'll try decorate it a little differently before he comes, since I have two-three months before his Dad arrives. I tell Tre don't worry about it, things will be perfect for him, besides, I don't have anything else to do and I don't want to do the nursery just yet, it just seemed too soon.

WHAT'S GOING ON?

I was sitting on my bed today thinking about all the things that we have gone through and how we handled them all, sometimes things happen in life that just make you yell out to know one in particular "WHAT IN THE WORLD IS GOING ON!!!"

Tre informs me that he has to go to LA for a video shoot day after tomorrow, he tries not to travel much anymore, but this artist he is producing asked him to be a part of the video so he has to go, plus he said the pay is really good. I'll be fine I tell him, I promise that I'll take it easy. Then he informs me that it's in New York and Nick is off this week so he's going with him. I just roll my eyes, I don't trust Nick, and for some reason, I got a bad feeling about his going – I don't say anything though, because Nick is "his boy".

"Okay," I told him. "But just be careful."

That dag on day...

Tre arrives in New York right on schedule. He calls me from his cell phone, said he has a busy day ahead and probably wouldn't get to talk to me until really late tonight or tomorrow. He said he's going to check into his hotel, go to the video shoot, then go to the club where they'll be performing, doing a sound check, and that they'd be there for most of the night. He also told me that if I needed him, to just call on his cell phone, leaving Nick's cell phone number as well, just in case there was some kind of emergency.

"Okay baby." I tell him, "don't work too hard and don't let no ho get you in trouble."

He laughs, kisses me through the phone and said, "I love you" and hangs up.

I go about my day as usual, but by the evening I was kind of bored and decided to sit down at my computer and see if I could find my father. I know he lived in Texas and North Carolina for a while and the last I heard he'd moved back to Maryland or Virginia. His name is Nathan Armstrong. I brought a box from my mom's house with old papers, and other stuff in it. Maybe now is a good time to go through it and see if there is any information about him anywhere. I go to the closet and pull the box out and start to look through it, there is all kinds of stuff in here, it may take a little longer than I thought. After about two hours between the box and the computer, I get tired so I shower and climb into bed, I call Tre's phone and leave him a message to say goodnight.

Around four in the morning, I'm startled with a phone call from Ray, who's a friend of Tre and Nick. I'm surprised to hear from him because I didn't know he was with them. He explains to me that he was at the club with Tre and the whole crew. He said something went on and

Nick and Tre were involved. I think my heart stopped beating for a couple of seconds, but I couldn't say anything. I got that same feeling I had when I saw my momma laying on the floor.

"Where are they?" I asked.

He said, "They are in the ambulance on the way to Mt. Sinai Hospital in New York City."

"I'm on my way," is all I managed to get out.

I jump up, throw on some clothes, grab my purse and hop in my car, I drive to the airport and go from counter to counter until I can get a flight, I manage to grab a six thirty am flight to New York. This had to be one of the longest plane rides I have ever experienced.

When I arrived at the hospital, Ray was outside smoking a cigarette. He saw me running towards the door and walked out to meet me and gives me a hug and tells me I should not be running. I ignored him. All I wanted to know is where my husband was and I can tell he was stalling. When I entered the lobby of the hospital, I signed in and he took me to the intensive care unit, where I knew this was not going to be good. When I got off the elevator, I saw Fuzz and his whole entourage, and he looked devastated. He was a good guy and this wasn't his type of thing. He walked over to me and hugged me and shook his head. I felt the tears rolling down my face and no one was saying anything. When I finally came out, "someone please tell me something", I said, so Fuzz walks me outside of the waiting room.

"Nia," he said. "Tre and Nick are both in critical condition. Tre was trying to look out for Nick and he was shot."

So now I'm not only scared I'm pissed, but I keep listening, "He was shot in his lower back twice."

"What! What!"

"And Nick was shot in the head and he isn't doing well at all."

I go to the desk and let them know who I am and ask to speak to the doctor, "No problem Mrs. Whitmore" the nurse said, "we have been waiting for you."

She takes me into a room and Fuzz asks if I want him there.

"Yes, I can't do this by myself I'm terrified."

Two doctors come in and ask me to sit down, they close the door, they tell me that Tre is in critical but stable condition, and that the first hour he was there they were trying to stabilize his vitals. He was shot in one of his kidneys, one bullet exited through the side of his abdomen and they are not sure yet how much damage it did. The other bullet is still in the kidney and that they have to do surgery to save his life, but could not do it until they got him stable. They tell me they need me to make some decision about resuscitation etc. and have me sign all this stuff. They ask me if I am in charge of Nick's medical care as well because there was no next of kin listed on anything for him except Tre, which I thought was weird because he had a girlfriend.

"Well he has a girlfriend," I said, "but what do I need to do?"

My head is spinning and I feel sick, but I try to keep it together and Fuzz is right there holding my hand – which is weird, cause I really don't know him all that well. I mean I've been around him a lot because Tre produces for him, but no personal conversations or anything but he seems so concerned. Well I call Nick's girlfriend, who explains to me that she is sorry to hear that, but she and Nick are not together anymore and have not been for about two months, but if I want her to come she will.

"I don't have time for this", I tell her that's up to her and hang up.

I go back to the desk and tell them, I'll be responsible for both of them and ask if I can see Tre before he goes to surgery. The nurse said yes but only for a moment, then she tells me that there are a lot of tubes and things so I should be prepared for what I was about to see. Nothing she said prepared me for what I saw, my husband looked a mess, he had tubes coming from everywhere and he was unconscious, all I could say was OH MY GOD and the tears began to flow. I think Fuzz who was right behind me was overwhelmed by me and Tre because I saw tears in his eyes as well, I try to get it together and walk over to him. I kiss his cheek because there was a tube in his mouth and I hold two of his fingers because there are all kinds of IV in his arms and hands.

I just say, "I love you and me and this baby need you. You gotta come through this."

I tell him, "You are strong and you'll be fine."

That's all I could get out before the nurse tells me that they need to prep him for surgery, Fuzz and I walk out. Fuzz goes over and talks to the nurse. I guess he told her I was pregnant, because she comes over ask me if I was okay and how was I feeling, I can't answer her because I don't know. I realize that Tre and Fuzz talk more than I realized because he also knew that I was on semi bed rest and he must have told her because she insisted that I sit down, but I refuse. I need to talk to the doctor about Nick, although he irritates me, he's family cause Tre loves him and he would want me to do right by him. The doctor told me that he was shot in the head and that the bullet is lodged a few inches from his brain, but he was also shot in his lower abdomen and the bullet hit his spine upon exiting, it appears that in the midst of all this one of his lungs has collapsed as well. To sum it up, he ain't doing so well. They need to operate but can't yet because his vitals aren't stabilized. They say it's been touch and go for about four hours now. I go in to see Nick, who doesn't even look like himself because the medication they are pumping into him has made him swell and there is a tube in his head draining something and tubes in his nose and mouth. I thought to myself, *'what did you do? This is crazy how did you get here and why did you have to involve my husband'*, but I quickly change my thought and I walked over to talk to him. I tell him it's me and that Tre is fine, not to worry, and that I'm here for him and I'll make sure he is taken care of him. I kiss his cheek as well and I walk out.

I go back to the waiting room and sit down. It was going to be a long night. Fuzz sends everyone home except his body guard and Ray, which I'm surprised, I look at him and tell him, "You don't have to stay."

"Are you kidding?" He said, "I know I'm a celebrity, but I'm a person first and before Tre is my producer, he is my friend, my music ain't my music without him. Secondly, he would kill me to know that I left his pregnant wife alone to deal with this, you stuck with me baby girl."

I smile. To be honest, I'm glad someone is here.

After about two hours Fuzz and Ray doze off, I'm sure they were tired at this point it's like eleven in the morning so they have been up for who knows how long. The body guard though, who doesn't say much was still wide awake, he came over sat down next to me and introduced himself. His name was Tim. He had been with Fuzz since he got started rapping, said that Tre was cool and that he was always talking about his princess. He asked how I was doing and I told him that I didn't know. He suggested that I take a nap. Said he would be up and he would wake me if the doctors came out, I thanked him but told him I doubt I would be able to sleep. The nurse comes over and said that Nick is finally stable enough to go into surgery, my God I think – this is too much so both of them will be in surgery. Ok I tell her and she tells me the doctor will be over soon to explain everything to me. About ten minutes later Dr. Matus comes over and tells me they will be removing the bullet from Nicks head, and survey the damage the second bullet did to his spine and lower abdomen, that's all they can tell me right now. I asked if he had brain damage, they say the bullet is inches away from his brain, but they don't know how much damage was done, plus he stopped breathing several times before he was stabilized, so they don't know if that caused any brain damage and we won't know until he wakes up.

"Okay," I said.

I come back out and Tim had gone to the cafeteria and gotten me some tea and crackers, "thanks" I tell him, "that's really sweet."

"I remember when my sister was pregnant that's all she could eat, so I figured this may help you feel a little better."

"Thanks," I tell him. I try to eat it, but I don't have an appetite at all.

The doctor comes out about an hour and a half into the surgery and said that Tre is doing well and that he seems to be pretty healthy and that's a big help – but they wanted me to know that they will have to remove one of his kidneys because the bullet did too much damage. They say he also had some internal bleeding but they were able to stop it tells me that the surgery will probably be about four-five more hours. All I can say is okay and thanks. When I sit back down I ask Tim if he knows how all this happened.

"Yeah," he said. "You don't know?"

"Nah," I tell him. "I was home in Georgia"

He said, "I mean I know that, I thought maybe Fuzz told you or Ray when he called."

"Nah – what happened?"

He said, "From what I saw and heard, Nick was in the club – up here in New York where he don't know these dudes up here, ya know you gotta be careful who you mess with. He had no business here for real, he wasn't in the video and he ain't part of the promotion, but nevertheless he was at the club anyway. Everything was going good, the party was Hot, and Fuzz and Tre were doing their thing. Well after the set, everyone was just chilling and enjoying the club. Nick meets up with some girl and decided that he wanted her. I mean I think he had been drinking cause he was all on her, well apparently she was the girlfriend of some dude. Anyway she says they weren't together, but he said they were, anyway, he ask Nick to stay away and of course he don't listen and he keep pursuing her. Well Nick steps outside to get some air and the dude approaches him and they start arguing, someone sees the argument, and tells Tre that Nick is outside and he better get him cause he drunk. Well this fool, instead of just leaving the girl alone tells the dude to step off and some mo. Tre comes outside and is like hey man, you know just let the girl go man, but Nick ain't listening . Tre tells him to come back in, Nick comes in and the dudes stay outside. Around three thirty, Tre and Fuzz decide they done and want to get to the hotel and get some rest cause there is work to do, you know they weren't done with the video. Well we put Fuzz in the limo but Tre decide he better drive Nick back cause he drunk, so they walking

157

across the parking lot together and we see the car ride up behind them and fire about 8 shots. When the shots start Tre starts to run, but he grabs Nick to try and help him cause he's drunk and so as a result they both got shot. I'm sure the bullets were for Nick but Tre got caught in the middle of all this mess."

I just shake my head, Tim is like, "What's the deal with those two – you know we can't figure it out, you know. Tre's a good dude, you know he know how to play hard, but he about business, but Nick he seem like a leech. He always hanging on and throwing Tre name around, he always want you to know that he is with Da ONE", which was Tre's producer name.

"I know," I told him. "You have no idea, but they grew up in a group home together and Tre sees him like a brother and nothing can change that."

Tim is like, "OH alright I get it now – well you can't mess with a bond like that – it's like his only family."

"Yeah" I said.

"I get it now, that's cool. It's sad though because Nick mind ain't right he is always doing stuff – this time it caught up with him."

Finally Dr. Gustav, another one of the surgeons, came out of the operating room.

He comes over and said "Mrs. Whitmore, your husband's surgery went very well, we removed a kidney, and stopped some internal bleeding."

He said, "Trevon is a lucky young man, because the first bullet should have killed him, it entered his kidney and existed through his abdomen, but it missed all his other vital organs; if not he would not be here."

I feel blessed to hear this, but what's next. Dr. Gustav said, "his recovery will depend on how strong he is. He is sedated right now because he was in a lot of pain, the surgery was major and we have him on a lot of medication. He will be sedated for the next couple of days because when he was shot, he fell to the ground and hit his head so he also has a minor head injury. We are not too worried about that, but we are watching him very closely. You are a lucky woman."

The Dr. said, "Most gunshot cases like this have a different outcome. We are hopeful that he'll be fine, but at this point he is still in critical but stable condition."

At this moment I feel a pain in my stomach, but I'm guessing it's just stress. I sit down and put my feet on the table in the lobby, maybe elevating them will help me. I feel light headed too and I guess Tim notices, so he asks if I'm okay.

"Yeah" I tell him, but really I'm getting really concerned.

I wake Fuzz up and tell him what the Dr. said, he looks a little relieved but still concerned. I told him to go to the hotel, get some rest and get back to work. I had his cell number and I'd call if I needed to. I told him Nick is in surgery and there is no word yet. At this point his publicist is walking in the door.

She said, "The press got wind that Da ONE was shot and they are all over this. They want to know what has happened and what his condition is."

"Aw man, I knew it."

He asks, "Nia what do you want?"

I tell him "I can't handle this and I don't want to be in the press,"

Tre had done a good job of keeping us out of the spot light and I like it that way. Fuzz said, "Tell them I'll issue a statement this evening and do your best to get rid of them. Tell them DaOne is in stable condition, that this incident is not related to Fuzz in anyway, and that the family would appreciate some privacy at this time. Let them know that Fuzz himself will issue a statement later on today."

The publicist leaves. Fuzz, Tim and Ray leave to go straighten out all the business matters. They tell me that they are all staying at the Waldorf Astoria and since Tre already had a room I should stay there. I thank them, but I'm not going anywhere until I see my husband. A while later, the nurse comes over and lets me know that Tre is in recovery, and that I can go and see him.

I walk in the recovery room and my big strong husband looks so helpless laying there, it's so hard to see him this way. He doesn't even know I'm here, it's weird, he has taken care of me since we met, and I can't remember how I lived without him. I can't see my life without him in it, I just break down cause he has tubes everywhere. He seems so weak, I have never seen him look so weak. I feel sick looking at him, it's like I'm losing him, I just want to hear his voice, and he can't even speak to me. I lay my head on the bed beside him, and I put my hand on his chest and I beg GOD to make him better. I can't be in this world without him, I won't make it, I don't know how I ever survived without him. The nurse comes in and tells me to try and keep it together in the room with him cause he may be able to hear me they are not sure, and you don't want to upset him if he can hear you or have him worry about his condition, cause that won't help his recovery. I try to get it together but I can't, so two nurses come in and take me out of the room. They were good nurses, they let me cry on their shoulders. They ask me is there anyone I can call, and I cry even harder cause my mom is gone and that was my best friend. I don't have anyone else really, but Tre. Basketball season is at its peak so I can't ask Wayne to walk away from that, it's an important time for him. As I'm standing there I feel a really bad cramp so the nurse asks if I'm okay, I tell her I'm pregnant and I should be on semi bed rest – supposed to stay away from stress etc; she looks concerned. I go to the bathroom and I see spots of blood, not a lot but spots. Oh my GOD I think, this can't be happening, not now. I can't go be in the hospital I gotta be around for Tre. I come back to the nurse's station for the operating room and ask about Nick. No word yet – wow I think what is going on. I ask her where labor and delivery was and she pointed me in the right direction, they offered me a wheel chair, but I refused. I go to labor and delivery and check myself in. After they check me out they say I'm showing signs of stress and that my blood pressure is elevated. They understand the situation, but somehow I have to relax, and that I need to go to the hotel, get some real rest and put my feet up. They tell me that this doesn't look good and it concerns them, that I really need to be laying down. I will I tell them, after I make sure Tre is okay. They tell me if the spotting turns to bleeding to make sure I come back.

Tears again, I think I have taken over the market on crying...

I walk back to the operating area and the nurse said that they have taken Tre up to intensive care. I ask about Nick and she said the Dr. will be over shortly to talk about his condition.

I wait... and finally the doctor comes over and said they removed the bullet from his head and that went very well, they won't know how much damage if any he has had to his brain until he wakes up, right now it seems that he should be okay. As for the bullet that hit his spine it did some damage they were able to repair it but he will need a lot of therapy to walk again, etc. His recovery will be long and hard, but because he is young they believe he will make it. The doctor said it was touch and go for a while with him, his lung had to be repaired as well; he is on a ventilator right now as a precaution. I have nothing to say, I feel so overwhelmed and alone.

I leave and go back upstairs to the intensive care waiting room; I stay there until they finish getting Tre settled into his room. As I'm sitting there I see Nera come through the door, I have never been so happy to see her in my life, she comes over and hugs me.

"Nia, why didn't you call," she said. "You know I was in DC performing at a club, I would have come sooner but I didn't know that Tre and Nick were involved. Fuzz called and said you probably needed me so I hopped on a plane and came as soon as I could."

"Thank you so much Nera,"

She looks at my arm – and notices the band they put on you when you go to labor and delivery – "is the baby okay?" she asked.

"I don't know Nera everything is a mess, I'm cramping and bleeding. They say I have to relax, but I can't – I can't do this – I am so scared."

"I know Nia, but you gotta rest and do what the doctor said."

"HOW?" I ask. "How am I supposed to relax when my husband has just had a kidney removed, and he also has a head injury?"

Before I could finish she said, "Okay, it's okay, we'll get through this. I cancelled everything I had to do, and I'm here,"

I just take a deep breath and sit back.

163

I finally get the opportunity to see Tre and at least they have taken that tube out of his mouth so he is breathing on his own – they say it was only there as a precaution. I stay for a while, but the cramping gets worse, so Nera decides I should go lay down at the hotel. I finally give in and agree to leave, but not before we stop by to see Nick.

She just looks at me and said, "This is too much Nia, Nick don't have no one to take care of him? Where is his girl?"

"Who knows," I tell her. "She finally got tired of him, when I called her, she say they been broke up for two months."

"Well who can blame her, Nera said. It's too bad though ,seems all his mess done caught up with him at one time, and the one person he talk bad about has to take care of him."

"Don't say that Nera."

"Whatever, it's the truth."

We get to the hotel, and it seems that Fuzz's assistant had spoken to the hotel because everything was all set for me. They had even upgraded me from a room to a suite on the same floor as Fuzz. I go to the room and shower, and I look in Tre's bag and grab a t shirt and some boxers. I have no clothes, I just hopped on a plane and flew here, I didn't even pack. Nera tells me to lie down and she'll run to the store to get me something to wear. I thank GOD for her.

I am awakened by Nera coming in from the store, when I look at the clock she had been gone for about two hours. I must have been tired because I don't even remember falling asleep, as I sit up I feel a huge gush and I scream. Nera comes running in the door and just stands there, I look down and there is blood all over my thighs and on the side of the bed. We both just kind of freeze for a moment cause I know she was thinking the same thing I was thinking – NO GOD Please, not my baby too – this just can't be happening…

Nera calls the ambulance and calls Fuzz too; she couldn't get him so she leaves a message on the cell phone. I am once again whisked away in an ambulance. This time, I already know what's wrong and I'm trying to be positive. The EMT workers are all telling me it's going to be okay, but all I could think about was Tre and how devastated he's going to be, and how my life as good as it appears seems to be emotionally falling apart. I get to the hospital and they rush me in, hook me up to the monitor, no heartbeat, and the cramps are horrible and I heard a nurse say my blood pressure was dropping…

The next thing I remember, I wake up in a room and Nera is sitting next to me looking like she has been crying, but she smiles a huge smile when I open my eyes.

"Nia" she said, "oh my GOD you scared me girl, I've never been one to pray much, but I sure prayed today."

165

"What happened?" I said, and she didn't say anything, she changed the subject and said "Fuzz is here. He dropped everything and came right away when I called and told him I was taking you to the hospital."

"Nera, stop changing the subject! What happened?"

She walks out and get the doctor. When the doctor came in – she was really nice she sat on my bed and held my hand.

"Hi Nia, it's nice to meet you with your eyes open," she said. "You scared us for a moment. You lost a lot of blood, and unfortunately, you lost your baby too, I'm so sorry, honey"

She said, "but we are sure glad you made it through – this was a pretty bad miscarriage. I was briefed on your history and I think that because you should have been on bed rest, the flight and all the stress was too much for the already fragile state you were in, and during all of the bleeding your body expelled the baby."

I could not speak, all I could do was cry and this doctor just held my hand and wiped my tears. She told me that I passed out from the loss of blood, so they had to work hard to take care of that, she also said that once they stabilized me, they went in and did a D&C to clean everything out.

She said, "You are blessed honey; this could have been a lot worse. Once things get back to normal, you should be able to try again," and she sat there for a while, and then she left.

I lay there and I refuse to think about how I feel. I decide I have to get out of here, and be there when Tre wakes up, and somehow, I have to figure out how to tell him that I lost his baby. I literally feel like my heart is aching, I don't know what I did to deserve such pain. I really wanted this baby, I feel so empty and so alone. I can't lean on Tre, this is so hard, I wish I could hear him say it's going to be okay, or call my name or something, this feels unbearable. Nera and Fuzz come in, but neither of them say much, they just sit, no one has any words. Fuzz said that he is so sorry about all of this and Nera just sits, I ask him if he can go and check on Tre for me.

"Of course," he said and then he leaves.

I ask Nera to find out when I can get out of here, "Nia" she said, "why are you worried about that you need to heal."

"I'm fine," I tell her. "I need to be here for my husband, can you find out for me please?"

She leaves out, when she comes back she said, "In the morning, but they want you to go home and lie down,"

I just look at her cause I'm getting dressed here, getting on the elevator and going to sit in the intensive care unit with my husband. She also informs me that she called Peaches, because she felt that someone else needed to be here to take care of Nick. I just look at her, and she goes on to say that Peaches was over in Japan on tour with some rapper (she is a back ground dancer) but that she would be home as soon as she could.

Then she said, "You'll be happy to know that I also called Wayne and that he was pissed and upset that you didn't call him. He sounded like he was about to lose it with all this news, and said he would be here as soon as he can."

"Thank you" I tell her.

Inside I was so happy, because I really needed him. I don't call on him much anymore because he is married and I have Tre, but right now I sure do need him.

Fuzz comes back and said Tre is still sedated so he doesn't really know that I have not been there. The nurses say his vitals are stable and if he stays this way he should be out of the intensive care in about four days and they'll move him to intermediate care and see how he does there.

"Okay thanks" I tell him, and then I remember – Nick – and I ask about him.

Fuzz said, "Ray checked on him, even stayed there for a while. The doctors say that miraculously his vitals are stable and that his brain activity is excellent so they don't think he has brain damage, but of course they'll know for sure when he wakes up. They do say that they were able to repair the injury to his spine, but he'll need a lot of physical therapy to walk again like he did before."

"Well at least he is alive," I think.

The nurse comes in with pain medication for me, I take it and in a few minutes I start to doze off.

I stayed in the hospital overnight and was able to go home the next day. As I was leaving the hospital Wayne calls.

"Nia I am so sorry you are going through all of this, I don't know what to say or do, I feel so bad."

"It's okay, I understand that you have a family of your own and that your team is in the playoffs. Keep playing, win a championship."

"Nia if you need me I will not play another game and I'll get on a plane and come to where you are, I don't care what anyone thinks or said. I am always here for you I will always be here for you."

"I know you would I tell him, but I'll be fine."

He informs me that as soon as his season is over he would be here. He said "I love you" and hangs up. I have to admit that was really hard and strange. I guess our relationship really has changed because there was a time that only the world ending would have stopped him from coming to see about me, and on the other hand I did tell him not to come. But I guess this is good – his focus should be his family.

I went back to the hotel, showered, got dressed, and made my way back to the hospital. When I arrived Tre was awake, very drowsy but awake, he didn't say much, but his eyes said he was thrilled to see me. They were moving him from intensive care to intermediate care a lot sooner than we expected, which is a great step in the right direction, if he continues to heal like this, he'll be home soon.

Once he got to his room it took a few hours for him to fully wake up because he had been unconscious for a while and then sedated for several days. But the doctors wanted him to wake up so they could start to get some food into him orally instead of through an IV they would start with liquids first. When he finally got himself together he realized how much pain he was in and he said that I look worried so he asked me what in the world was going on. I had to remember that he doesn't know all that happened to him. He said he remembered walking to Nick's car hearing gun fire and that's it. I told him everything and he just kind of set there stunned, I told him I know this is a lot to take in at one time. He then asks me to come a little closer to him, I got up slowly, hoping he would not notice that I was moving really slow and walk to the bed. He put his arms around me and held me so tight, then he rubbed my belly, and the tears started to flow. I couldn't help it; I didn't know how to tell him that I lost the baby.

He wiped my tears and said, "Baby I'm okay and thank you for being here."

I was so glad that he thought I was crying about him. I have to tell him I just don't know how. And then the big question.

"How is Nick? I mean is he okay? Princess, please tell me Nick is okay."

I sat on the bed next to him and explained all about Nick. Tre really looked like he was in shock, but he kept it together. He asked me if I could ask the doctors if he could go and see Nick. I do what he asks and the nurse came in and told him they would allow him to see Nick, but not today, they want to monitor him first for a while and they would take it from there.

The next week went pretty good and Tre was doing great. The doctors said he could go home soon, but was to take it easy for about three weeks and then he could start getting back to normal. Nick was doing well also; he was awake, not saying much, but awake and expected to make a full recovery with a lot of physical therapy. My challenge was to get Tre home and find a facility for Nick close to our house because now he was our responsibility. Overall, I was happy that everyone was recovering fine, but inside I was feeling pretty overwhelmed. I had not told Tre yet about the baby and I was trying to mentally prepare myself to take care of him, Nick and get things ready for his Dad.

Life Back Home…

We flew home today and I cried the entire flight, Tre slept and I was glad about that because he didn't see me. I feel so sad and I can't shake it, I don't know what to do. I'm hoping that once I tell Tre about the baby I will feel better. I just feel lost and empty and alone and I know I'm none of these things, but I really wanted the baby and losing him or her really hurt, especially how and when it happened.

Once we landed, Fuzz had a limo sent to pick us up and Nera was at the gate waiting for us so that she could help. She has been such a blessing through all of this; I'll have to remember to do something for her. She hugs Tre and me and asks about Nick. I told her he was on a medical flight because he was going straight to the Rehab hospital. We arrive home and get Tre upstairs in the bedroom. I tell Nera thanks and she gives me a look. I shake my head no, the look she gave me was the big question, did you tell Tre yet.

She hugs me tighter and whispers in my ear, "Tell him Nia, he can handle it."

I gave her the address to where Nick was and she agreed to go check on him for me to make sure he was settled. Then she said, "after that, I'm off duty boo, I got to get back to work."

"I know and thanks again, please call if you NEED ANYTHING."

I go into our bathroom and run a tub of water for Tre, he gets in the tub and I sit at the vanity and fill in the schedule for when he should take all his medicine, when his doctor's visits are etc. While he is in the tub I shower, I get out and then I help Tre out of the tub.

"Princess, you don't have to do all this I'm okay a little slow but okay."

"You had major surgery," I tell him.

"I know, but I'm fine and I feel really good looking at you in that towel,"

I just smile and dry him off. He looked so good to me. I'm like, "boy you sure are one sexy patient."

172

He smiled and those dimples show and for a moment, the world seemed right and fair. And then I'm snapped back to reality by one statement.

"Princess, how have you been feeling everything has been about me, and we haven't talked about you and the baby at all."

I just look at him and say, "come on in the room and we can talk."

We both put on our PJ's and sit on the bed.

"Tre, I need to talk to you about the baby."

"Okay," he said and sits up with his back on his pillow.

"Well you know the doctors said I should be on semi bed rest."

"Right," he said.

"With no stress, etc."

"Yeah I know."

"Well Tre," and I just burst into tears and he sits up next to me and grabs me.

"Princess, what are you trying to tell me – stop crying what are you saying" and I looked into his face and I couldn't speak – I felt like I failed him like I let him down.

"Nia, please don't tell me you lost the baby – baby talk to me…Oh my GOD, OH MY GOD." He gets up and slowly walks away from me.

"Tre, I – I lost the baby while you were in the hospital."

"Oh my God," he just kept saying over and over again, he walked back over and knelt down in front of me with his head in my lap – and I have never seen him this way, HE CRIED I mean not loudly but just tears rolling down his face and he held me so tight I felt like I couldn't breathe.

"I'm so sorry Tre, I'm so sorry Tre – I tried hard" and he looks up at me and said, "Nia you have nothing to be sorry for – I'm sorry, I'm sorry I put you through this, I can't imagine what that call must have done to you. I'm sorry that I stressed you out and caused you to lose our baby."

He tries to get himself together and said, "tell me what happened," so I explained everything to him.

He looks me in my eyes with tears still rolling from his and said, "I apologize for allowing you to go through something so painful alone and I'm sorry that I let my love for a friend, put you in jeopardy. This is my fault. I should have never walked Nick to that car."

"No" I tell him, "Tre it's not your fault you didn't do it, my body just couldn't handle it. I was so scared that I was going to lose you that I stressed and my body couldn't take it, it was just a combination of the flight and the stress, but it's okay – I promise I'll give you a baby."

He just looked at me and his eyes said so many things, he was hurt, shocked, but most of all apologetic. He got in the bed and pulled me close to him with my head on his chest.

"Nia thank you so much for being there for me, and for Nick, I know you don't like him, but I know that you made sure he was taken care of for me and that means a lot. I am so sorry you had to lie in that hospital without me."

"It's okay, I'm just glad you are alive, my life would be so empty without you."

We just kind of lay there holding each other, not saying much and finally we both drift off to sleep.

I wake up to Tre sitting up in the bed, staring at me, he was just sitting there staring at me. He had pulled the covers off me while I was sleep and he was just watching me. I wonder to myself if he wants to make love, but I know he has been in a lot of pain and I don't want to make him move to fast, plus I'm sure I should not be engaging just yet for at least for another week. It was just strange he didn't say anything he was just staring.

So finally I said, "Good morning, are you okay?"

"Yeah," he said. "Good morning."

"What are you doing?"

He tells me, "I was watching you and thinking. First, I'm still so blown at how beautiful you are to me. I could look at you all day. I mean you just do it for me. And then I was thinking about how you must have felt when you got a call in the middle of the night like that, I think I would have lost it. I can't imagine my life without you, so I know it must have really hurt to think you might lose me, and then to watch me lying in that hospital, and then to lose the baby all at the same time. I just feel so bad that you went through this, but I'm watching you sleep, and looking at you, even after all that happened, looking at you and being here with you makes me feel like the world is still okay. Nia I want you to know that I want to have babies with you, but if you want to wait it's okay. If we have babies' great, if we don't, I'm fine. You are more than enough for me. I realized that I need you. You know I laid there in that hospital and I could hear you talk to me. All I wanted to do was open my eyes and see you, I kept telling myself no matter how much pain I was in, that I had to live because I had not loved you enough, there is so much more I need to give you."

I'm just speechless, I lay there and I said nothing, there are no words for how this man makes me feel, he leaned over and kissed me like it had been years since his lips had touched mine – it felt like time stood still for a moment.

"Nia, I know you need to heal, but I need you so bad, I feel like I'm going to explode. I laid in the hospital thinking about being with you, I watched you in the shower last night and I know we should wait, but I want you to know that there is no injury that could keep me from wanting to be with you."

I sit up and take off my night gown, and he took a breath that sounded like he was seeing something amazing for the first time.

"Tre it has not been that long."

"It feels like years Nia, you don't understand."

He laid me down and just stared at me – "I laid in that hospital and I thought I would go crazy, I'm like I can't die and have somebody else make love to my wife – I feel like you were created for me. I just can't get enough."

He slid down in the bed next to me and turned me over on my stomach, he rubbed and kissed every inch of me from the base of my neck to my ankles. Then he flipped me over and slid his body very gently into mine and he made love to me like he had not been with me in years. (I'm thinking I guess he was not in as much pain as I thought). When we finally come up for air, he held me and asked if I'm okay, if I feel alright.

"I'm fine," I tell him as I lay on his chest. "Tre you amaze me, sometimes I think you are too good to be true."

"I'm not perfect Nia – I have flaws, but I have just figured out that having a wife is a gift and you treat your gifts well. I feel like I owe you for all you went through, and I'm going to make it up to you."

"What, you are the one who was shot."

"Yeah I know, but I'm fine. You almost lost your husband and you lost your baby and you did it all alone without your husband, the man that's supposed to always be there for you – and I'm mad at myself for this, cause it didn't have to happen. I'm going to make it up to you, I promise."

I guess the conversation must have somehow turned him on, cause the next thing I know he was flipping me over and sliding right back into place.

COMFORTABLE IN DARKNESS

We had a storm today and all the power went out for a while. I just sat in the dark and I thought about how sometimes life pushes you into a dark place and we can just get comfortable in the darkness and stay there. Sometimes we get so comfortable with pain that we expect it and we hold on to it because it becomes such a big part of you, it's what we know.

It's been about 8 weeks since Tre has been home and our lives seem to be getting back to normal. He's been spending about two hours a day in the studio down stairs and plans to really get back to work in another two weeks. I started fixing up the bedroom at the end of the hall for his dad and we turned the study on the first floor into a bedroom for Nick when he comes home, so there are contractors down stairs adding a bathroom there for him. Our lives are going to be different and a little strange for me living in the house with three men. But we'll see how this goes.

The doorbell rings and its Wayne – I'm really glad to see him, I open the door and I get the biggest smile and warmest hug from him. He kind of held on for a while, and I know him so I know that this was not just cause he was glad to see me – he comes in and sits his bags down.

"Wow, boo it's good to see you."

"You too Nia, I'm sorry it took me so long. I had games to play and I couldn't get away, but as soon as I was able I hopped on a plane and here I am. How have you been?"

"I'm fine," I tell him. "Holding on, every day is easier."

How is Tre?"

"He's good – he's down in the studio."

He gets up and goes down to see him, so I follow. Tre smiles when he sees him and they do their man hug.

"Thank you for coming out to visit man – how is everything?"

Wayne tells him life is fine, but something in his voice tells me otherwise. They talk for a while and Tre decides that we should all go out to dinner. We have been home for a while. We should get out and do something. Good idea, I think. I show Wayne to the guest room, we decide we'll leave for dinner around 7pm.

Tre gets dressed before me and he sure looks good in his cream outfit, I always love to see him in cream. He goes downstairs and said he would wait for me there. I got my figure back, so I decide I'll show it off a little. I have this brown strapless stress that kind of just clings to your curves its ankle length with a split up to mid-thigh and has the cutest bronze belt that kind of just dangles off you. So I put on these cute bronze shoes, grab the matching bag, of course and I grab the jewelry to match and a jacket. As I walk into the kitchen where Tre and Wayne are, Wayne stands up and grabs my hand.

"Girl you look good – oh my goodness," and Tre just looks at him out the corner of his eyes.

"Yeah you do princess," then he walks over and takes my hand out of Wayne's and is like "let's go."

We decide to take Wayne's rental car – only because he insisted he had rented this Bentley and wanted to show it off.

"Wayne, I'm not in the mood for no celebrity stunts today, so let's go someplace quiet. I don't feel like being mobbed by your fans or Tre's for that matter."

"Me either" he said, so he calls a friend he knows that owns a restaurant in down town Atlanta and lets him know that we are coming. We arrive at the restaurant and are whisked away to a private room. Dinner was great, and surprisingly the conversation was fun and easy. I was proud of Tre because I know hanging with Wayne is sometimes awkward for him – only because he whole heartedly believes the man is in love with me. We leave the restaurant and decide that we'll go home and sit in the hot tub on the deck for a while.

We got home, changed and all jumped into the hot tub, it was a beautiful night. Tre went in and got drinks and snacks for us to nibble on while we sat out there. Wayne asked a ton of question about Tre being shot, and me losing the baby. We filled him in on everything and I was glad that he asked about it with Tre there, it made him feel included. It was getting late and I could tell Tre was getting tired – so I told him to take his medicine and go to bed. I could tell that he was hesitant about leaving me alone in a bathing suit with Wayne, but I lean over, kiss him, and tell him it's okay, I promise to be up shortly. He reluctantly gets out the hot tub grabs his towel and goes inside.

Wayne just looks at me and I'm like, "What?"

"Girl I have missed you so much – you have no idea."

"Really, I can't tell."

"Nia you know why I stay away"

"Yes I do," I said. "But how are you really – I know something is bothering you, besides what went on with Tre and me."

"Well, my life is screwed – it seemed to have been that way since you have not been around."

"Wayne, I have not gone anywhere."

"I know, it's just different, but the best thing in my life has been my daughter."

I'm stunned, "what is going on with Lisa?"

"Nia, she is cheating, I know she is."

I'm stunned, "after all these years – why cheat now?"

"I don't know," he said. "I guess I'm on the road too much."

"I'm so sorry boo," I tell him.

"It hurt so much to find this out you know, I work hard I have loved that girl since we were kids. You know I do all I can for her, and this is how she repay me – if it wasn't for the baby, I would've put her out."

"Have you talked to her about it?"

"Yeah, she knows I know."

"How did you find out?"

"I caught her."

"WHAT!"

"Yeah I caught her, you know she said that her and a few of her girlfriends were going to Hawaii for a couple of days to stay at our beach house – kind of a girls weekend. So that's cool, cause I can spend time alone with Paris, but what got me was that she pack up and left, but one of the girls she is always hanging out with called the house looking for her. So I got the nanny to watch the baby and the next day I flew out there and when I get to the house, she down stairs in my beach house cooking for some dude and he upstairs in my shower. You know what Nia, I didn't go crazy or nothing I just turned around and left. I flew home the next day and so did she. She apologized, said all the right stuff, and we are supposed to go to counseling."

"Wow Wayne, I don't know what to say."

He leans over and lays in my arms, "There is nothing to say, this is good enough."

I just hold him. I know Tre would have a fit, but I didn't know what else to do. He stays there for a while.

"Nia – I miss being able to do this – our friendship was always my safe place. I guess I never worried about a lot of things because I had you."

"I know Wayne."

"Tre is a good man, I'm glad he loves you like he does. For real, he has every right to look at me like he does."

"What?"

"Yeah, I see him look at me and if I were him I would too. You turned out to be my perfect woman; you are the only girl that never hurt me. I can't have you and I should have tried to get you when I could – I just took you for granted."

"Wayne – look you feel that way because your life is a mess right now, but you love Lisa and this will work out. She loves you too, and she put up with a lot, if she doesn't make a mistake again try to work it out with her. Does she know you are here?"

"Yeah she knows."

"Is she worried?"

"She said she wasn't cause Tre was here."

"Wayne," I said. "I guess us not seeing each other is good"

"Yeah," he said. "Right now it's very good – and right now I'm going to get out of your arms, cause I've had all I can take and I'm going to bed."

He gets out the hot tub and stands on the side to help me. I feel a little awkward right now cause I'm all in my bathing suit, but I got to get out the tub. I stand up and his face said it all, he grabs me and hugs me and it was WRONG.

"Wayne – hold up – this is my house."

"I know Nia. I just wanted to hold you one more time. I'll leave in the morning. I know that in the frame of mind I'm in I can't stay and I don't want to disrespect Tre, and I know every time you walk in the room – my face said it all."

"Wayne," I tell him. "I want you to go to counseling and save your marriage. Work it out, I know you love her."

"Yeah I do, but she broke my heart and this ain't cool and looking at you right now I wonder if I love her like I love you."

"I can't handle all this right now." I tell him, "I'm trying to keep my own self together."

I tell him to have a good night and I go upstairs to my room. When I walk in my room, Tre is still up.

"Why you up baby?"

"Do you really think I was going to sleep while my wife is in a hot tub with a man that I know wants her? Why it take you so long to come to bed?"

"Tre, why are you yelling at me?"

"What are you talking about? Nia I'm not stupid, you are going to tell me what's going on with you and Wayne, or I'm going to talk to him myself – cause this ain't cool and I know what I see in his face when he looks at you."

I don't say anything I just go in the bathroom and shower, so he comes in the bathroom while I'm in the shower and just goes off.

"This been going on long enough and I know something is not right. You better start talking now."

So I get out the shower, grab a towel and go to the bed with him following me. He grabs my arm and snatches me close to him. Now I'm about to be pissed.

"Tre, stop man handling me."

"Answer me now Nia. You got one minute or I'm going down the hall to talk to him myself."

"First of all, if you felt like this you should have just stayed out there with me and secondly, his wife is cheating."

"WHAT – LISA?"

"Yes, his wife is cheating. He caught her and he is all messed up in the head about it."

"I'm sorry to hear that, but that's bull. What's in his eyes ain't got anything to do with Lisa."

"Okay Tre – sit down – a long time ago, well when Wayne called me to tell me that him and Lisa got married he told me something else."

"I'm listening," Tre said.

"He told me that he realized that he was in love with me but" – Those big brown eyes look like they were going to jump out of his head.

186

"I knew it you knew this all this time and you never told me. NIA how could you keep that from me? That man in my house down the hall, looking at my wife. What else he say – have you ever?"

Before he could finish I said, "Tre, now you going too far you know you were my first."

"I'm talking about after that."

"Now you talking crazy – are you accusing me of cheating?"

"I'm just asking a question."

"Tre don't play victim here, I have never been with Wayne and you know that, and I didn't tell you because I knew you couldn't handle it. But don't act like you ain't put me in the same place with Peaches and you just expect me to understand. I mean you had sex with her and she still be sitting at my dinner table eating my food and you expect me to just grin and bear it."

He calms down, "Okay princess you got a point, but I didn't have sex with her."

"Tre please, oral sex is sex."

"Well Nia you may be right, but I can't handle it I'm not you."

"Like I like this mess – I don't even understand why you feel like you have to take care of her."

"I'll tell you about that later, right now I'm going to talk to Wayne."

"You can come too, but I'm going to talk to him and he has to leave my house. I'm not having this."

So I put on my night gown and start to follow him – "Umm I don't think so get a robe Nia and stop playing with me."

I grab my robe and we walk down the hall. Wayne was already standing in the door; I guess he heard us because Tre was real loud, even though the guest room is on the other side of the hall.

"Hey man, can you come down stairs, we all need to talk."

Wayne agrees and we all go to the kitchen and sit at the table, I feel so embarrassed because I have never seen Tre like this, I really don't know what to expect. So Tre don't waste no time he looks at Wayne and is like, "Are you in love with my wife?"

Wayne just kind of looks at him and then he looks at me and his eyes said yes I love you with all my heart. I just turn my head.

"Don't look at her man, be a man and tell me to my face dude – you in my house – you send my wife expensive gifts, you tell her in front of me how she look all kinds of stuff. I know y'all WERE best friends, but I'm her best friend now. You got to understand and RESPECT that, so tell me you in love with my wife?"

So Wayne looks at him and said, "Tre man – you know I love Nia."

This crazy man hits the counter, "Don't play with me you know what I said – ARE YOU IN LOVE WITH NIA WHITMORE?"

So Wayne looks at him and said, "Yes, no, yes, but its not like you think. I don't really know what to say."

I could have crawled into a hole in the wall. So Tre sits there for a moment, because I think it was different hearing him say it.

"Yeah man, I guess... but it's different. I have loved Nia my whole life, but I didn't realize how much until she met you, but I respect you man. I'm not trying to mess up your home. You know I don't want to cause any problems. That's why I stay away."

I am surprised at Wayne's tone and demeanor and I know his temperament is all about me – because Wayne can be real hood when he wants to.

"You know she is like my family and I don't know how to let go."

"Well," Tre said. "You letting go now dude cause you can't come around here no more."

"Tre," I said – he looked at me like he was about to slap me, so I politely shut up.

Wayne looks at him and said, "You know Tre I understand and I can respect that cause it's probably best. Cause every time I see her, I realize just how much I love her and I really miss her and being away is really hard, but I do it because I really do want her to be happy and she is happy with you. She loves you – you are the only man that she has ever loved really and I'm glad she got somebody she deserves. It's just hard for me because that's the best friend I got in this world, right now. But, you are right – I don't need to come around – but I ask you to please let me call her for her birthday and at holidays, can I do that?"

Tre looked like he was about to explode, "You talking about calling and birthdays and I'm stuck on you being in love with my wife and I know I heard you say underneath all that crap that basically the more you see her the more you know you want to have sex with her."

"I didn't say that."

"Yes you did man – come on dude I'm a man just like you. I know what you see when you see her. Just admit it, you want her."

At this point I have had enough, "Tre this is too much."

"Then LEAVE NIA.., GO TO YOUR ROOM", he yelled.

"Tre I'm not a child and you need to calm down."

Wayne looks at us and said, "Look, I'm leaving, I never unpacked anyway, I'll get a hotel room tonight and fly out in the morning. I just wanted to come out here and make sure both of you were okay. I'm sorry that I caused a problem; I guess my life is a mess and I just brought all my drama out here to y'all, and that was not my intention. Tre man I'm sorry, I won't be in your way. I would never do anything to hurt Nia and she whole heartedly loves you. She has nothing to do with how I feel about her, she didn't do anything, and I know you are thinking it. I never slept with her man – you were her first and only – I hope you know how special that is"

"I don't need you to tell me nothing about my wife" Tre said and he gets up and leaves.

I'm just sitting there, lost, confused, sad, mad – all kinds of emotions. Wayne gets up, he walks over to where I am at the table and

said, "I do love you, I always will, I'm sorry I caused confusion because
of it, I can't help it and I'm not mad about it. I understand how Tre feels
and he's right to feel that way. Just know that I will always be only a
phone call away."

He kisses me on the forehead gets his things and he leaves. I am in
shock, what kind of a day was this. I just sit at the table until Tre comes
downs stairs, gets something to drink, looks at me, and goes back upstairs
he said nothing. So I get up finally, I go to my room. Tre is in bed and he
is ANGRY.

So I said, "Why are you so mad at me?"

He won't answer me. He just looks at me with no words. I just
shake my head take off my robe and lay down. He gets out of the bed,
goes to the closet grabs a blanket goes to the sitting area of our room and
lays on the couch and sleeps there for the night.

Peaches ...

Tre had not spoken to me in two days and its really starting to hurt.
I've tried talking to him, but he said he can't talk to me right now, he is
not ready. There is a knock at the door and Tre answers it and its Peaches

Oh NO! When he opens the door she jumps on him to the point
that he falls on the floor and she kisses him all over his face.

"Tre I'm so glad you are okay, I'm so sorry it took me so long to
get home, I was out of the country."

"Its okay," he tells her with this big smile on his face. "I'm glad to see you now."

I walk in the foyer and she looks at me and said, "Hey ne – sorry to hear that you lost your baby."

"Our baby," I said.

And that was it and he picks her bags up and takes them up stairs to the guest room and I'm thinking to myself – is she staying here. So she goes in the guest room and I'm like "Tre is she staying here?"

"Yes," he said. "I told her she could."

"For how long?" I ask.

"I don't know," he said. "I guess until she goes back on tour, she don't have her own place yet."

My heart sank – he is really trying to hurt me – he's never been like this before. I go downstairs and peaches is in my kitchen in her booty shorts and a bra top, so I tell her, "This ain't the ho house you are used to staying in. This is my home and you can't walk around my husband like that."

"It's cool Ne she said I'll put on something else."

So she goes into her room and puts on a T shirt. Tre comes down stairs and said, "Peaches I made dinner reservations," and then he looks at me and said, "Nia are you coming?"

"No thanks!"

A few hours later Tre gets dressed and him and Peaches go to dinner.

Lost It...

When Tre and Peaches walked out the door to dinner it felt like every bad experience I had in the past year just came to the surface. He's never hurt me before, but seeing him walk out the door with her, broke something in me, because I knew he was deliberately trying to hurt me and that's something he said he would not do. I felt like I wanted my mom, but she was not there. I could not call Wayne, I felt so hurt and just broke like I could not wrap my mind around why he would do this and think it's okay. The pain I felt was not about them going to dinner it was the intent behind it that hurt and I began to cry I felt like from my soul. I lost my mom, I lost my best friend, I lost my baby, I can't believe I lost my baby it just hurt so bad , nobody will ever understand what it felt like to lay in that hospital alone . I don't know how to handle this.

Tre and Peaches came home around two in the morning, said they went to dinner and to the club for a while, they even took some pictures. He has not slept in the bed with me in two days and he hasn't touched me either. I don't have the energy or strength to fight – emotionally I feel I have nothing left I got to get it together somehow.

I get up early cause I have to go and sign some more papers for Nick, so I go to the rehab center. Nick is doing pretty well, he is talking and able to get around in a wheel chair, he can even stand now. Physical therapy for him is very intense, but the doctors say he will recover at some point, they just don't know how long it will take. They are going to release him soon, so that's what I have to set up because he'll have a therapist come to the house three days a week. When I arrive he actually looks happy to see me and concerned.

"Hey Nia."

"Hi Nick."

"What's wrong with you girl, you look depressed."

"I'm fine," I tell him.

"You are fine girl." Then he said, "Hey Nia, I know we aren't the best of friends, but I've been around you long enough to know you don't look like yourself. Sit down, there is something I want to tell you anyway."

I sit and he starts talking, "Thank you for taking care of me all this time – I know you made sure I had the best care and I appreciate it. I know you probably would have preferred that I was dead, but I know you took care of me because of Tre."

"That's true, but I don't wish you dead, I just wish you didn't cause so much trouble."

"Look Nia." He said, "I guess Tre never told you huh?"

"Told me what?"

"The reason Tre looks out for me and Peaches like he does. It's because he always has, see he was at the first group home before us. My parents got locked up, my dad was a pimp and they ran a prostitution ring, but after she got out she left me she just didn't want me. She just decided that I was too much trouble so she left me with a neighbor – well the neighbor was a woman with a liking for young boys so she decided I should be one of her "men". She had a live in boyfriend and later I found out that he had a thing for little girls. She made me do stuff – so you know I decided that no woman would ever make me do anything again that I would always be in control. Well Peaches was her daughter and that's why she acts like she do. When you a little girl having sex with a grown man, it messes with your mind.

The school found out I was living with her and reported us to CPS – well when they came to check out my situation they found drugs in the house and Peaches told them about the abuse, so they removed us. When we got to the group home the older kids you know they use to try and make you do stuff, but Tre was a fighter and I guess he felt bad for us, so from day one he would defend us. He taught us the ropes, like how to survive and I think he just felt sorry for us, you know once we told him our situation. It was like an instant bond between the three of us, we went through a lot you know. We been in some tough situations together, we went from group home to group home until we ended up at the last one, and that's where life really started for us, but we vowed we were family, you know and that nothing and no one would change that. So when you came along, you seemed like an intruder. You know Tre was our family and you seem like you were taking him away and you know Peaches she loves Tre. Nia I ain't going to lie to you – you got to watch her. I love her like a sister, but she loves Tre, she always has, she'll do anything for him."

I was stunned again – that's like my new middle name, "Thanks for sharing that with me Nick – it explains a lot."

"Well now that you know about me, what's up with you?"

I told him about Wayne and he was like, "Yeah – Tre don't like to feel threatened."

Then I told him about Peaches.

"WHAT! That's over the top, it ain't like him. He must really be pissed with you girl."

"I know this."

I ask him if he knew I lost the baby – and for the first time I see some emotion in him.

"Naw Nia, I didn't know that I'm sorry. Wow girl you been through the ringer and he acting like this, you want me to talk to him?"

"Nah, it's okay," I tell him.

I tell him it's getting late and I got to go, I tell him about the room I had done for him and that I'll see him in a couple of days. I kiss him on the cheek and tell him thanks for the talk and I leave.

When I get home, Tre and Peaches are in the family room watching TV.

"Nia come here," he yells, so I walk in the family room. "Where have you been?"

I just look at him and I turn around and go to my room. Peaches gives a giggle. I guess this is making her day. I go to my room and shower, when I walk out the shower Tre is sitting on the sink in the bathroom.

"You look good."

"Whatever," I said to him.

"You do Nia, just cause I'm angry don't mean I'm blind. You look like you lost weight, you haven't been eating"

I just ignore him and go into the room – he follows me.

"What do you want Tre?"

"I want to know where you were."

"I went to the rehab center to take care of your friend."

He gets quiet, "I forgot those papers had to be signed today."

"Yeah," I tell him. "You were too busy, ignoring me, and taking care of Peaches."

All of a sudden tears start to roll down my face, and I'm angry at myself for crying ... he don't deserve my tears, but I can't help it. In that moment the anger leaves his face.

"Nia, I'm sorry."

"I don't want your apology Tre, you did something to me that I can't explain. You waited until I was at my lowest point and you turned on me. Here I am trying to take care of you, your friend, get things ready for your father, keep my emotions under control cause I lost my baby in the middle of one of the scariest times of my life and you get mad at me and shut me out at that moment when I had no strength of my own. I needed you and you weren't there, and this time it was your choice." He just sits there. "I know Wayne freaked you out and I can handle that, I lost my best friend and I didn't do anything wrong, but I was okay with that because you are my choice, but you just ... I can't explain it – it feels like you broke my soul and I can't seem to get it together."

"Nia – wow – I wasn't thinking. I was just so MAD and so hurt and I felt threatened cause I know you love Wayne and that messed with my head. You are my everything, and to think someone else was moving in on that I could not handle that. It hurt too much."

"No one was moving in on you, you could be mad but you didn't have to treat me like that and then you bring the one woman in my house you know would hurt me. I know how she feels about you and you had sex with her! You crossed a line – after you told me you were going to do everything in your power to make it up to me for having to go through all this stuff by myself. I don't know if you know what it feels like to have the person you love most shatter something on the inside of you."

He tries to touch me, but I can't right now, "I don't want you to touch me, I need to get it together."

He just stands there, I guess, reality was setting in. "I know sorry is not enough huh?"

"Nope I tell him. Don't worry about me Tre – I'll be okay."

I put on my pajamas and got into bed. Tre leaves out of the room and is gone for I don't know how long. I'm awakened by him climbing into bed and tapping me.

"Nia, please wake up."

I turn over, "what?"

"I can't sleep I need to talk to you."

"About what Tre?"

"I got to talk to you."

"Okay", I sit up in the bed.

"I'm sorry I hurt you, I won't ever hurt you again. I mean that, I want you to promise me that you won't leave me."

"What"

"I got to know that you won't leave me."

"What makes you think that I would?"

"Nia, I have never been so angry in my life. I felt like I could have killed Wayne – that man looked me in my face and said he was in love with my wife and I know you didn't do anything, but I felt like you should have told me. I couldn't handle it, I felt like he was going to steal you from me."

"Tre I'm here with you because I want to be. If I wanted to be with Wayne, I would not have married you, I don't plan on going anywhere, but I'm just not in a place right now where I can deal with all this stuff. I can't take care of you, Nick, get ready for your father, get my self together and look at Peaches too. I would never ask you to live with a man that I have been intimate with."

"Why you say it like that?"

"You don't think oral sex is intimate?" He nods his head yes. "Plus I talked to Nick and I know that girl loves you."

"You talked to Nick?"

"Yep, he told me the whole history"

"Really?"

"Yeah – I mean I understand, but when you put her before me you crossed a line. You went out with her that's not right."

"Well Nia I felt like you cheated on me."

"WHAT!"

"I know you didn't, but to hear another man say he was in love with you felt like you were cheating and I wanted you to know what that felt like."

"Well it hurt – and I didn't cheat – and I would never deliberately hurt you. But if that's what you needed to do to me then you succeeded. I'm hurt and I feel really bad, I hope that makes you happy."

"Actually Nia, it doesn't. I feel really stupid and I asked Peaches to go and stay at Nicks place since he'll be here, so she packed her stuff up and left."

I just look at him. "I'm going to make it up to you."

"You can't." I tell him, "and don't make me anymore promises."

I guess for the first time in this relationship I had a revelation, Mr. Trevon Whitmore is not perfect ...

THE BIG MOVE

It's been a month since Tre and I had our fight, things seem to be getting back to normal. Tre has done everything he can think of to make it up to me, and I appreciate it. Really the issues I have don't have anything to do with our fight, I forgive him whole heartedly for what happened, he had every right to be upset. I just feel like something is missing in my life and he can't fix it, I appreciate his trying, but he can't fix the way I'm feeling. It's weird, I'm a counselor, I am normally able to help everybody else but I can't seem to help myself. Losing my mom was hard and it made losing the baby that much harder, and then to once and for all give up my best friend was much harder than I thought it would be. I guess I figured he was like my emergency plan if things didn't work I always had someone to run to. Plus he'd always been there, so it was hard to walk away from him and that really hurt, and it's not something I can really talk to Tre about. With all of this going on inside me, I have to put on my best face and try real hard to be a good daughter in law because Tre's father is moving in on Friday.

Daddy's Home...

Tre's father is moving in today and he wanted everything to be perfect for him, so I had the suite at the end of the hall done for him, and Tre insisted that I prepare a big soul food meal. We decided that he would drive down to pick him up and I would stay to make sure everything is prepared. Tre got up early and left to go pick up his dad, so I got started cooking – all this and it will only be three of us here at least that I know of, but this is what he wanted. I put balloons on the gate outside and on the door, I put a big welcome home banner in the foyer and one on his door. Then I get in the kitchen and get started cooking – since he wanted soul food that's what he will get. I pin up my hair, jump into some comfortable clothes and start cooking I decide that I will prepare, fried chicken, ribs, roast beef, sweet potatoes, greens, potato salad, macaroni and cheese, homemade corn bread, sweet potato pie, peach cobbler, and I baked a chocolate cake. I figure by the time all this food is done and I set the table, Tre and his dad should be home.

The time seem to fly, before I knew it Tre was calling me on the phone saying he and his father were about twenty minutes from the house. I was done with the food and the table was set, but I was a mess, so I run to my room, jump in the shower and throw on some jeans and a nice shirt. There was nothing I could do with my hair so I redo my pony tail, as I am coming down the stairs I hear Tre's father saying, "GOD has been good to you son, this house is gorgeous" and he looks up and said, "so is the lady of the house, Hi doll baby."

"Hi Mr. Whitmore."

"Please Nia, call me Trent."

"Well Hi Trent," I said. "Welcome home."

Tre of course has a big grin on his face that just means he is happy with the effort I made to make things look festive for his father's arrival. His dad meets me at the bottom of the step and gives me the warmest hug.

"You are little Nia, you didn't seem that small the first time I met you."

"I know," I tell him. "That's because I was pregnant and had put on some weight,"

He got quiet for a moment and said, "Oh that's right, I'm sorry about that Nia,"

"Don't be," I tell him. "Let me show you to your suite."

"My suite?"

"Yes," I said. "Your suite"

"Wow, I was expecting a room in a nice house, not a suite in this mansion."

"This is not a mansion" I tell him – "we are working on that."

I lead him to his room and Tre follows carrying his bags. When he enters he has a bedroom nicely done, a small sitting area with a recliner and a TV and stereo, DVD, etc and a computer desk and computer and a book shelf. He also has a walk in closet and a private bath, he almost looked overwhelmed.

"WOW" he said again. "Did this house come with all this?"

"No." Tre said, "Nia had this room redesigned so you would be more comfortable."

"Are you hungry?" I ask.

"Yes," he said. "It's been years since I've had a home cooked meal."

"Dad, Nia is a REALLY good cook – you are in for a treat."

We go down stairs and into the dining room.

"I'll show you the rest of the house after dinner," I tell him. He sits down at the table and just really looks like he can't believe what he is seeing. We hold hands and his Dad prays – he thanked GOD for everything and then we ate, and this man ate like he had not eaten in years for real. I was happy that I did prepare that much food.

"Nia, I can't believe you can cook like this, you are so young."

"My momma taught me," I told him.

Tre said, "Yeah dad, she can make anything."

We ate and talked and laughed it was a nice time and Tre seemed so happy – it was nice to see. But again it got me to thinking about my own father and wondering why he was not around and where he may be.

When dinner was over, Tre and his Dad retreat to the family room and I of course head to the kitchen to clean up, but after about ten minutes Trent comes in and starts to help me put the food away and put the dishes into the dishwasher. I told him he didn't have to, but he insisted.

He said, "After all that cooking and I know that took a lot of time, the least I can do is help you clean up."

As we are cleaning up he asked me a lot of question about my life, where I was from, he told me all about his child hood and how he met

Tre's mom. We take our conversation into the family room and Tre joins in – Trent said I remind him a lot of Tre's mom and he can see why Tre fell in love with me so fast.

He said, "It's so weird how much like her you are. You don't look like her, but your mannerisms and attitude are almost identical to hers."

"Thanks" I tell him. "That can only be a compliment."

We decide that now would be a good time to show him the rest of the house, but I let Tre do that. Tre shows him the house and then they come back. Trent decides he would like to see the video of our wedding. We all watch that, and after that was over I was tired and so was Trent so we all retreat to our rooms. He asked if we had plans for tomorrow, Tre said yes, going to take him shopping so he can get clothes and things that he may need. Trent just looks overwhelmed, he didn't even say anything he just hugged us both good night and went into his room.

Once Tre and I are ready for bed, out of the blue he just starts talking about how he wished he knew his father growing up.

"I understand," I tell him.

He looks at me and then he said, "Nia – you want to find your father?"

"I have been thinking about it, even started looking, but when you got shot I put all that on hold."

"You should continue, and let me know if you need help. I will do whatever I can."

"Thanks" I tell him.

"Tre don't forget that Nick is coming home soon."

"Oh Wow, I completely forgot. I was so caught up on my Dad that I forgot about Nick coming too – I should let my father know about that."

"Yeah" I tell him. "I'm done with his room."

"Nia you have been wonderful, taking care of my family – I know this is not easy."

"NO." I tell him, "and it aint cheap either. We have spent a lot of money lately on remodeling and doctor bills, etc. Do you think I should go back to work?"

Tre sits up quickly, "Nah why Nia, you think I can't take care of you? I'm back at work now and financially we are doing fine. Our investments are doing great and we are making money off the rent for the condo. Is there something you want, or need that you feel you can't get?"

"No Tre, I just know that we have spent a lot of money lately and I was wondering if I should go back to work to kind of make up for what we spent."

"No way," he said. "I don't want you to work a nine to five anymore, but if you want to do something Fuzz asked me how I felt about you dancing in his knew video. He's looking for a lead dancer for his new single."

"What did you say?"

"I told him I didn't know and that I would talk to you about it to see if you were interested. I also told him that you CAN NOT dance in no skimpy outfit."

"Good." I said, "cause I'm not doing that but I may be interested in dancing though – is the song positive?"

"Yeah," he said. "It's got a tight beat too, you could probably have a lot of fun with it."

"Okay – it will be nice for us to work together – as long as you can handle it Tre."

"I'll keep my cool," he said.

"We can talk to Fuzz on Monday."

"Oh one more thing," I said. "The money is good? Right?"

"Heck yeah," he said. "I already told him that, if you dance he got to pay you professional money."

"Good."

Tre and his father were gone most of the day on Saturday out shopping. While they were out I decide to work out and then to start choreographing a dance to one of Fuzz's songs in case he wants me to audition. I didn't worry about cooking dinner. I figured they could eat leftovers, which is exactly what they did when they got home. I left them alone for most of the evening – it seems the two of them were having a good time playing catch up.

Tre comes in and asks me what I think of him giving his dad his Escalade since its old and he had it since college.

"It's in excellent condition."

He said he can give his dad that truck and he'll go buy himself a new one, it's about time anyway.

"That's fine, but let's shop around for the new car cause we don't do car notes. So if we are about to kick out a lot of money then I want the best deal out there."

"Great," he said and he goes to tell his dad he can have his truck.

Sunday morning, I get up at about 8 am to go and make breakfast, as I pass his father's room I hear him up. He had on church music and he was praying. Wow I thought, I guess he was telling the truth, he does live his life differently. As I finish breakfast he comes downstairs all nicely dressed."

"Where you going Trent?" I ask.

"To church," he said. "I got on the internet and looked for this church I saw on TV when I was locked up. The messages the Pastor preached really helped and I always said that I would go there when I got out. It just so happened that his church is in Georgia only about twenty minutes from here. You want to go with me?" he asked.

"Not today." I tell him, "but I'll go with you sometime."

Tre was still sleep so he and I ate breakfast and he left. I put Tre's breakfast on a tray and take it up to him so he can have breakfast in bed.

Once he was done eating, he thanked me and told me that he and his dad had talked about a lot of things and he wanted to run them by me. His father had decided that he wanted to let his family know he was out and to have them over for dinner mainly so that he could meet them and know who his family was.

That's fine, but can we get through one thing at a time. Let's get Nick home and settled and into his routine and then we can concentrate on your 'family reunion."

He laughs and agrees.

Nick moves in...

Time seems to goes by pretty fast and I have to admit I have enjoyed having Tre's father around. Tre took him earlier in the week to meet Nick, just so it won't be too awkward when he moves in. He also sat him down and explained their whole relationship to him. I was happy to see that Trent didn't look too happy after hearing about all the trouble that Nick had caused, but he understood the bond, so he didn't make a comment. I am okay with taking care of Nick, what I don't like is that if he moves in, I know Peaches will find her way over here on a regular basis. The way I see it something has to be done about her, if I can let go of Wayne then Tre can let her go.

Tre insisted that I give Nick the same kind of welcome that his dad got except Nick likes seafood, so he wanted me to cook for him. I stay home while he goes to the rehab to pick Nick up, and his Dad stayed home with me, said he wanted to watch me cook. He sat at the breakfast bar while I prepared all the food.

He just kept saying, "Nia you just don't know how amazed I am that you cook like this, most young ladies your age can't boil water."

"I love cooking," I told him.

"You should cater," he suggested.

'I think about it sometimes, I do minor stuff, just haven't started a business yet."

Trent tells me that Fuzz offered him a job as a bouncer at the club, but that he refused it because he can't afford to be back in that life style. He didn't think it was a good idea for him, he said he had been praying and that he believed GOD would give him a good job.

"What do you want to do?" I asked him.

"Well I have a degree in Psychology. I got it while I was in prison."

"Wow." I told him, "I'm a counselor by profession, I know of an organization that does rehab for ex con's if you are interested. Maybe I can make some calls and see what I can do."

"My angel," he said. "Please if you don't mind I would love that."

"Sure, give me a few days and I'll get back to you."

While I was finishing up dinner for Nick, I had Trent go and hang a welcome sign on his door. That's all he get I thought to myself, this is something else. Since he still has to use a walker to get around, we turned

212

the study into a bedroom for him so he wouldn't have to go up the steps and we added a bathroom.

Trent sits back down after hanging the sign and said, "Nia I can tell you don't like Nick."

"I don't know how I feel about him Trent, I don't trust him. He free loads off Tre, but Tre loves him."

"How does he treat you?"

"He has been rude in the past, but after the shooting he has been kind of nice to me, I don't know what to think." I tell him," I just take it one day at a time with Nick."

"Tre told me about Peaches too."

"Wow, he got you all up to speed, did he tell you that I DON'T LIKE HER."

"Yeah he did."

"Did he tell you why?" I ask him.

"He just said the two of you don't get along.

"That ain't why Trent ... they were intimate in the past, and she still make passes at him. She's in love with him, you can see it all over her, wait till you meet her." I said.

At this point he is frowning, "I'm not lying," I tell him.

He just shakes his head, doesn't say much. I figure, he is going to see for himself.

"I'm sure she'll be over here today so you can definitely see for yourself."

R. Gaskins ~ BROKEN

Nick, Tre and Peaches arrive just like I suspected. Peaches was at the rehab center when Tre got there and she followed them home. Nick comes in, speaks to Trent and me, and then Tre introduces Peaches to his father. She hugs him and puts on her sweet act and then looks at me and said, "Hey Ni Ni how are you – and what did you cook – I don't get invited much so I'm looking forward to this."

Then she just walks her butt right on into the dining area.

Tre shows Nick his room and he has the nerve to say, "It's kind of small, but thank you."

I tell you some folks just can't be satisfied and Tre don't even say nothing. He puts his bags down and helps Nick into the dining room for dinner. He is walking pretty well on the walker. The doctors say it will be about 6 months before he can walk normally again, but he is strong. I don't think it will take that long, at least I hope it won't. We sit down and eat dinner, Nick of course enjoys it, me cooking is the one thing he never complains about and is always appreciative of – said I can cook for him anytime. Peaches, of course gets on my nerves and at dinner I sat on one side of Tre and she sits directly across the table from him so she can stare at him the whole time. Trent didn't say much, he just kind of watch this whole ridiculous soap opera.

After dinner, Peaches has to leave – thank GOD – she said she has a plane to catch in the morning. She is auditioning for some show in New York. I am so relieved I did not want to have to deal with her the whole night. I clean up the kitchen and Tre, Nick. and his Dad sit in the family room and talk. When I come in, I see Nick staring at me, but I just ignore him. Funny thing is I see Trent notice it and he frowns, but still he said nothing.

Then this man said, "Nia, girl you seem to look better every time I see you."

"Um thanks," I said. "I guess."

"You do girl, maybe it's because I ain't really seen no girls in a few months or something, but you look good."

Tre is like, "Alright Nick that's enough."

"What man? I mean you know I'm right, that's why you with her cause she look good."

"That's not all man."

"Whatever," Nick said and then he laughs.

He ain't funny to me I don't know what's wrong with him tonight. Tre said to all of us, "I'm back at work and the label is thinking about signing this new artist – they want me to go and hear him."

"Where is this?" I ask.

"He's from Jamaica."

"What you going to Jamaica?"

"No Nia, Miami we going to meet him in Miami, I leave on Thursday and I'll be back Sunday. I said all this to say, we are family and I'm trusting yawl – no offense Dad– here with my wife. I expect her to be respected."

"I'm not offended Tre," Trent told him. "You doing what you supposed to do."

Nick said, 'If she yours you ain't got to worry about me right? – Nia, look girl you dangerous, just stay out my room at night and you safe," and then he grins.

"Nick man, don't play that's not funny – I let you in my house and I fully expect that you will respect my wife and my marriage."

"I'm joking man – dag."

"Alright man, just respect me. That's all I ask."

We all went about our week as normal as possible and I made sure that we sat down at dinner time together. Tre was loving this and his Dad seem really grateful. Nick of course was being himself, but for the most part he behaved. Nick seemed to be getting back to his old self. The physical therapist was scheduled to come to the house twice a week, but after his first session she said she felt that with exercise, that he would be on his own in no time, and that he really only needed a therapist once a week and maybe just for the next month or so.

Nick decides to celebrate his good news from the therapist by having over some friends. He catches me as I'm walking past the door and said, "Nia I invited a couple of the fellas over to hang out and kind of celebrate my good news and my recovery."

"Umm I guess that okay." I said. "When are they coming?"

"Friday night," he replies.

I know he is only doing that because Tre will be out of town. He is no good, no matter how much I try to like him, I don't trust him.

"Just let Tre and Trenton know," I tell him.

"Alright," he said. "Oh and do you think you can cook for us?"

"WHAT! Are you crazy cook what?"

"Never mind."

"Nope," I said. "I can order pizza for you and pick up some junk food."

He looks at me like he is kind of mad, but said, "okay."

I know he is not going to tell Tre so I will. I go down to the studio and tell Tre about Nick's party and he said, "It should be okay, I will talk to him."

"Thanks," I said.

Tre leaves on Thursday and it's kind of weird because he has not left me overnight since he went away and got shot, but I'm thinking it won't be so bad because Trent is here and he and I have really began to bond. It's kind of nice having a Father in the house. He seems to be a good man. Nick on the other hand seems to be doing very well. He put the walker down and is using a cane. He said he feels more and more like his old self every day. All I can think about is great, maybe he can get back on his own soon.

Trent comes in and tells me that one of the job leads I gave him turned out really well and that the pay is not bad either. He will be a counselor at a center for young men out of prison, it's a place they go like a half-way house, to gain some skills and some independence.

"Great," I tell him. "We'll have to go out and celebrate, maybe this weekend when Tre comes back."

"Well Nia, the thing is I start training on Friday night and I'll be gone until Saturday. I told them I can't work on Sundays."

Oh no I'm thinking I'll be here alone with Nick and his crew. He sees the look on my face and said, "if anything happens' call me on my cell and I will leave and come home, I promise."

He goes on to say that the job is a three day on, four day off position so he'll be away from home three days a week because you stay at the center all day and night during your shift.

I just say, "okay."

I'm a little uneasy about being here alone with Nick during his little 'party'. I wish I had some friends here I mean I know people, but no real friends because if I did I would sure hang out with them on Friday.

The next day goes along as usual I do my normal house work and I check on Nick from time to time. He is doing fine doesn't need much, hopefully it's a sign that he'll be out of here SOON. Trent was gone most of the day, doing some last minute running around before he starts his new job Friday night. Nick asked me to order some food for his little get together, so because Tre said this shindig was okay, I ordered the food and made sure that the house was in order for his gathering. I suggested that he have his party out on the sun porch, it's a nice size room with seating and room to set up food. He agreed, it's right off the kitchen and there is a bathroom right next to the kitchen, so folks won't be roaming all over the house. He said he invited a few girls and asked if I would at least drop in to say hi and meet his friends. I told him I guess so, but I was thinking to myself I will have to ask Tre first.

The Party…

I spoke with Tre several times before the party just to let him know about everything that I had done. He told me thanks because he knew this was something Nick really wanted, he also said that he thought it would be okay for me to meet his friends and mingle for a bit and then if I decided not to stay it would be okay, but that he thought I should see the people coming into our house. I said okay tell him I love him, and can't wait for him to get home on Sunday and we hang up. Once everything is set up Nick seems very pleased and asked again if I would hang around.

"Yes," I told him and then he tries to tell me what to wear.

"Put on something sexy," he said.

I just look at him, "You ain't my man and I'm not getting sexy for no one around here but Tre."

"Gone girl," he tells me. "You ain't no fun."

"Whatever," and I leave to go upstairs and get dressed. I just throw on some jeans and a cute shirt and call it a day. I'm not getting fancy for none of these jokers, I don't trust Nick and I sure don't trust his friends.

When everyone starts to arrive surprisingly they seem like a decent group of folk, guys and girls. I introduce myself to everyone as they enter the house and then I show them to the sun porch. By the 7th person it dawned on me to just put a sign on the front door that tells them to go around the back of the house, walk up the deck, and come into the sun room. I think to myself this way they don't have to walk through my house. By about ten at night, all twenty of his guests had arrived. There were about twelve guys and eight girls and they seemed to be mostly folks he grew up with and a few co-workers. Everyone was cool except this one guy named Mack that just kept following me around and talking to me. Nick told him I was off limits, but it was with a snicker. I just ignored the guy, around midnight I noticed that everyone is or has been drinking and I'm thinking to myself I should probably go because I know they are about to get out of hand. I ask Nick if he was okay and tell him that he knows he can't be drinking because of his meds.

"I know Ma," he said jokingly and then he said he is fine I told him I'm out of here, going to my room. I go into my room, close the door, and head for the tub. It feels like a bubble bath night, I light my candles, turn on the jets in my tub, sit down, lean my head back and relax. It has been a long day, but hasn't turned out to be as bad as I thought it would be. Once I'm done with my , I step out of the tub, grab my robe, and walk back into my room. When I walk in the room I notice that my bedroom door is cracked open and I know I closed it. I walk over to my dresser and as I'm reaching in the drawer to get my pajamas I see dude standing behind me in the mirror and I think to myself this cannot be happening you only see this stuff in the movie. I scream and he runs over to me places his hand over my mouth pushes all the stuff on my dresser on to the floor with one hand. I'm kicking and trying to scream, but I can't cause he has his hand over my mouth. I try to fight him, but this dude had to be about 6'6" and 290 pounds I can't beat him. I kick and everything, I can smell liquor and weed on him and he is still stronger than I am and the look in his eye was just scary.

He kept saying to me, "Look baby I just want a little bit, I promise I won't hurt you. Don't fight me, I've been watching you all night and I can't help it."

He forces me on the dresser and pushes my legs apart and forces himself into me. I can't believe this, I try to fight and I don't know what's going on, this can't be real. He is moving and making noise like this is something I asked for, and finally I hear Nick come in the door and he freezes for a second and then is like "MACK NO oh my GOD! Nia! Mack what are you doing!"

He pulls out and just leaves me on the dresser and this bastard takes off running. Nick walks over and pulls my robe together, and where he got the strength to pick me up off that dresser I don't know, but he does it and takes me over to the bed and lays me down and I'm numb no words and no tears. I'm hoping that I wake up from this bad dream. I think Nick felt the same way because he just stares at me like he was afraid I was going to die or something.

Finally he said, "Are you okay?"

I just look up at him cause there is no way I'm okay. He goes down stairs and I assume he tells everyone to leave because I hear cars start to pull off. He was gone for about fifteen minutes. He said he called the police to come to the house. I hear him but I just can't say anything and he just sits down on the bed next to me. I can't speak I just lay there. When the police arrive he brings them upstairs to my room, but I can't say anything. I just lay there and the officer suggests that they get an ambulance to take me to the emergency room.

I did find a way to say, "No I don't want to go the hospital."

The officer asks Nick if he would sit me up in the bed and Nick does so. He asks him if he was my husband and he said no and explains his relation to me. Next the officer sits next to me and said "I know this is difficult but you have to tell us what happened."

Nick said, "I can tell you part of it."

He explains how Mack had followed me around all night despite the fact that I kept telling him no thanks, and then he said around thirty minutes after I left to go to my room he noticed that he didn't see Mack anymore so he went looking for him. When he couldn't find him downstairs anywhere or outside, he came upstairs to see if I was okay. He never thought he would find him raping me, just thought that maybe he would have followed me and still be bothering me. So the officer asked me to walk him through the attack, and somehow I found a way to get the words out to describe what happened. The officer told me they needed me to go the emergency room so that they could get DNA evidence, but I feel so nasty. He told me to get dressed without bathing. I told them okay, they offered to take me and I said I would have my father in law do it. So they told me they would meet me there and they left. Nick asked me if I wanted him to go with me.

" NOPE," I said. "Can you just call my father in law," and I gave him the cell number.

I don't know what he told Trent but he was home in about twenty0 minutes. He walked in my door, looked at me, and then ran down the stairs to Nicks room and after I didn't hear a noise I got scared and went down the steps slowly. I walk to Nicks room and Trent was in there with his hands around Nicks neck choking him!!

"Trent!" I tell him. "No please, please, don't kill him, please."

That's all I could get out, finally he let him go and I know it was about fifteen sec before I heard Nick take a breath he just looked terrified.

Trent looks at him and said, "You better pray she is okay, cause I will KILL YOU and I mean that and happily go to jail for your murder."

"Trent," I tell him. "He didn't do it,"

"I don't care Tre left him here and he didn't take care of you like he asked. This is a mess boy, you always causing trouble, you are getting out of my son's house and I mean that. I'm taking Nia to the hospital and when I get back you better be gone."

Trent walks me out of the room and to the truck and we head for the emergency room. In the car he asked me what happened and strangely enough through tears I was able to tell him. He looked disgusted and angry. He said he felt guilty because he had a feeling he shouldn't have left me there at that party. I get to the hospital and go through the exam, answer more questions and we leave.

Finally Trent said, "Nia you haven't called Tre?"

"NO" I said. "Oh my GOD I can't tell him this, this is disgusting, what if he has something. All those tests I had to take and now I have to sit and wait for the result. This can't be happening to me."

Trent just looks at me as we are driving and takes my hand and starts to pray out loud. I know it's the right thing to do now, but I feel like I'm not even worthy to talk to GOD, like he let this happen to me cause I ain't been living right.

"Nia" he said. "GOD can heal all things."

I know he's right, but I don't want to hear that now, I don't want to hear nothing.

Trent said, "I'm calling Tre when we get home, I will tell him."

We were at the hospital for about three hours and when we got back Nick was gone. He left a note saying, he was so sorry, that he never meant for this to happen and that he would be back later to get his stuff, that he had his cell phone if we needed to call him. In a weird way I feel bad because he didn't do this and actually he was very helpful, so I tell Trent all this but he doesn't care. He walks me upstairs to my room and tells me to take a bath. I don't want to go in that room, but I think to myself this is my house and I have to live and I can't let nobody steal that from me, he already took enough. So I go in the bathroom and close the door. When I come out, Trent has cleaned up the mess and changed the sheets on my bed. Tonight I figure out that I really love my father in law. He is like the Dad I don't have and I feel safe with him here. I lay in the bed and look over at the phone and I know I have to call Tre, but before I can call him the phone is ringing. I said hello as calmly as I can and it's Tre,

"Nia Baby, oh my god I'm on my way home."

"Tre hi baby, I'm fine," I said.

He said, "Where is Nick?"

"I don't know."

"Who did this?"

"Why?"

"Nia what happened?!"

"What, Tre your dad called?"

"Yes," he said.

"Just calm down and get home safely, we can talk then."

He sound so crazy and furious and hurt just all over the place. He said, "Nia I love you and I'm on my way."

A few minutes later Trent comes in with some hot tea hands it to me and sits on the bed next to me.

"Thanks." I said. "And thanks for telling Tre for me."

"Nia" he said. "You know Tre better than I do, but he didn't sound right to me, do you think he will try to find this guy?"

"Yes unless you talk him out of it, but he'll come home first."

I drink the tea and Trent leaves out for about ten minutes and comes back in his pajama's carrying a pillow and a blanket. He plops himself on the floor next to my bed reaches up to hold my hand and after a while I drift off to sleep.

I'm awakened by the sound of the alarm being turned off and Tre bolting up the stairs. He opens the door and walks in the room like he is going to see someone in critical condition. I'm so glad to see him I feel tears start to run down my face. He comes in and climbs in the bed with me and just holds me.

"Nia I'm so sorry, I am never leaving you alone again. I'm sorry, this is my fault if I were here this would not have happened."

"Tre it's not your fault," and finally I can say it. "It's mine. I should have locked my door instead of just closing it."

Trent sits up and said, "Nia it's not your fault."

"Hi Dad, thanks for taking care of her," Tre said.

Trent grabs his pillow and blanket and leaves out of our room. Tre is holding on to me like he is afraid I'm going to slip away.

"Tre I'm okay, but we have a lot to talk about."

"I know, but first we have to talk about how I'm going to kill Nick and Mack."

"Tre, Nick didn't do it."

"Nia he let him in here, Mack had been drinking and smoking, I don't care he knows that guy has problems."

"You know him?" I ask

"Yeah I know who he is and he ain't never been no real fan of mine which is probably why he went after you like that. He was Nick's friend from way back and they were like brothers in all the same group homes together before they ended up in the one where I met Nick. He never like me too much cause Nick and I got to be really good friends, he just weird. But he has issues he has attacked people before, he supposedly got help for it, but it seems the help didn't help him."

I said, "Tre there are a lot of things I need to tell you."

He is looking at me all funny.

"What?" I ask.

"The bruises on the side of your face and on your neck."

I hadn't even noticed, and then I see tears run down his face and he just shakes his head. I feel so nasty so I cover myself up and he is like, "Nia no don't do that, I'm not mad at you just at all you have gone through within the past year. This is too much and I feel like I have not been a good husband, I haven't been able to protect you from any of it."

"Tre you can't protect me from everything, but I need to tell you," and I just blurt out " I had to take test for all STD's including HIV and the police said that once they catch him, they'll have him tested as well just for my peace of mind. The hospital said they can have my test results in three days so I will have them all back by Monday, but that I need to see my OB/GYN in four weeks to have another exam."

"Okay," he said. "I understand. Do you want to move Nia?' he asked.

"I think we should move."

"No Tre," I said. "You love this house, we just got it,"

"Not no more." He said, "I don't know if I can stay here."

"I'm fine, this is our home, and I'll be okay."

"How can you be okay Nia? I'm not, this is crazy, you always say you okay, HOW?"

"I don't know Tre. I don't know how else to be or what else to say, I am just trying to keep it together."

"WHY?" he yells. "You don't have to!"

"What do you want me to do Tre?"

"I don't know Nia, all I know is that I'm mad as HELL and I don't know how not to be. This aint' fair, we didn't ask for this and you don't deserve this. My life been hard enough and I finally got some happiness and stuff just kept happening."

I just listen to him because honestly I think I'm just numb, I don't feel anything. When he finally comes over, he pulls me close to him and he begins to kiss me, but I pull away. I'm scared, not for him to touch me, but what if I have something I don't want to give it to him.

"Nia, please don't shut me out, I can't handle this. If you need time I understand, but I just want to hold you and kiss you."

"Tre its not that. I'm scared that I may have something."

"Well if you do Nia, I don't care. My life aint nothing without you anyway."

"I can't baby, I love you too much I can't put your life in danger, the test results will be back on Monday."

He said, "Just kiss me then."

So we kiss and just hold each other. Actually I'm glad cause I don't want to have sex right now, I still feel nasty. I feel like someone reached on the inside of me and snatched something out.

The next couple of days are like a blur I think I slept most of the time. Tre and Trent left me alone mostly, on Sunday evening Trent came into my room to tell me about the message at church, said it was about understanding salvation. I listen to him, but I know all about salvation I was raised in the church.

He asked me if I am saved, first I said, "yes" then I said, "No, well I'm not sure, I was saved before."

I tell him, "but I know I have not been living right at least not like I know I should, I just haven't thought about it."

"Well Nia," he said. "I think you should think about it. GOD loves you and at this point in your life I think you need him."

I just listen and don't say much. When Tre comes to bed, he said his dad talked to him about the message and it made him think. Maybe GOD is trying to get our attention again and I just listened. He said he thinks he will go to church with his Dad next Sunday.

Three weeks go by really quickly and I do my best to get back to normal as much as possible. The police department calls to inform me that Mack turned himself in. My hope is that he pleads guilty or whatever, I just don't want to have to go to court. Nick has been calling, but Tre said he is not ready to talk to him. He knows he didn't do it, but he feels betrayed by him and said it's just one too many times. Nick knew that Mack didn't really like Tre, so he doesn't understand why he would even think its okay for him to have been at our house. According to the message Nick left, it was him that convinced Mack to turn himself in. He said Mack was high and drunk and didn't really know what he was doing. I disagree, but whatever, it's done now. The good news was that my test results for STD's was negative and so were Mack's, so I don't have to worry about that. My four week follow up is on Friday and after that I'm guessing that my life can really get back to normal. I'm worried though because I just feel really nasty and I know that after four weeks Tre is going to want more than hugging and kissing, and I don't know how I'm going to get through it. Trent has been watching me and checking on me and I know he is praying for me. He said he wants me to talk to the counselors at his church, for some reason he thinks I need help. I don't think so I think I'm fine, I'll get through this just like I have everything else.

Friday morning I get up, get dressed and Tre, Trent, and I head off to the doctor's office. I told Trent it was not necessary for him to be there, but he insisted and since his work nights were Monday – Thursday, he was available and wanted to come. When I get there Tre and I talk to the doctor first. They give me all this information about life after rape and then they explain that I'll be getting a pelvic exam and they will also give me a urine test to see if I'm pregnant and another blood test, which is all just standard procedure. So I go in the room and Tre goes with me (Trent is waiting in the sitting area). They give me the cup for a urine sample once I'm done they go on with the pelvic exam. When the exam is over I get dressed and they tell me to go back to the office to talk to the doctor.

My doctor comes in and said, "Well the good news is that for the most part you seem to be healthy. The only issue is that Nia your pregnancy test was positive."

Tre just gets up out his seat and kind of walks around the room and I just sit there. The doctor , "Mr. Whitmore before you get upset, it looks as though you are four-five weeks."

So I said, "So now I don't know who's the father, my husband or the rapist."

I just think to myself, this cannot be happening. If I were not living this, I would swear it was a horror movie. What in the world?

The doctor said, "You can terminate the pregnancy or you can carry the baby, do a DNA when he or she is born, and at that time you can decide to keep him or her or you can place the child up for adoption."

Tre walks over and kneels in front of me, "Nia we lost one baby, and if you want this child, I don't care what has happened. If you have the baby, I'm the father. We don't even have to do DNA. Whatever you want to do I'll stand by you."

"I can't have an abortion because what if it's your baby, this is awful. I want to have a child but I want my husband to be the father."

The doctor said, "At this point you don't have to decide. Go home and take it easy and think about it."

Tre grabs my hand and we walk out of the office and just keep walking through the waiting area, so Trent sees us and jumps up to follow us outside.

When we get in the car he said, "What happened, y'all both look like you saw a ghost."

Tre said, "Dad, Nia is pregnant."

"That's not bad news is it?"

So I said, "Yes, cause now I look like a slut because I don't know who the father is."

"NIA!" Trent said, "What are you talking about?"

"Four to five weeks could be Tre's baby or it could be the rapist's baby."

"OH MY GOD!" Trent said.

"Yep," Tre said. "That about sums it all up."

When we get home Tre and I go upstairs and there are really no words to describe how we were feeling. But Tre being the awesome man that he is said, "Nia I love you and I will love this baby no matter what so I don't want you to think about it like it's not ours. If you carry a baby it's ours."

That makes me feel a little better. He then grabs me and pulls me close to him like if he could he would have climbed inside my body and he kisses me as if he was trying to regain his possession like someone had taken my lips and he was snatching them back. He was not forceful, but it was like I could feel him saying that I belonged to him and he was not letting go. He removed my clothing piece by piece and very slowly like he was afraid I would say no or freak out, I let him do it. I just closed my eyes and asked GOD to help me not run from my husband and to help me continue to be the wife he needs. I think this was my first sincere prayer in a long time. Tre touches me like he hasn't touched me in years – I still don't know how he does that and it makes me feel so special. He pulled the covers back laid me down and slowly very slowly slid his body into mine, and it was weird because I remembered the way Mack just intruded and he had no right and Tre being my husband had every , but it felt as though he was asking if it was okay to be there. After a few minutes I felt my body begin to say yes and I just let go and decided to trust Tre and do my best to enjoy this moment with him and I hoped that I would again desire to make love like I had before. It didn't take long before I was able to get lost in this place with him and it actually felt good not to think about anything, but to just allow him to make me feel good. He seemed to be enjoying himself as well. It was like we had been on a long unhappy vacation and were finally back at home. When we finished I turned over and I began to cry and I tried not to, but I could not help it. Tre didn't make any comments or ask any questions he just held me and let me feel what ever I was feeling he didn't intrude on that moment I was having. I think he knew that I needed to cry some things out and that there was nothing he could say so he just let me do it and he held me while I did and that was good. It made me feel safe with him which was what I needed.

For the next couple of weeks I try to take it easy and wrap my mind around being pregnant, but it just doesn't feel right and it's too heart breaking to think I could be carrying another man's baby. I wish there was a test I could take that would tell me before the baby is born who the father is, but I guess that just wishful thinking. Trent gave me a Women's devotional bible and I actually started reading it and surprisingly to me I find comfort in some of what I read. I know I need to get back to church, I guess now is a good time. Tre has been going to bible study with his Dad.

I'm not sure if he enjoys the bible study or if he is going just to make Trent happy. Nevertheless, we all seem to be trying to live a normal life no one really said anything about me being pregnant except they ask how I feel. I know this situation is stressful on everybody, but I'm the one who really has to live with all of this. I don't say anything though cause there is nothing to be said.

De ja vu…

In the middle of the night I hear Tre say – "what in the world" and he leans over turns the lights on and lifts the cover, by this time I'm opening my eyes and he said "Oh no" kind of softly. At this point I turn over to sit up and then I feel a really bad cramp and something wet, and I think to myself, this must be de ja vu cause I've seen this before. Tre calmly picks up the phone, calls the ambulance, and said, "I think my wife is having a miscarriage."

I just lay there with all these emotions going on and part of me was sad cause this IS MY BABY. Another part of me is relieved because it was hard carrying a baby from a rape, and the other part of me is scared cause I don't know why I'm now losing my second baby. Tre tries to help me clean up as much as we can, but I was bleeding all over the place so he just grabs my robe to help me cover up. He leaves to go down stairs to let the medics in, they come in ask a few questions take my blood pressure which at this point is extremely low put me on a stretcher and I'm off again to the emergency room. Still I have said nothing I'm speechless. I feel so lost and so helpless, at this point I really believe that for some reason I am being punished.

I hear the same song and dance I heard before from the doctors, "sorry – you lost your baby."

I didn't even listen. I just don't know what to feel so I decide not to feel anything. Tre is of course very supportive I think he was even a little hurt, although I know deep down inside he was relieved not to have to go through a whole pregnancy not knowing if it was his baby I was carrying. They tell me they'll keep me overnight, give me some pain medicine, send me home, and that I should rest for about a week and then I can slowly resume my normal routine – whatever that is.

REMININCING

I was doing some cleaning today and I came across a box with a bunch of my old journals in there. I decided to grab a cup of tea and sit in a corner and read through a few of them. Sometimes remembering where you came from helps you appreciate much more where you are...

It's been about six weeks since I had the miscarriage and life for me is kind of getting back to normal. Tre and I decided that we would sell this house and start new, though I love it dearly there are too many tormenting memories here and it's not helping me to move on. I mean I'm doing it, but it's so painful – we don't even sleep in our room anymore cuz though I said it was fine – I always felt really sad when I was in there, it's weird what memories do to you. Tre has gotten back to work full time and so has Trent, the good thing for me is that I'm busy looking for another house which seems to be something I've really turned out to like. I like it so much that I signed up for Real Estate classes, I think I'll get my license and start my own business.

While I was out today, I picked up a journal. I remember telling a lot of my clients way back when I was working, that writing down their feelings was a very good therapy, so I decided that I would take my own advice.

Tre has been going to church with his Dad every Wednesday for bible study and just about every Sunday. I've been going too and the funny thing is I grew up in church and Tre didn't, but he seems to be getting way more out of it than I am. I mean I hear the preacher but it's like he's not saying anything that I want to hear. I want to know why my life is the way it is, it's like I have everything I could dream of, but way more pain than anyone deserves and this makes no sense. I think I'm figuring out that I'm angry anyway, no time for anger I have to find us a place to live.

A Surprise from Auntie Sasha...

I checked the mail upon my return from house hunting today, and to my surprise there was a letter from my Aunt Sasha – very strange she normally just calls. I go inside, put my things away, go into the family room and make myself comfortable to read her letter. When I open it; there is a letter from her in another envelope. The letter from Aunt Sasha stated that she remembered that I told her right before Tre was shot that I had decided to try and find my father. She said that she contemplated this for a while, but decided that it was not fair that she should withhold information from me, and that since I was an adult she didn't see any harm in telling me the truth about my father and his whereabouts. As I continue reading my stomach starts to feel sick, my auntie Sasha's letter said that my dad lived on Corley Court and that my father was married but didn't have any other children. I feel sick because Corley Court is around the corner from the house I grew up in – you mean this man lived around the corner and NEVER contacted me. She said that the reason I didn't know him or see much of him was because he dated my mom and never told her he was married and that when he found out that my mother was pregnant he told her about his wife and asked her to get rid of the baby. Being the woman my mother was she refused to have an abortion and told him to have a nice life and that he didn't have to worry about her telling his wife. She said that he has always known my whereabouts – in fact his heart softened when I was about seven or eight and he gave my mother the money to buy the house I grew up in, but that she had to agree never to come around him or acknowledge that she knew him in any way. For me my aunt said my mother agreed because she wanted to raise me in a decent neighborhood. Wow, how I wish my mother were alive as I read this letter – there are so many things I would love to ask her – I'm sure she must have been devastated to find out that a man she loved was married. This would explain why she ran to church like she did and why I never really saw her date anyone. She would always say Nia, Jesus is all I need. His love has never lied to me or hurt me, so many things she used to say make since now. When I was younger and would ask her about my father, she would always say things were complicated and that she had enough love for me to be my mom and dad. My aunt Sasha said she called him when my mom died and told him that he needed to contact me and when he was ready to let her know. Low and behold she said out of the blue he called and said he told his wife after all these years about the affair he'd

239

had over twenty years ago with my mom and that it resulted in a child. She said his wife forgave him and said she would love to meet me – if I were willing. So he was calling her and she had enclosed in the envelope his contact info and that when I was ready I should open the envelope. Her letter said to please not be upset with my mom and that she believed my mother made the right decision. Tears began to roll down my face because I know my mommy very well and I'm sure that she was very hurt to have been deceived like that. Then a part of me felt for his wife because what was so wrong with her that he had to date my mom while he was married. So many questions, so many things I wanted to know about.

I decide to open the contact information, I knew his name was Nathan Armstrong, but when I read his full name I realized that my mother was really in love with this man when I was born despite the deception. His name was Nathan Isaiah Armstrong and his initials spelled Nia WOW! My mom named me after my father. The letter with the contact information stated that he no longer lived on Corley Court, that he moved from there a few years ago and lived in Myrtle Beach, South Carolina. She gave the address and phone number and said that his wife's name was Rachel. I fold the letter up, put it in the envelope, and leave it on the end table. I dry my face and go into the kitchen to make dinner. I will talk to Tre about all this when he comes home.

When Trent comes home he comes into the kitchen, "Something smells good as usual Nia, whatcha cooking?"

"Nothing special, I just made some Chicken Marsala, potatoes, and a salad."

He said, "Are you okay, you look a little down."

I contemplate telling him about my dad before I tell Tre, but since he is home first and he asked I go ahead and tell him all about the letter and the information. Trent doesn't say anything at first like he's thinking and then he said, "I think your mom did the best she could and I think it's wonderful if you could meet your dad now despite the past. After all that you have been through it may be good for you."

"I don't know. I keep having different emotions about it," I tell him.

As I'm saying that Tre walks in, "Hi Nia."

He comes over and kisses me and then said, "Hi dad."

He looks at me and said, "different emotions about what?"

I tell him all about my aunt's letter and the information, but he frowns and looks a little pissed off, "He was married? What in the world and lived around the corner and you still want to meet him?"

"Yes I mean my mom is gone and I thought I had no parents and now I find out that my dad is still alive and that he now wants to meet me."

"I don't know Nia," Tre said. "You have been through enough, what if this doesn't turn out like you are expecting? I don't know if I like this, I got to think about it."

Now I start to feel a little angry, "What do you mean Tre? I mean when you wanted to find your dad in PRISON – sorry Trent – I didn't object. I wasn't thrilled, but I supported you."

"Yeah Nia I know, but you and I are different and it's a different situation."

"How," I said as I'm fixing plates and setting the table. "You wanted to meet your dad and so do I."

He still looks pissed, but doesn't respond. We all sit down to eat and no one is saying anything.

Finally Trent looks up and asks, "May I said something about this situation?"

Tre looks over at him and I said, "Yes Trent go ahead."

"Nia, Tre is just feeling very protective of you because you have been through so much and he doesn't want anyone else to hurt you, but I understand your desire to have a father in your life."

Tre said, "I don't think you can take any more disappointment Nia. I mean you are already at a breaking point."

"I am? What do you mean?"

Trent looks down at his plate and Tre just stares at me.

"WHAT!" I said. "Why y'all looking at me like that?"

"Nia, you take those sleeping pills all day unless you out looking for a house. You have lost way more weight than you needed too," Tre said.

"I lost baby weight that's all."

242

"No, you lost more than baby weight Nia," Trent said.

"Huh so okay I take some pills to rest and I lost weight."

"That's not all" Tre said. "I worry about you all the time – I hear you crying in the bathroom."

I just look at him cause I didn't know he knew that, "So what are you both saying?"

Trent said, "Well, we think you may be depressed."

"DUH, who wouldn't be?"

"No" Tre said. "We mean like you need to see a doctor."

I just look at both of them, "How did we get from me wanting to meet my father to me needing to see a shrink – and all of this comes out because I want to see my father."

"That's not the issue," Tre said. "I just want my wife back and if you have one more disappointment I'm afraid I may really lose you Nia that's all. You haven't been yourself in a long time and I miss you."

Trent gets up to leave, "Dad you don't have to go," Tre said.

I shake my head in agreement – but he leans over and kisses me on the forehead and said "no I think this is a private conversation I'll finish my dinner in the family room, wanted to watch TV anyway."

Tre goes on to say, "I know things have been hard for you, so I didn't say anything. I just pray for you, but you haven't smiled in 6 weeks and you cry every night and you haven't done your hair in 6 weeks. Though you are still extremely beautiful, you are not yourself and so many things have happened that I could not help you with, so meeting a man that deserted you on purpose your whole life at this time concerns me."

I understand what he is saying, I really feel like this is something I need. He just shakes his head.

"What if I call and ask him to meet me for dinner at a hotel on Myrtle Beach this way he doesn't have to know where I live and if things don't go well I don't have to see him again. Plus you and I can get away for the weekend at the same time."

Tre just shakes his head and said, "I don't like it not sure if I like him, but if it's important to you, then alright but you have to promise me that you'll slow up on those pills."

"Agreed," I tell him.

Once things are cleaned up and we settle down for bed I grab the journal I picked up and I make my first entry:

Today was a good day ... I think I managed to cry only twice today – that's good for me and I didn't cry tonight before bed. I think tomorrow I will make the call to Nathan and see if he is willing to meet me for dinner. I drove past a gated community today that caught my attention. I will go there tomorrow to see if I like the houses. It's only five miles from here so that's not too bad. I like this area just don't want to live in this house anymore. I thought about a lot today as I was looking at houses and decided that I do want to be a mommy. A few weeks ago I was not sure about that, but now I am – I just got to get past being scared to try again.

Meeting Nathan and Rachel…

      I decide to go check out the houses when I get up in the morning and then once I do that I would call Nathan. When I get into the community I really like it, beautiful landscaping, gorgeous homes, and I fell completely in love with the model and decide this is it for me; I will tell Tre about it and move from there.

      When I get back home it's about noon so I decide to go ahead and call Nathan. I pick up the phone, dial the number, and a woman answers.

      "Hello," I said. "May I speak with Nathan or Rachel?"

      "This is Rachel," the woman on the phone said.

      I tell her my name is Nia and she gasps and said, "I was wondering if you'd really call – Nathan is in the den I will get him for you."

      A few minutes later a gentleman answers the phone and said, "Hi Nia I am pleased that you decided to call."

      I said, "Hello" and we talk for a few minutes. Before I could suggest it, he asked if I would like to meet in person.

      I tell him yes and he said he lives right on the beach I tell him that I'd like to meet him for dinner over the weekend. He tells me to hold on, I assume he was checking his schedule with Rachel and he comes back and

245

said, "Take my email address down (which I do) and email me where you would like to meet and what time and we'll meet you then. We have no plans for the weekend."

"I will do that," I said. "Thank you." and hang up.

Immediately I get on the computer and make reservations for us at The Diamond Hotel right on the water, I decide to get a suite that will be fun. This hotel had a five star restaurant called Shelby's, it's supposed to be excellent. I actually find myself feeling a little excited about this meeting.

When Tre comes home I give him all the details and though he is not thrilled about this, but he is supportive. We decide we'll leave Friday morning so we'll have some leisure time at the hotel before dinner.

Tre gets up early Thursday morning to catch a flight to Orlando for an appointment with a potential new artist. He wakes me up to remind me that he'll be home later than his usual today – since his flight won't get back in until seven o'clock in the evening. I get up, walk him to the door, and kiss him bye. I look at the clock it's five am. I decide I'll lie back down and get up around 8am and start my day. The first thing I decide to do is check our bank account to see if we can really afford the house I want. I am shocked to see that I have really been out of the loop and my husband has been working really hard cause we can afford to pay cash for the house I want without even selling this one and it won't hurt us at all.

Then I think – what a blessing, my mom would be so proud, and then I think WOW because this is just one of the accounts Tre has for us. For a moment I forget about all the sadness I have been feeling and I feel very blessed – not because we have money, but because I married a man that promised he would love me unconditionally and take care of me and he has done that. Outside of all the material things we have – I would still be in love with Tre even if we didn't have all of that. I will have to tell him that and thank him. I decide that I need to get it together, so I call my hair stylist who I haven't called in I don't know when, and she is so glad to hear from me that she tells me to just come and she'll fit me in. So first I go and put some money down on the house I want just to hold it. The house isn't built yet, but I loved the model and I wanted the lot with the lake in the back of it, so I give the builder a check for more than enough money to hold it. I don't want to pay cash for it until I'm sure that Tre likes it. I finally get to Moni's, which is where I get my hair done and she puts me right in her chair. She takes my hair out of the pony tail and proceeds to lecture me about how long it has been since I've had a touch up, etc. I just tell her to make me look pretty – she smiles and does her thing. I get out of her chair and realize my hair has grown a lot it hangs midway down my back. This is the first time I've ever let it get this long, it looks nice. I just got a roller wrap, simple but pretty. I go get my nails and toes done and I head to the mall and shop a little. I haven't done that in I don't know how long either. While I'm there I pick up a few things for Tre. I hadn't noticed the time, but it was already close to 6pm when I start heading home. I need to hurry up and get home, find something to make for dinner, or at this point I guess we'll be ordering out because I also have to pack for our drive to South Carolina in the morning. Trent is pulling into the drive way right behind me as I'm in the back of my truck to get all my bags he walks up.

"Nia you look gorgeous – oh my GOD." and hugs me.

I think to myself I must have really been looking a mess for a while. "Thanks Trent – did I look that bad before?"

"No!" He said, "You are a beautiful girl no matter what, but you just hadn't been looking like yourself, and your hairs looks really nice I see you let it grow."

"Yes," I said as we both grab my bags and head into the door.

Trent and I decide we'll just order pizza tonight for dinner – he orders while I head up stairs to unpack my shopping bags and pack our suit cases for the trip tomorrow. When I return downstairs I remind him that we'll be gone for the weekend – gone to meet my father.

"I know," he tells me. "I'll be praying for you while you are there."

Thanks," I tell him.

It's about eight thirty at night when Tre comes in. By this time I have showered and I decide to lounge in one of my VS lounging dresses – very form fitting and spaghetti strapped. I look at myself and realize I have lost a lot of weight, but not too much. I look like I did in college which is not bad. Tre had just gotten use to me being bigger because I gained a little weight after we got married. He walks in and the biggest smile comes over his face and Trent just cracks up laughing and leaves the family room yells "good night" as he continues to laugh his way to his room.

"Hi baby, what are you smiling at?" I ask.

"NIA wow you look soooooo good to me – I mean you look like that girl I fell in love with at Camp Over Comers."

I of course blush, "What," I said.

He just grabs me and kisses me. I remember I haven't kissed him like this in a long time, I mean I think I have just been gliding through. We didn't stop having sex, but at this moment with this kiss I realize that with all that's happened I was kind of going through the motions of things and not really there, but it feels good to really feel this, and I can tell that Tre is happy. He steps back from me and there he goes again, he looks at me like he can see through me.

"I'm pleased and thank you," he said.

"Thanks for what?"

"You listened, you listened to what I said at the table last night and that means a lot to me."

I fix him a plate and I fill him in on all that I'd done today including putting money down on the house, but mainly he just stared at me and nibbled on his food. I don't think he heard much of what I said, and when we got upstairs I figured out he didn't care what I said. In this room and in this bed with me naked is all he was thinking about and I realized I had way more energy than I realized, taking those pills had really slowed me down. By the time both our bodies slid apart and collapsed, Tre was looking at me with awe and he smiled and said, "You didn't take any of those sleeping pills or sedatives the doctor gave you did you?"

"No," I said. "I told you I would ease up on them – why you say that?"

He actually blushed and was like, "Cause you were out of control – I could hardly keep up – I mean I forgot just how much of a bomb you were in bed. Not that it was ever bad, but now I remember why I lose my mind every time I get to touch you. You amaze me Nia."

We both laugh, "Get some sleep, we have to get up early," I tell him.

We get up and hit the road at about nine in the morning. Check-in was at three pm and dinner with Nathan and Rachel will be at seven pm. I wanted to get there and have time to relax and get my mind together before we meet them.

On the drive Tre begins to tell me how much he is thankful that his Dad is in his life and how grateful he is that he invited him to church. He said giving his life to Christ was the best thing he's ever done and he feels like it can only get better from here. He said he knows that serving GOD will make him a better man.

I said, "Where was I when you did all this? I mean I always knew you believed in GOD and prayed, but this is new."

"I know," he said. "I talked to you about it, but when you take those pills you don't remember much."

He said "A few weeks ago – after all that's happened I just felt angry and I went to bible study. The Pastor was teaching about vengeance and you know it was for me because I was angry and was thinking about how I could get back at Mack for hurting you , and just mad at everyone who had ever wronged me. I mean all this stuff was bringing back memories and anger and all kinds of stuff and then the pastor read this scripture that said, "Vengeance is mines said the LORD I will repay" and something in me clicked. Then he said that the battles in life are not ours to fight, but GOD's it did something on the inside of me and from then I just realize that all I have to do is trust GOD. That's not something I had in the beginning of my life, but I realize it sure does make living a lot easier."

"That's good Tre," I tell him. "I'm proud of you."

He was like, "Well I don't know about being proud because I have a long way to go. I'm far from perfect, but I just understand that I need GOD – I guess that's where I am."

"I understand. I grew up trusting GOD for everything and he took good care of me, but somewhere in life I think I got lost and I'm not sure if I'm ready to come back. I mean Tre you know I feel very angry and I'm not sure why. I mean you are a dream come true and on the other hand I feel like I have suffered pain that I don't deserve, some of it so hard that well never mind. I just felt mad, but thankful at the same time just confused I guess. I love GOD, I do and I got saved when I was younger, but I don't know. I don't feel like I left GOD or anything, I never stopped believing – I don't know what I'm trying to say it's just that right now I feel like he forgot about me or something. Like why did so much good happen to me and at the same time so much pain? I don't know, sometimes I feel like I have everything and nothing at the same time."

Tre looks at me and reaches over to grab my hand and said, "Nia I know you have been through a lot, but I realized that the only person that could help you and heal you is GOD cause I tried and I still try it's my daily desire to make you happy. But all of this made me realize that there are some things I can't do for you."

I get quiet for moment and then I said, "Okay – well how do you think tonight will go?"

"For your sake, very well."

It takes us about six hours before we arrive at the hotel. It's beautiful, we spend about two hours looking around before we check into the hotel and walk into our suite and there was all kinds of stuff in there. Special things from the hotel and a note from the manger to Tre saying they are pleased that he decided to stay with them and that they hope our stay is enjoyable. Since the manager was a woman I pick up the phone and ask to speak to her. She comes to the phone and I pleasantly speak to her and she is very polite.

"Hi Mrs. Whitmore is there anything I can do for you?"

I ask very politely, "How did you know who we were?"

"I'm a big fan of Nera. I have her CD and your husband's name is all over the album. He produced a lot of the music and I recognized it from there, don't worry I didn't tell anyone."

WOW I think this is something – I guess because Tre is so much behind the scenes I never think that anyone knows who he is and I completely forgot that Nera is really doing her thing now and that her CD was released and doing very well. It seems everyone is walking out their dreams.

"OK thanks," I tell her and hang up.

Then for a moment I think to myself, "What are my dreams – I use to have them – oh well I guess I better get myself together and get ready for tonight."

Tre walks over and grabs me, "This place is nice princess – what do we do now?" – with this sly smile on his face.

"There is no time for that," I tell him.

"Whatever" he said. "There is always time for Tre and Nia."

Of course I can't resist – this crazy man starts to do a little dance for me taking off his clothes. As silly as it is to see him dancing around, I realize just how sexy he is – it's like I haven't paid attention in detail in a while. I am really a blessed girl, so I join in he slides over to the radio and

turns on some music and keeps dancing his way out of his clothes and I
follow suit. Pretty soon he has gotten down to his boxers and is just
watching me, before I could slide my panties off he was already pulling
them down for me.

"You can drive," he whispers to me, which I know means – I can
ride.

He's a trip. We cruise for a while before I collapse from delight
and fatigue. He is of course smiling at me from ear to ear, which always
makes me laugh. Who smiles like that after sex – he's crazy.

Anyway, I look at the clock and I'm like, "Tre we have to hurry up
we need to meet Nathan and Rachel in one hour and look at me you
messed up my hair."

"Your hair is fine," he said and rolls over to doze off.

Oh boy – I let him sleep while I run to the shower. I shower, plug
up my curlers, and start pulling clothes out my suit case to find the perfect
outfit. I want to look pretty, but not too sexy – (meeting my father) and
this restaurant is very upscale so no jeans. I finally decide on this pink
linen sundress not too fitting but not to big either. Very elegant and I have
the cutest sandals and bag to match. Before I get dressed I wake Tre up to
shower and I go in to do my hair and makeup. Once we are both dressed I
grab Tre and hug him real tight.

"What's that for?" he asks.

"For loving me, and for agreeing to this – I appreciate it."

"No problem," he said.

We leave our room and head for the restaurant, we get there we tell the Hostess our name and she said, "Welcome Mr. and Mrs. Whitmore – you'll be seated in the VIP section of the restaurant per the hotel managers request – we have already seated your guest."

They are here I think to myself and suddenly my stomach feels nervous and I think it must have showed on my face cause Tre turns me toward him.

"Nia there is nothing for you to be nervous about – you don't need his approval, he needs yours. You are a beautiful young woman inside and out and if he doesn't realize that than he is just stupid."

We follow the hostess to our table and as we approach Nathan and Rachel both stand up to greet us – we both walk over and speak and shake their hands. Nathan is a very handsome older man I can see why my mom would have liked him. Rachel is a very nice looking woman, but doesn't come across very warm at all. Nathan just stares at me like he has seen a ghost, I know I look like my mom, but I'm guessing I must be the spitting image of her at this age cause he almost appears speechless. I introduce them both to Tre and we sit down and our waiter comes over and we place orders for the first two courses of what will be a five course meal.

Rachel looks at me and said, "So Nia it's nice to finally meet you after all these years. I have to tell you I was very shocked to find out that Nathan had a daughter, I was never fortunate to have children."

"I'm sorry to hear that," I tell her.

"I'm over it now" she said. Then she said, "You must look like your mother I don't see any of Nathan in you."

Nathan chimes in and said, "You are beautiful Nia, you do look just like your mother – how are you? Tell me about yourself."

Tre looks annoyed, but I plan to make it through this dinner, so I tell him I have a dual degree, but that right now I stay home and that I'm planning to start a few businesses.

"That's great," he said.

Rachel asks, "Why are you wasting time at home, shouldn't you be out helping Tre pay the bills?"

"I don't need any help paying the bills, she can do whatever she wants. I can take care of my wife – she works if she wants."

"That must be nice, but in these days both people need to work to have a nice life. This is a very expensive restaurant, will you be splitting the bill with us or are you expecting Nathan to pay?"

Nathan chimes in, "Rachel there is no need to be rude. I'm happy to pay the bill, but it occurs to me that Tre and Nia know some people we don't because we certainly have never been seated at the managers table in this restaurant before and these folks if you have not noticed have been at our beck and call."

"The manager knows Tre," I said.

"Really," Rachel said. "Have you seen her Nia, beautiful, YOUNG, woman. Very successful, works hard – how does Tre know her?"

I ignore her and I see Tre's hazel eyes start to look brown which means he's getting angry – not good – I lean over and kiss his cheek and say, "I'm fine."

Although I'm thinking to myself, no wonder he cheated with my mom, she was probably not the last one either cause this chick is a mess, seems to be hatting on me big time. Anyway the conversation finally gets better when Nathan tells me that he is a real estate broker. He has been for a long time and he owns his own business in MD and in SC. He said he just always loved houses and property and decided when he was younger that's what he wanted to do and built himself up a nice business.

Tre laughs and said, "Well Nia is about to take real estate classes, she loves looking at property – now I know where she gets it."

Nathan smiles – he seems very nervous and sad and happy all at the same time. He just keeps staring at me, Rachel notices it and said, "Why are you staring at her like she may disappear at any time," and rolls her eyes.

"I apologize Nia," he said. "I just have never seen you and until this moment, it never dawned on me that I really have a child."

"It's okay," I said – I don't know how to respond to this.

We get through our meal finally with a pretty pleasant conversation. Nathan told us all about his real estate business and talked about Rachel whom we found out was a lawyer and that her law practice has done very well even after they left MD and moved to SC. After we order dessert and are waiting for it to arrive I excuse myself to go to the ladies room – and Rachel pops up and said, "I'll come too I need to powder my nose."

After I use the rest room, wash my hands, and am reapplying make up, she comes over and abruptly said, "Nia what do you want from Nathan, I mean what can he do for you now he missed your whole life?"

"My life is not over" I said.

"Well if it's money you want I suggest you stop being lazy and get a job."

To my surprise I giggle – "I don't need Nathan's money," I tell her. "We do just fine."

"How fine can you be doing, you are both very young, barely out of college."

"We are doing fine enough, don't worry I don't need any money from you, but on the other hand I'm starting to see how I got into this world – if this is the way you always behave."

Then I catch myself because her demeanor started to change, no need to hurt her the way she is trying to hurt me. There are obviously some serious issues here. I grab my bag and head back to the table; she follows a couple of minutes later. Rachel is quiet through dessert, but Tre and Nathan seem to be getting along pretty good.

Nathan said, "Nia I would like to see you again if it's okay – maybe you can come visit or I can come visit you and we can really sit down and talk. I would also like to have lunch tomorrow after we all check out before we go home any place you would like", I look over at Tre and he nods ok.

I said, "I'll call you tonight after we settle back into our rooms and say where we should have lunch."

Then he said, "Actually – I have some friends that own a restaurant right down the board walk, right on the water – really nice and the food is great. We could eat there and you could meet them."

"You want to introduce her to your friends?" Rachel said.

"Yes I do," he replies. "What's wrong with that?" – she just turns her head.

"Sounds good to me," I reply.

When the bill comes Tre takes it, looks at it, and pays cash for the bill and tip. Nathan was a little surprised, but I could tell he liked that.

"Thank you Tre." He said, "but I was going to take care of it."

"It's okay," he said. We shake hands again and tell them good night and leave.

Once we got back to our rooms and settle in for the night Tre asks me what I think.

"I'm not sure, something seems very weird to me between the two of them and Rachel is plain mean, but she sneaky with it."

Then I tell him what happened in the bathroom, "WHAT?" Tre said, "She tried to corner you in the bathroom, I was wondering why she went with you – something about their relationship ain't right."

"I know, but it's not our business. I'm not going to get my hopes up though cause I don't think she want me around and Nathan don't seem like the strong type. It's like she holding something over his head or something, she seem like she trying to control him and he lets her. Oh well its not my business, I'm just glad I got to meet him, it would be cool if we could at least be friends, but I don't know where this is going. I feel sad too cause it's like I finally found him, but he still won't be in my life cause his wife won't let him because of the way I was conceived."

Tre just pulls me close to him and hugs me. He said, "Nia it seems as though you are searching for something. I mean I know you wanted to find your Dad and partly because your Mom died, but it seems like you just keep trying to fill some kind of void.

"I don't have any voids," I tell him. "I have everything I dreamed about."

"I know Nia, but you still seem like you searching for something. I'm just saying that I'm here and it's my pleasure to be whatever you need to the best of my ability, but I know for a fact NOW that there are some voids not even all the love I have for you can fill."

"Tre you are all I need," I tell him and I kiss him on the forehead – when truly deep down inside I do feel so empty. It's like I have pieces of me missing, like there are holes in my soul and I don't know why, I really don't. I decide to write in my journal tonight:

I met my biological father today – and he seems like a nice, but I'm not sure – he didn't even hug me when he met me – I always thought that when I met my father for the first time he would just grab me and hug me because he felt the way I did, but it didn't happen. I didn't tell Tre I was disappointed though, I don't know why I didn't tell him, I just didn't. I feel like there are parts of me all over the place and I can't seem to get it together, on the outside I look fine, but I feel like on the inside I'm a mess and I know there has to be a way to fix me. Maybe I just need to focus on my marriage and starting my business, I'm sure I would be fulfilled in doing that. Oh well, tomorrow we meet again for lunch. I'll see how that goes...

Just as I'm closing my journal the phone rings – its Nathan. He said, "Nia the restaurant is called 'Belle's' it's nice I think you will like it. Can you meet us there for lunch at one in the afternoon?"

"Sure," I tell him.

"Good night, he said.

"Night."

I hang up the phone, close my journal, snuggle up to Tre who is already dozing off and I fall surprisingly right to sleep.

In the morning we get up kind of early, grab some fruit for breakfast and decide to take a walk on the beach and around the hotel. At about ten thirty we go back to our room, shower, and take a nap. We are up by noon so that we can get dressed and get to the restaurant on time.

When we arrive at the restaurant we are greeted by a young lady who introduces herself as Malina. She asks for our names and shows us to our table – Nathan and Rachel are already there. Later we find out that Malina is Belles' daughter. "Belles" is a really nice place it sits out on the end of a pier and has two areas, one upstairs that is open only for dinner and looks a lot more formal. I would love to come back because all the tables upstairs are next to windows that overlook the water and there is a stage there for entertainment. We sat at a table overlooking the water as well and this area also had a small stage. There was a guitarist playing, which really gave it a nice atmosphere – I would later find out that he was Belles' son – seems like a family operation here. Nathan stands to greet us and Rachel never looks up from her menu. After we are seated, Malina tells us that as a special request from her mother she will be taking care of us tonight and that her mother would be out later to greet us.

"This place is really nice," I tell Nathan.

"Yes," he said. "We have been coming here for years – I was very pleased when you picked a hotel so close to this place."

Rachel finally looks up and looks at Tre and said, "When will you two be going back to Georgia?"

"Tomorrow," Tre said.

"That's good," she responds.

When Malina comes back with our drink order she said, "So Uncle Nathan, who are these important people that you wanted mom to meet?"

Before he could answer, Rachel answers, "These are some friends of ours – Nathan knew Nia's mother."

I shake her hand and say, "It's nice to meet you, and Tre follows.

Nathan looks shocked, but does not correct her. I almost wanted to cry because I think to myself you mean he is not even going to acknowledge that I'm his daughter – that really hurt, but I try to keep a smile and just keep the conversation going. Tre on the other hand now looks pissed, but I can tell for me he is trying to be civilized. She takes our food orders and walks away. Nathan just looks at Rachel and she is looking past all of us out at the water – like we are not even there.

He turns to me and said, "I met Belle in college, we used to party together and got to be very good friends and have been ever since then. We have always kept in touch ,we even partnered up in the real estate business for a few years, but when some of our investments made a very good return – she got out of the business took her earnings and opened up this place – this is her dream."

Rachel chimes in, "This place is nice – I just don't know if I would have walked away from my real estate business to do this – but Belle is a nice lady."

Finally a very nice looking full figured woman comes over to our table followed by a gentleman pushing a cart with our food on it. Nathan gets up to greet her, she smiles, and gives him a big hug. She walks over to Rachel and leans down to hug her because Rachel of course did not move out of her seat.

Finally Nathan said, "Belle I would like you to meet Tre and Nia."

I stand up to greet her and she hugs me, which kind of caught me off guard. Then she stares at me for a moment and looks at Nathan – like she is wondering if she knows who I really am – she also hugs Tre.

Malina comes running back over and goes, "I know I recognized you, you are Da One – I was thrown off by Nathan introducing you as Tre."

"Tre is my real name," he said.

She was like, "I'm a huge fan of your work – can I have your autograph?"

"Sure," he said and he signs a small note pad she had for him.

"Mom you should take their picture and hang it on the wall with the other celebrities."

"What – celebrities?" Rachel said.

"I wouldn't say I'm a celebrity," Tre said. "I like being behind the scenes."

"But you are," Malina said. "Oh please let mom take your picture."

"Sure," he said.

So he grabs me and we pose with Belle for her wall – can't hurt I think. It's strange though, I still don't think of Tre as a celebrity – like he said he does a good job of working hard and staying behind the scenes. Our food is served and Belle walks away to greet some of her other customers, but she promises to come back and sit with us during dessert. Lunch is going pretty well, we have a pretty pleasant conversation. I excuse myself to go to the ladies room and of course Rachel follows. Once we are in the ladies room she said to me, "Look Nia I have been waiting all afternoon to tell you this. I don't know what you are trying to pull, but I don't believe you are Nathan's daughter period, although you seem to have him pretty fooled. But in the event you are, you aren't getting anything from us."

"I told you Rachel, I don't need anything."

"Whatever," she said. "I have made it my business to make sure he doesn't even name you in his will – to me you don't exist. You should have stayed invisible, that's the way I see it – why would you want to know a father that abandoned you anyway. My father left me and I made it a point to become somebody just because he left me."

"Good for you Rachel," I tell her. "I don't want anything from Nathan except the love of a father, he owes me that."

"He don't owe you nothing and I'll make sure of that – I'm not only his wife but I'm his attorney and I'll make sure that you never get anything."

"What in the world does he have that you are trying to protect? I didn't ask him for anything, Tre takes very good care of me and if he didn't I can take care of myself. Look Rachel, I don't want anything from him and you know I'm his daughter, but I don't force anyone to like or love me. So you don't have to worry about me asking you or Nathan for anything."

I use the restroom, wash my hands, and return to my seat. After we are done with our meal – Belle sends over a cart full of specialty desserts we each pick one including her and she sits down with us and we all chat for a while. Belle is a really sweet lady, but I can tell there is more to this history than what has been said and you can tell by the way Nathan looks at her. Some things occurred that Rachel does not know about. Seems to me Nathan may have had more than one affair, anyway the conversation with Belle was great. She even brought Jay, her son, over for us to meet and Tre gave him a card, he was a very good guitarist. Nathan finishes his dessert and asks Tre, "Do you mind if I take a walk with Nia?"

"No, not if she doesn't." Tre said – "excuse me Rachel."

She she rolls her eyes and said "I can come with I would love to take a walk."

"No," he said. "I want to talk to Nia for a few minutes before she leaves."

Nathan gets up from the table and reaches for my hand, we get up and he holds my hand as we walk down the pier toward the beach. I must admit it was nice and strange at the same time to have my father holding my hand for the first time in my life. As we began to walk the first thing Nathan said is, " I apologized to your mother a long time ago and now I want to apologize to you. It was never my intention to betray her or hurt her, I was sincerely in love with her. I was just young and stupid and I was not happy in my marriage and decided to find love and happiness someplace else. I know now what I did was wrong, but I have always felt that the one thing I did do right in the entire situation was you. Although when it first happened I didn't think so – over the years as I've gotten older and wiser I see myself for the man I am and I'm not happy. I don't know how to fix all the wrong I have done. I tried to do right by your mom later in life by buying the house you guys lived in. I know that could never make up for the hurt I caused her, but your mom was a class A lady and all she wanted was the best for you. So she never said anything she took the house and the money I sent from time to time and kept

silent about everything else. Nia, I want you to know that Rachel is
a very hard woman and part of it is because she's had some horrible
things happen to her, and the other part is just that she's a mean
woman – and then part of her can be so loving and so caring until
she can be almost confusing. You may wonder why I stayed with
her; in the beginning it was because of financial reasons. She
invested a lot into my business and threatened to take most of it if I
left her – her being a lawyer, I knew she could do it.(I just listened it
seemed he really needed to say all this stuff). Later on I stayed with
her because I felt guilty from the pain I had caused her from all the
affairs I have had – though your mom was my first and one of the
most meaningful ones I have ever had, she is not the only. And I
know you see a lot between Belle and I – I will just share with you
that Belle is and will always be very very special to me. Do you
have any questions?" he asked me.

     I looked at him and said, "No."

     I really didn't have any questions – I felt that there was
nothing to ask – he was not around for me because he didn't want to
be in the beginning and later he felt he couldn't – so what was there
to ask. Since I didn't have any questions, we turned around to start
walking back down the beach towards the restaurant and he turns to
me and said," I want you to take this envelope and put it away."

     "What is it?" I ask.

"It's my will," he said. "I had it amended when I first talked to you – I had it done by an attorney that Rachel doesn't know about, its notarized and everything. In the event that I pass away this will is legitimate."

"Why are you giving it to me?"

He faces me and said, "I have never done right by you and I don't know how at this time because my wife is just not going to let me without a fight, but the least I can do is do right by you in death. My will states that all my houses are yours, half of my life insurance policy is yours, if you have children at that time it will be divided equally between you and them, my stocks are yours. I left Rachel my business and my retirement money, the house we live in and the cars."

"You don't have too," I tell him. "Tre and I are fine, he takes real good care of me."

"I know I can see that, but this is from my heart. If it were up to Rachel, when I die if she is still alive you would get nothing."

"I know. She made that clear to me."

"So you take this Will and you put it away. She doesn't know about it, but my other attorney does and it's legitimate and it has the latest date on it and he has the amendment papers that I filed to change it – so she can't fight you on this."

"Okay," I tell him. "It's kind of creepy, but I understand," I thank him and we start to walk again.

"Nia, I don't know if I'll ever see you or talk to you again – I hope I will, but if I don't, I'm sorry you had to grow up without a father, and I'm sorry I was not man enough to love your mom the way she deserved. Please forgive me and know that I love you – and I'm very proud to have a daughter like you."

I just say thanks and okay because I don't know what else to do at this point. The walk back to the restaurant seemed to be very long and it felt so sad, it was like I had found my father and lost him all at one time. As we walked back he didn't say a word, he kept a straight face as if he didn't want Rachel to think he had any emotions when it came to me. As we got closer Tre noticed us and he got up and begin to walk towards us to meet me and I was really glad about that, I look at Nathan and told him "bye" and kissed him on the cheek, he didn't say anything. I looked up the pier into the restaurant and waved at Rachel. Tre grabbed my hand and we began to walk along the beach, it was if he had read my mind because I didn't want to go back in there. I had no words for Rachel and I didn't want to see them leave. We just walked, Tre didn't say anything until I began to talk, I told him all that Nathan had said to me and he just listened. We walked for a while and then we decided it was time to go home.

FALLING APART

I was sitting in our garden today and I looked around and everything was so beautiful and I was very thankful to be able to appreciate this, but it also made me think, there was a time in my life that everything around me was beautiful and well put together, but everything in me was broken and just falling apart...

When Tre and I arrived home from meeting my father, he went ahead and bought that house I fell in love with and after it was built we moved. He thought that it would be best if we left the house where all the drama was, rape, losing babies, his shooting, the house was nice, but just too many bad memories. So we moved and once we got settled we were very happy with the decision and the investment.

Tre had spent a lot of time away from producing and touring with all that had gone on with me, so once we were all settled in, he threw himself back into producing and left me to fix up the house and basically do whatever I felt I needed to do. Trenton had done so well on his job that he'd been promoted and so he spent more time at the center than he did at home, I must admit I missed having him around. With all this time on my hands I began to really realize that I had nothing to do. I had a dual degree that I was not using, I had not danced in over a year, I was not doing anything with my real estate license, I had not completed the research I started on how to start a catering business, I had all these things I could be doing and yet I was not motivated enough to do anything. I felt so sad and just so empty inside like there was something missing, but I didn't know what it was. It was times like these that I miss my momma, I could always pick up the phone and call her and she knew just what to say. I wish I could just hear her voice...

This sadness I'm feeling is so overwhelming at times, sometimes I feel like I can't breathe like I could just roll myself into a ball and stay there like I have no reason to live, and then I have days where I feel like I could fly. I don't know what's going on with me, I feel so confused and yet I don't know what I'm confused about. I think I just need something to keep me busy. I decide I will call an agency and get myself hooked up with a decent company to work for and sell real estate. I loved looking for this house and I have a license so I may as well put it to work, besides this way I can have a very flexible schedule and can still travel with Tre sometimes and this is a job I can keep when we decide to have a baby. I get started on making that happen that will keep me busy and my mind off my life.

Later...

It has been a while since we moved and got settled in and everything seems to be going pretty well. Tre is mega busy and is on Tour with four of the artists from the label he partnered with. He has been gone for three weeks now, seems like it has been much longer than that. He doesn't plan to be on the road the entire tour just off and on, but wanted to be there for the first month to make sure things get off on the right track. Trenton is busy as usual, but comes home more often since Tre is gone to make sure I'm not home alone, I told him he doesn't have to do that, but he insist and I do love the company. I have not heard from my father since we met except he sent me an email just to say if I ever need to reach him to do so at this email address and he wanted me to know he was having some health issues and if I don't hear from him at least once a month by email to call his home and check on , I just replied okay. I hope he is okay, that crazy wife of his probably did something to him for wanting to meet me. I just think I'll stay away, would love to have him around but not at this price – besides Trent is a great substitute and he definitely treats me like I'm his daughter.

Wayne...

I don't have any appointments today so I slept in late, worked out a little and decide to do some shopping. My picking up a few items turned into a day of shopping so I stop off and get my feet and nails done too, might as well. I had nothing else to do besides I like to look well put together when I meet clients, it's all about first impressions. I get home and decide I will take a shower and watch some television. I go into the kitchen grab me a sandwich and go into the family room, I turn on the television and as I'm switching channels I see the breaking news blurb on the screen and there is an over turned SUV and rescue vehicles are everywhere and they say they are waiting for the medi-vac team to arrive so I sit to see who this is and my phone rings.

"Hello" – all I hear is crying – "hello," I said.

"Nia – Nia is that you?"

"Yes who is this?" My heart starts pounding cuz I can't take another accident with Tre. I just can't.

"This is Lisa."

"Lisa what's wrong!" I said.

"Nia I need you to come to LA."

"Why?" I ask her.

"Have you seen the news? I was trying to catch you before you saw the news" – and as she is saying this the newscaster said we are at the scene of the accident where NBA player Wayne Nelson has been critically injured – all I could do was scream – I felt like I was about to pass out.

"Nia!" Lisa said, "don't panic, I know you and Wayne have not been talking much, but a lot has gone on and you have to come.

You know him so well I know he would want you here and I can't do this alone. I have so much to explain to you" – as she is talking my other line beeps.

"Hold on Lisa," I manage to get out and its Wayne's mom and she sounds like she is crying, but holding up well enough to talk.

"Nia – this is Juanita."

"Hi," I said to her.

"Look baby," she said. "Wayne had an accident in his truck in LA and we need you to come. He told me all about what happened and I know you have not been talking to him much. But I know in my heart that if anyone can give him reason to live it's you, please come."

"I'm coming," I tell her. "I just got to get a flight, Lisa is on the other line I have to go."

When I click back over, she is still there, "Sorry Lisa that was Ms. Juanita."

"Okay," she said. "I spoke to her before I called you."

"I'm coming," I tell her.

"Thank you so much," she said. "We'll have a limo pick you up from the airport, just call me with your flight info."

"Lisa how bad is it?"

She sobs, "Nia they took him to the hospital by helicopter and they say his truck hit the guard rail and flipped over several times. He is unconscious, his heart had stopped when the rescue workers arrived, but they revived him. I just don't know Nia it doesn't look good, Oh MY GOD Nia" she yells. "What am I going to do?"

"I'm on my way," I tell her. "I'm on my way, I will call you from the airport."

I hang up and I think I screamed for about a minute because all I could think about was this was my best friend for the first twenty0 years of my life. He was always there, I had to be there for him and he could not die not like this, I had to get to Cali. I try to pull myself together enough to call Tre and sound like I was keeping it together. I call him on his cell and he doesn't answer, I leave a message telling him what's going on and that I hope he is not angry with me and Lisa and Ms. Juanita both asked me to come. I said I love him and hang up. I then call Trent who answers the phone.

"Hi sweetie are you okay?"

"No," I tell him and I burst into tears.

"What happened?" he said and he sounds alarmed.

I explain about Wayne and before I could finish he said, "Go Nia, and I will talk to Tre if there is a problem. You call me if you need me to come out there with you okay, I will be praying for Wayne."

"Thanks love you," and I hang up.

I grab a bag throw a few things in it, put on some traveling gear grab my keys and head out to my car.

When I got in my car it seemed that every memory I had of Wayne came rushing to me all at once. Wow I didn't realize how much I missed him until I thought I was going to lose him. Not talking to him was okay because it was like we had an understanding, but thinking of him being dead was unbearable. I just started to scream out to GOD – "GOD I don't understand. I gave him up why you want to take him from this earth I stayed away from him, please don't punish me, my momma is gone, I don't have a real relationship with my dad I lost two babies, I was raped I have had enough – what did I do to deserve this – why are you angry at me?"

I just screamed and sobbed – where is Tre I really need him right now. I pull myself together enough to get to the airport, park my car, and get on my flight.

The limo that Lisa sent picked me up from the airport and drove me to the Medical Center where they'd taken Wayne. When I arrived there were reporters and camera's everywhere, the Limo driver said that Lisa told him to take me around the back of the hospital through the delivery entrance and that someone would be there to meet me, so he did just that. During my ride Tre called.

"Nia" he said "are you okay?" I did my best to put on my calm voice, but he knows me so well.

"Nia I know you must be very upset and scared and that's okay". He was in Europe right now, so far away. I told him I was okay, just arriving at the hospital, didn't have much info and I asked him if he was angry at me for going.

"No Nia, I wouldn't expect you not to go, "I know you love Wayne and I wish things could have been different so that you could have stayed in his life, but he couldn't handle it and neither could I. I don't expect you to hate him at all, I know he'll always be a part of you, you go and see about him, and as soon as I can get home, I'll be there. Love you"

"I love you too," I tell him and hang up.

At the Hospital…

Ms. Juanita meets me as I'm getting off the elevator and gives me the biggest hug. I haven't seen her in years although I have spoken to her by phone. She is like my other mother and I forgot how much I missed her until this moment.

"Nia it's so good to see you," she looks like she has been crying her eyes out, "we've been waiting for you, the doctors have just called they are on their way to give us an update."

She walks me to the small counseling room where Lisa is already seated. She gets up and gives me a big hug and said, "Nia, the doctors will be here in a few minutes to give us an update and I hate to spring all this on you at once, but you have to know that

Wayne and I have been separated since he left your house. We are dating just not living in the same house right now, we were doing good, really working things out and getting back on the right track. I know you know what the separation was all about."

I just nod, "Well when the separation became legal, he had all this paper work done just in case something happened to him. What I'm trying to say is that , he added you to all his living will request – I know you knew you were in his WILL" I shake my head no, "but he didn't want to leave any decision to just me or Mom I guess."

"Huh?" I said.

"I know this is a lot, but I wanted you to know that before the doctors came in and that's why you had to be here. When he arrived at the hospital he was barely conscious and had internal bleeding, they have been working on stabilizing him and are coming in to discuss with us the next course of action."

Once we all sit down, two doctors come in, they have already met Juanita and Lisa and I introduce myself, and they begin to explain that Wayne's condition right now is critical but stable and that they need to do surgery on him to fix the internal bleeding, but that though the surgery is necessary they can't promise that because of the severity of his injuries he will survive. Ms. Juanita just loses it at this point, but I think Lisa and I both were in shock and just wanted to hear what they were saying. The doctors said it's just a matter of wait and see now, and that they were getting ready to take him to surgery because if not, he definitely would not make it through the night. They said we had about fifteen minutes before the surgery and that we should each go in and see him before they take him, they said that his level of consciousness keeps going in and out. We all get up and they lead us down the hall to his room. Lisa said she wanted to go in first and so she does and then Ms. Juanita, when Ms. Juanita came out she said he squeezed her hand and so she knows he is aware that she is there. So I get myself together and I go in to see him and wow he didn't look as scary as I pictured in my mind that he would. He had just a few scrapes and bruises on his face, but the doctor said most of his injuries were internal, so I go over to the bed and I lean over and kiss his forehead, and then I said, "Wayne its Nia, I got here as fast as I could. I want you to know that I love you and I need you to make it through this surgery, you still have a lot to do and I still have some things I haven't done that I need you to be a part of. I need you to be strong and get better, you can't leave me not like this okay, so you have to get better,"

I kiss him again and he slightly opens his eyes, I can't tell if he even knew it was me, but I sure hope so, as his eyes close again I lost it I just really lost it. He couldn't talk to me, he was on a machine. This was not my best friend. He had always been the strong one and able to do just about anything, I couldn't believe this and I was at a breaking point and everything just exploded right there and I could no longer hold it and I just cried and sobbed and cried some more until I think the nurses heard me and two of them came running in and took me out of the room. Once I walked out I realized that the waiting area was full of his team mates and coaches. They'd all seen the news and came straight to the hospital, once I got it together a hospital rep came to me with papers to sign, LAWD have mercy what is going on shouldn't Lisa be doing this. Lisa and Juanita were talking to his publicist who was about to go make a statement to the press.

About thirty minutes into the surgery the waiting room started to clear out the press had left and things seem to be calming down. Lisa came over and sat down next to me.

"Nia, I guess now is as good of time as any to tell you what's going on."

"Okay," I said.

So she said," well where do I start, Wayne and I have been separated ever since he caught me in Hawaii."

"Why" I ask her.

"Why what," she said.

"Why did you do that?" I ask her.

"I don't know Nia – Wayne had done his dirt and I felt like secretly he always compared me to you. I felt though he never said it out loud I always felt like I was in your shadow and then he was always busy and this guy just made me feel really special."

"Wayne didn't?" I asked her. Y'all have been together forever."

"As I look back I was just being stupid and once we were married Wayne treated me like a queen, and he was not cheating I was just stupid at the time and I have paid for the mistake. The thing is whatever happened when he went to visit you set him off and he started drinking real bad after he got back, and from what the doctors are saying they think he had been drinking when his truck flipped over. Anyway, we recently went into counseling and have been dating to see if we could work things out – funny thing is he said you made him promise that he would try to work things out with me and I guess I should say thank you because he said he never broke a promise to you so he wanted to try. The ironic thing is I was pissed about him going to visit you – whenever there is trouble or a problem he runs to you and comes back like the world is great. I don't get you two and I guess I never will, during the separation he put into writing that if anything happened to him, no life decisions are to be made without yours mine and his moms consent. Ms. Juanita said she understood. I didn't, but it was okay. I figured out during counseling that Wayne was in love with you at one point and it has taken him all this time to admit it and get over it, but that it doesn't mean he doesn't still love you and that you are so much a part of him that you will never go away and that's something anyone in his life will have to deal with."

I just sit there, and think why is this so hard, we have never slept together or anything and we were friends before all these people came into our lives and complicated things I wish we could just ALL be FRIENDS!

"Lisa I understand why he would make that choice with y'all being separated, but you have to know that I am not a threat to your relationship. I love Tre, he is a wonderful man and I wouldn't trade him for anything. Thing is and you know that Wayne and I have been friends since we were very young and we did everything together and when you have that kind of history and bond it's hard to break, but I would never come between him and his wife and I respected that you didn't want me to be around. I can handle that, all I want is for him to be happy and safe and to know that he is okay and that he knows if he needs me I am and will always be here."

"I know," she said. "Well you should know that he is definitely getting it together emotionally and he was working on the drinking too. He had been out with the fellas the night of the accident, I guess he had a little too much that night, but before that he was doing well with trying to stop drinking. You know he is a great father, and we were heading in the right direction, Nia I can't make it if he doesn't make it."

"He is going to make it – I just know it"

"I hope you are right," she said.

"Lisa you should know that Tre didn't feel comfortable with Wayne and I being so close and the last time he was at my house they kind of had it out and we all decided that it was best if we had no contact. As hard as that was for both Wayne and I because I love Tre and respect you, I agreed and Wayne did too. We said our goodbyes and left it at that, I didn't hear from him for a while until a few months ago, I got an email that said – 'I'm alive' with a smiley and doing okay, just wanted you to know that, love you always Wayne.' It felt good to know that he was okay and so I sent him one back that simply said, thank you and ditto. So now once a month we do send an email that said all is well that's it, just so that we know that we are alive and well – that's it, we have both given up a lifetime friendship for the people we are in love with – you can't ask for more than that."

She just nodded her head. "Since we have time," I ask her, "you say you don't get us – there is nothing to get – have you ever had a best friend?"

"Yes," she said. "Of course, you know that."

"Well," I said to her. "It's no different, people just have a problem with it because he's a man and I'm a woman."

"It's different," Lisa replies. "He fell in love with you."

"I don't deny that, but I know it's different because he wanted to marry you – since 9th grade! And I was there all the time, so you think about that."

She just smiles and nods.

Seems like time was standing still…

The doctors return and inform us that Wayne surgery went well and that it would just be a wait and see from this point on, they tell us he is heavily sedated and that we can go in for a brief moment and after that we should go on home for a while. None of us responded, we just wanted to see Wayne.

For the next several days we spend all our time at Wayne's bedside with no change in his state of consciousness. The doctors finally say that he's in a coma and it's up to him to wake up. The good news is he is no longer on a ventilator so he is breathing on his own and his internal bleeding was fixed in the surgery, they believe that the head injury he suffered caused the coma. I don't understand because he was somewhat in and out when he arrived here and now he is just out, but what can I do, it has been over a week and reluctantly, I'll have to go home.

When I arrive home I immediately call Lisa to check on Wayne – still no change. I get caught up with some of my clients and try to stay occupied so I don't worry, but I am worried and I don't know how to feel about this. I feel like there are pieces of me just breaking and falling off day by day and I can't understand what's going on inside me, I feel so empty and yet, I have such a full life. I really want Wayne to be okay, I just feel that I don't know what I would do if he doesn't or how my reaction would affect my marriage. I'm lost right now and I don't know what to do.

When Tre comes home, he looks extra good to me for some reason, maybe it's because he has been gone for so long. We spend the entire day and night together and emerge, very happy but tired from our room. When we enter the kitchen, Trent welcomes his son home and asks him if he wants to go to revival with him – and Tre jumps at the opportunity. I don't understand GOD right now, I ain't going.

I filled Tre in on Wayne's condition and he said he will pray for him.

"Pray for him" I said.

"Yes Nia," he said. "I will pray for him, I don't hate Wayne Nia and actually I need to talk to him and I pray I will have the opportunity to do so, I should not have handled the situation with him the way that I did, and I realize after praying that I allowed myself to go somewhere I should not. I should have just prayed with him and talked to him because he was going through something I could not imagine having to deal with."

I just say, "okay."

He gets dressed and goes to church with Trent. And again I have time to sit and think and the more I think about Tre and this change he has made, the more I begin to remember when I was younger. I got saved and I loved GOD and I tried really hard to live the way he would desire me to. I don't know how I got to this place, I don't even really talk to GOD anymore and I think he is mad at me. I feel like if he really loved me why did all this bad stuff happen to me, I have so much, but I still feel like I have nothing. At times I feel I can fly and at times I feel like I could just die, I don't know what to do, and now I feel like he's trying to take Wayne away from me to punish me more. I don't want to go to church cause I don't understand right now. I know GOD is real; I just feel like I don't know my way back to him or even if he wants me back.

I grab the remote and lay on the couch with my blanket, I figure I'll wait here until Tre comes home. As I sit there I said to myself *'Jesus if you are not mad at me, please heal Wayne and then I just start to talk to him.'*

"Jesus what did I do to deserve all this and why are you trying to take Wayne and why can't I have a baby, and why did you take my mom when she loved you so much, and why do I always feel so sad?"

Before I know it I'm on my knees just screaming, "GOD I'm so angry and confused and hurt! Why didn't I have a father? What's wrong with me? Why has life been so good and yet so painful, all at the same time?"

I think I cried and screamed until I wore myself out.

Life Changing Dream...

As I lay on the couch I drift off to sleep and I dream that I am in this huge beautiful building and there is this long hall and I see myself as a child and I start to walk down this hall. As I walk down this hall I grow and I see myself changing and growing up, and finally I get to this door. I walk through the door, as I walk through the door I pick up some jewels. They are beautiful and suddenly I have a cart to push and I put the jewels in the cart and as I put the jewels in the cart I see a piece of myself fall off. I get to another set of doors and I choose a door and I pick up some more jewels and this time nothing falls off. I continue through this building doing the same thing, some doors I CHOSE, a piece of me would fall off and others it would not. Finally as I approach the last door I notice that my cart is full, when I get there the door is huge and beautiful and it's covered in stones I cannot describe. It swings open and as it opens there stands this huge, beautiful Angel and she holds a mirror up before me and I'm a mess. There are only parts of me there but most of me is all broke off and left behind those doors I just came through and she asks me a question.

"What profited it you to gain the whole world and lose your soul?" and I wake up!! I jump up screaming and I just felt overwhelmed and I began to cry and it felt like the tears were rolling up out of the depths of my soul and all I could do was let the tears fall.

"God I don't understand what you are trying to tell me, I don't understand."

As I'm crying Tre and Trent return and Tre must have heard me because he came running into the family room with Trent two steps behind him.

"What's wrong baby?" he said as he rushes to me.

"I had this dream," and he and Trent both sit down to listen and I explain the dream through tears.

I said, "I don't understand why GOD is mad at me."

Trent said, "Nia may I explain the dream to you."

"Sure," I said. "If you can."

He begins to say, "Nia, GOD wants you to come home. He wants your heart and the dream was just his way of reminding you that you still have time to return."

"Come home?" I ask, "What do you mean?"

"HOME, is back in his will, you said at one time you were saved and had a relationship with Jesus. He wants that again with you, the dream you had was about the choices you made in life. Some were good and in his will and the others, where parts of you fell off were times when you were not in his will or when you made choices and the consequences of the choices you made, took a part of you away."

"Okay, but what about the rape and losses and my momma?"

"Nia," Trent said. "GOD did not do those things to you, and sometimes things happen in life that we can't explain. The thing is if you love GOD and allow him to call you according to his purpose – ALL THINGS NO MATTER HOW BAD THEY SEEM WILL WORK TOGETHER FOR YOUR GOOD. See think about it, you appear to have everything – you've got a great husband, a big house, nice cars, a big bank account, a nice career, degrees and all and you are still not happy. You say you feel empty that's because what's missing is a relationship with GOD."

At that point I really sob because he is right I do have everything and yet I feel I have nothing.

"What do I do?" I ask.

Tre said, "Baby all you have to do is the same thing I did and just let GOD do the rest."

"What did you do?" I ask.

He said, "I simply surrendered…"

Trent said, "That's all Nia, I can pray with you if you want."

"Okay," I said.

Tre holds my hand and Trent begins to pray for me and then he said just repeat after me.

"Lord, I need you, please come into my heart and use me for your purpose. I want from this day to have a relationship with you and be in your will. I ask that you forgive me for everything that I have done wrong and every decision I made outside your will. I confess with my mouth and believe in my heart that Jesus is Lord and that he died for my sins and that GOD raised him from the dead. I ask that from this day forward you lead me, where you lead Jesus I will follow, Amen."

"Amen," I said.

For some reason at that moment I felt like a weight lifted off my shoulders and the tears began to flow again and Trent kisses me on the forehead and said, "Congratulations Nia, your life will never be the same."

Tre smiles and said, "I am proud of you Nia."

I finally get myself together and I head to my room. Before I doze off I ask Tre if he minds if I fly back out to California. He hesitated, but he said, "I understand if you feel you need to go then go – it's okay – at some point I will visit him too."

"Ok," I said.

I don't want to push it I know he is uneasy about it, but trying to do the right thing and not be jealous. When he gets the chance to talk to Wayne again I really wonder what he will say.

SEASONS FOR A REASON

Some friendships are for a season and some are for a lifetime – I have found that some friendships are ordained by GOD and are for a purpose. There may be one incident that brings the whole purpose of the friendship to light....

When I arrived in California I rented a car and drove myself to the hospital, Wayne was still fighting for his life, though his condition had been upgraded he was still in danger of losing his life. I went straight to the ICU where he'd been for some time now still in and out of consciousness. When I entered the room Lisa and Ms. Juanita were there, Ms. Juanita jumps up and runs to the door.

"Nia I'm so glad to see you – I knew you would come back."

"Yes, I couldn't stay away with him like this."

Lisa comes over and gives me a hug – she looked like she'd been crying. She grabs my hand and we walk into the hall area.

"Nia it has been a rough night, his blood pressure was up and down all night. They just got him stable and he has not opened his eyes in about forty eight hours, whereas before he was just out and then in and out of consciousness – now he seems to just be out again. The doctors are saying that if there is not some change within the next seventy two hours the prognosis may be very grim."

"What do you mean?"

"They say if something doesn't stabilize soon he may be in a lot of trouble and…"

'Lisa, something happened to me when I went home – and I gave GOD my life."

"Really Nia," she said. "Wow – I have been praying, but I don't think I'm where you are."

"What I'm trying to say is that I believe GOD can fix this I don't know what else to believe and at this point we have no other choice"

I grab her hand and I pray with her and then I ask her if it's okay if I go in and pray with Wayne so he can hear me.

"Sure," she said. "You can do that while me and Juanita go get something to eat – it may do him some good to hear your voice."

Lisa and Juanita leave the room and I go over to the bed and lean over close to Wayne's ear, "Hi Boo," I said. "I'm here, you know I couldn't leave you like this."

I just talk to him and I tell him how much his family needs him and how different the world will be if he doesn't fight. Then I tell him all about my dream and how I gave my life to GOD and then I pray with everything in me for him. I think I prayed harder than I ever had before and I asked GOD to not only bring him back fully restored, but that he would have an encounter with him that would cause him to change his life. I prayed and prayed until I felt something happen within me, I said Amen, and then I grabbed Wayne's hand. I sat down next to his bed and I told him no matter what I believe GOD and you know something I really did – I had such a peace, one I didn't have before. About fifteen minutes after I prayed, Wayne opened his eyes and looked at me – not only did he look at me but he winked his eye. I wanted to scream, but I didn't want to scare him, I got up and pushed the buzzer and the nurse came in.

"Oh wow," she said. "His eyes are opened. We haven't seen those brown eyes in two days – welcome back Wayne."

She left to go get the doctor and I closed my eyes and said, "GOD I THANK YOU!!"

The doctors came in and checked him out and said he seem to be more stable than before, but of course not out the woods yet and yada yada yada. I didn't care what they said I knew GOD was in control. When Lisa and Juanita came, she ran in the room I think seeing the nurses and doctors startled her, but then she saw Wayne's eyes open and all she could do was cry. They'd put the breathing tube back in as a precaution so he had a tube in his throat and he couldn't talk, but you could tell he wanted to say something. The doctors said if he stayed stable through the night they would take the tube out in the morning and see how things went. We all camped out the entire night and he seemed to do well all night. He would doze off, but wake up ever so often – which was great – in the morning the doctors came in and took out the tube. His voice was a whisper, but he could talk, Juanita and I left the room so he could have a moment with Lisa. Once she came out, Juanita went in to talk to her son – I can only imagine how she felt. I called Tre to tell him how I prayed and how I believed that GOD had given me a miracle. Tre stated that he and Trent had also prayed for Wayne. I told him I would be home tomorrow.

"So soon," he said.

"Yes," I said to him. "I just wanted to come here and pray and I did that."

When I entered the room Wayne smiled and I went over and kissed him on the cheek. He grabbed my hand and he said, "I heard you – I could hear everyone – I heard you when I first got here I heard you break down and cry and I heard you yesterday. Thank you." He said, "I heard you pray. You sounded like your mother. She would have been proud."

Tears began to run down my face – I had not thought about that, but my mom was a praying woman.

"I'm so thankful that you are okay," I told him. "I'm leaving in the morning I just came back to make sure you were alright."

He looked at me with a long stare and smiled. He said, "I feel like you are saying good bye."

"Never good bye," I tell him. "I'm just stepping out of the way."

"Nia when I heard your voice I knew everything was going to be okay – just like when were kids every time something bad happened if I could talk to you I would feel better, I don't think that will ever change."

Well I'm glad you are going to be fine Wayne. I'm going home. Your wife loves you, you know?" I told him.

"I know," he said. "I'm glad I listened to you and worked things out with her, tell Tre I said thanks."

"I will" I told him.

"Oh and Nia, Congratulations!"

"For what?" I asked.

He said, "I heard you say you gave GOD your heart – Me too, right when you were praying for me I told GOD if he would bring me back – I would live for him – I figured if you can do it so can I."

"Good," I said to him. That means no matter what, we'll be friends for eternity."

I kiss him very gently on the forehead and I leave the room. I said bye to Lisa and Juanita – I leave the hospital and stop by their house to see their daughter. I took her shopping, spent some time with her, go to my hotel room to head home in the morning. On my flight home I had time to reflect on my life and everything that led me to this point and for the first time I felt totally at peace with myself, with my life, with my friendship, with everything. I was thankful, although I had some devastating moments if all that had to happen to lead me back to GOD then so be it. I had been broken from head to toe, emotionally shattered and GOD had put me back together and I was grateful and not only that, he had used me even when I didn't know I was usable to pray for someone and had given a friend his life back – my first miracle. I had witnessed my first miracle.

Epilogue

It's been two years now since I rededicated my life to GOD and he has blessed me beyond my wildest dreams. As I walk into the nursery in our home, I can't believe that I not only had one baby, but blessed with twins...a boy and a girl. Wayne is fully restored and back to playing ball. Although I don't talk to him much anymore, I am grateful to God every time I see him on the court and realize that a friendship that began when we were children was preordained for one specific moment in time. I was put into his life to pray for him that day at the hospital. What can I say? Tre is wonderful and he has been a gift from God from day one. He's truly a representation of God's love for me in the flesh. He loves me unconditionally and I praise God every day for showing me what he meant in his word about loving your wife as Christ loves the church. If I left this world today, I can truly say that I have been loved and though we have had our share of ups and downs, God has truly blessed our relationship. We have survived some storms and we kept pressing on. I sat down one day and decided that after all that I've been through, maybe I can help someone else...so I decided that I would write a book and I started it like this:

Human nature would have us to believe that being broken means that you are in a place of lack, being without material possession. However, I've learned on this journey called life, being broken doesn't necessarily have anything to do with lack or not having. Being broken comes from within. I realized that being broken is a painful position to be in...spiritually, mentally, and physically. When you look into the mirror and you don't even recognize the person you are looking at because you are a mere shell of who you use to be and this hollowness has come from a place of emptiness on the inside, this feeling of despair can thrust you into a place that seems so low and lonely, even almost hopeless. When you have hit your lowest and you have reached a point in which you see no way out, or when you've cried until you have no tears left, and yet you still have no peace, it's at that moment that you will allow yourself to call upon God.

You will find that He is more than able to help you begin to heal and see life with a clear vision. It's in that very place that your sight begins to become clear and you look into the broken reflection of yourself in the puddle of tears you have cried and see a reflection that almost looks perfect. What you will see is that God has begun to put you back together. When you have allowed God to chip away and tear down every wall that you have up when it came to relationships, love, trust, and friendships; when you allow God to break down every door that you have locked yourself behind; when you let him strip you naked of every layer of those things that you have placed upon yourself to cover up who you really are, is when you find that you have been broken. That's when you start to find real peace, love, strength, and joy like no other. It's at this point that you see that there is nothing left for you but to stand on the word of GOD. It's in this place that you find yourself rising and soaring higher than you ever have before. It's when you begin to prosper, which has nothing to do with material possessions. These things that you've lost and thought it meant you were broken, is when you realize that it was all a part of His plan. It's a state that you would not trade for anything else in the world. In your state of brokenness, you will find what it really means to be free. True freedom comes with the realization that all you really need is God and his word. And if you hold on to him and stand on his word, you'll be whole and begin to receive, give, and love freely, knowing that there is nothing broken that God can't put back together and make brand new.

Know that brokenness is not about what's missing on the outside, but what's missing on the inside. Let God in and allow him to pour his spirit into all of your broken places and make you whole again!

Have you been BROKEN?

From the Author

Thank you so very much for reading my first book. I wrote this book out of my soul hoping that it would touch some part of yours. It is my desire that you have learned from this book that it means nothing to have everything without GOD. I encourage you to find a relationship with Jesus – it doesn't profit to gain the whole world and lose your soul.
Your life is important to me – be encouraged and know that no matter what you are going through – Joy does come in the morning.
You are a jewel.

Much love.
R. Gaskins

Thank you for reading Broken!

We hope you've enjoyed it...

<u>ORDERING INFORMATION</u>

To order extra copies of *Broken*, please visit us at
www.obpublishing.com

Opal Book Publishing
"Treating Your Work Like A Precious Jewel"

1419 SOUTHERN AVENUE, SUITE 301
OXON HILL, MARYLAND 20745

obpublishing.info@gmail.com

Also visit & LIKE us on Facebook:
facebook.com/opalbookpublishing